“The first few p[illegible]
down. The actio[illegible], fast paced way the story unfolded had me and would not let me go until I got to the end. I was sure who the bad guy was early on, only to discover I was totally wrong. There are beautifully constructed twists throughout that did not allow me to stop reading. First, Do No Harm contains a fictional portion, which is told and intertwined with non-fictional background of medical facts, which I found fascinating. There are also thought-provoking notions as Dr. L. Jan Eira allows a sneak peak behind the scenes into the real world of medicine and medical doctors.”

Jane Crawford, Psy.D.

FIRST
P R I M U M
DO NO
N O N N O C E R E
HARM

A NOVEL BY

DR. L. JAN EIRA

FIRST

PRIMUM

DO NOT

NON NOCERE

HARM

TATE PUBLISHING & *Enterprises*

First, Do No Harm

This title is also available as a Tate Out Loud product. Visit www.tatepublishing.com for more information.

This novel is a work of fiction. Names, descriptions, entities and incidents included in the story are products of the author's imagination. Any resemblance to actual persons, events and entities is entirely coincidental.

The opinions expressed by the author are not necessarily those of Tate Publishing, LLC.

Published by Tate Publishing & Enterprises, LLC
127 E. Trade Center Terrace | Mustang, Oklahoma 73064 USA
1.888.361.9473 | www.tatepublishing.com

Tate Publishing is committed to excellence in the publishing industry. The company reflects the philosophy established by the founders, based on Psalm 68:11,
"The Lord gave the word and great was the company of those who published it."

Cover design by Lindsay B. Behrens
Interior design by Nathan Harmony

Published in the United States of America

ISBN: 978-1-60462-960-6
1. Fiction: Suspense 2. Fiction: Medical
08.11.14

Preface

The Facts

Over the last fifty years, heart disease emerged as the number one killer of Americans. This formidable slayer is capable of taking a life slowly, over many years of misery, or rapidly, in a matter of seconds.

The most important heart chamber, the left ventricle, can become weakened and inefficient by a variety of mechanisms, characterized by progressively incompetent heart contractions. This leads to congestive heart failure or CHF. Its sufferers develop fatigue, shortness of breath and physical activities become harder and harder to perform. This progression of declining quality of life is often paralleled by repeated hospitalizations and eventually death from pump failure. This may take years, sometimes decades, to transpire.

Some patients suffer from the sudden emergence of lethal arrhythmias, racing heartbeats caused by electrical short-circuiting within the heart's electrical system. Patients afflicted by these disorders collapse unexpectedly and suddenly, their hearts quivering uncontrollably. Effective pumping and circulation cease instantaneously and, without prompt resuscitation, sudden cardiac arrest (SCA) ensues. Rapid initiation of cardiopulmonary resuscitation (CPR) and quick defibrillation—delivery of a shock across the heart to bring to a halt these deadly electrical short-circuits—are necessary to save the life of a SCA victim.

Electrophysiologists are cardiologists that specialize in the care of patients with heartbeat disorders. Individuals at high risk for SCA are fitted with an implantable cardioverter-defibrillator (ICD), a small device that monitors the heart rhythm for the emergence of lethal arrhythmias. If these fatal arrhythmias arise, the ICD shocks the heart from within to normal rhythm, saving the patient's life.

Roughly, on average, one American dies of cardiovascular causes each minute. Unfortunately, for many of these individuals, a fatal SCA event is the first and only manifestation of heart disease.

Research dollars directed to the fight against heart disease have increased appropriately by government and private organizations alike. Institutions delivering results are held especially high on the pedestal of medicine and those directing the battle are widely revered.

Today

October 1

8:28 PM

It was a beautiful twilight in October—a perfect end to a perfect day—not too hot, not too cold. Everything was just right in Evansville. The moon was a crescent sliver. Around it, a million stars hung high with a perfectly painted deep blue sky as the background. All seemed in place and at peace.

Erratic footsteps and loud chaotic breathing suddenly assaulted the calm of the serene autumn evening. The approaching dark form was Dr. Jack Norris. At this time,

Jack was not sure of anything—he knew not who he was, where he was or even what he was doing. He wore an expression of utter panic and fear. He was a tall, handsome man with dark features and a square jaw. His hair was disheveled. He looked awful and felt even worse. His heart hammered powerfully inside his ribs and he had a colossal headache. He walked rapidly, occasionally looking back. Then he ran for several yards. Jack scampered away from the hospital's main building, unpredictably changing from a rapid walk to a mad dash. His vision was cloudy at best; for short periods, it would become exceedingly focused. He was sweating profusely and panting ferociously. Weary. Wild. His mind had become nebulous and he simply was incapable of logical reasoning. There were horrible images in his mind, but he could not explain or understand any of them.

He entered and zigzagged aimlessly through the meandering streets of the affluent neighborhood that surrounded the Newton Memorial Hospital. As he ran, confusion, thundering palpitations, breathlessness, and headache became exacerbated exponentially. Occasionally, Jack had to stop, but this made him feel dizzy and faint. He developed increasingly severe bouts of abdominal cramping causing him to bend at the waist. Doing so provided brief and mild relief. Sporadic stints of nausea also ensued. As these symptoms would wax and wane, a heightened feeling that he needed to run would overcome him. He would scurry again. Stumbling faster, and faster.

To lighten his load in his escalating bewilderment, paranoia, and desire to escape, he had shed his lab coat. The white jacket had been tossed carelessly on the ground of the doctor's parking lot, his nametag over his left breast pocket—

Jack Norris, MD, Department of Cardiology, Section of Electrophysiology, Chief of Fellows. The coat pockets were full of accouterments including a stethoscope, personal digital assistant, and a couple of pens. There were also syringes, needles, a tourniquet, and three large drug vials. The vials were nearly empty.

He knew he had to escape, but he had no idea as to where he should head. Primitive feelings of self-preservation persuaded him that something or someone was trying to find him. And kill him. He needed to get away as fast and as far as he possibly could. He didn't know how he knew, but he knew that he was being hunted. It was imperative that he start planning an attack strategy. He had to strike first or he would die. And soon. How do you plan an assault when you can't reason or analyze the situation? He was now totally incapable of thinking rationally and only instinct ruled his actions. Deep down, Jack just knew his life was imminently in danger and he had to strike first. And he would. He intended to fight. He would fight to kill.

He ran straight into a driveway as the street meandered to the right then left. He skirted around the beautiful house. The almost palatial domicile was one of many luxurious homes in the area. It was dark out. As Jack stumbled forward, a motion detector was activated and a spotlight automatically came on, dumping bright light onto the driveway. Jack's eyes stung with the sensation of a thousand needles. The sudden brightness heightened his confusion and disorientation. Inside him, primitive, self-conservation emotions overflowed powerfully and overcrowded his mind, sharply adding to his panic and aggressive idealization. He would kill whoever was after him.

A barking dog could be heard in the near distance. Jack looked around frantically attempting to hone in on the origins of the growls. Was that his attacker? Jack ran pointlessly and nervously, unpredictably gazing in different directions as he contemplated the question. By now, he had turned the corner of the ornate home submerging him back into the darkness of the night. Just like the sudden bright lights a few seconds earlier, the sudden dimness augmented his befuddlement. His breath grew increasingly short and labored. He perspired copiously and his heart raced thunderously. He was lightheaded and weak. Waves of nausea and abdominal cramping recurred. He knew he couldn't continue this way for long, now staggering unhurriedly in the dark.

Jack suddenly and unexpectedly felt a sharp pain across his forehead and neck as he struck a tree limb. He fell backwards and lay prone on the grass beneath the tree, grunting noisily.

"Who's there?" an old man's voice could be heard coming from the back of the house.

"Close the door, Harold. I'm calling the police," whispered an old woman anxiously.

"I think someone might be hurt in the backyard and—" the man continued, as the door slammed shut followed by the sound of a loud bolt solidly locking the entry.

Jack tried to stand up but found it hard to do. He was too weak to bear his own weight, his chest heaving in and out, furiously. With difficulty, he struggled to roll over. Gathering all the effort and resolve he could muster, he managed to get on his knees. Sapless, he fell again, sprawled face down on the lawn. As he did so, he felt an uncomfortable feeling, as his left thigh area hit the ground. It was his cellular phone, deep in his pocket. He managed to get back on his knees and extract the mobile device. Mesmerized, he hypnotically gawked at the Treo 650, a Palm Pilot and cell phone combo device, like a cow staring at an incoming tornado.

What is this? What is it for? Jack tried to recall, but the brain synapses would not oblige, his mind increasingly garbled and unconnected to reality. Jack gazed at the phone turning it side to side. Accidentally, he pushed one of the keys. The keypad illuminated. Startled, Jack dropped the device. A few seconds later, he bent down to reexamine the cell phone. As he picked it up, he fortuitously pressed the Send button. A moment later, a voice emanated from the small device.

"Hello." It was a woman's voice. "Jack, are you there? Hello! Jack, are you okay, honey?" No reply. Silence. "Jack, are you hurt? It's Claire. Are you there?" the woman's voice persisted.

She could hear Jack articulate deep guttural sounds in the distance. The words were incomprehensible, but the message was meaningful to Claire—Jack was in trouble.

Drops of blood from Jack's forehead wound dripped onto the lit cell phone pad causing him to grunt and again drop the device.

"Jack, I'm calling Susan. I'll get help, honey."

The woman's voice fell on deaf ears.

8:48 PM

The Evansville Police Department Central Dispatch received a call from an elderly woman requesting immediate help. The 911 operator, Nicole Gehring, was a jolly, overweight, acne-ridden woman in her early twenties, with dark hair and big brown eyes. Her voice was pleasant, calm, and soothing, the result of both her personality as well as training for this position.

"A man is trespassing on my property. I'm afraid he'll try to get into my home and hurt my husband and me. Please come quickly," begged the old lady.

Nicole reassured the woman and instructed her to stay inside and lock all doors. She promised the caller that help was on the way. She knew the address. It was displayed on the computer in front of her, obtained from the caller ID database. She took notes in her logbook and radioed for all available police cars with instructions to proceed immediately to 3076 Bell Road, giving them the details of the call. Three police cars replied, stating they were available and on their way to the scene.

A few moments later, Detective Susan Quentin's cell phone rang. She was in bed with a lover. A lover she hadn't known long. They had met a few months earlier on a money counterfeiting case consisting of a complex web of events, involving law enforcement agencies from multiple jurisdictions. Since the crime had crossed state lines, the FBI became involved. The Bureau sent out two of its best and one of them was Detective Lieutenant Michael Ganz.

Mike was in his early thirties, blond hair, blue eyes, well built and always incredibly well dressed. Not only did Mike have the looks, he was also very bright and enjoyed the reputation of always cleverly solving the case. His outstanding success with the Bureau had caught the attention of his superiors who rewarded the charismatic Detective Mike Ganz with relatively quick promotions up the ranks. Despite this, Mike continued to be liked by his counterparts, in keeping with his outgoing personality and demeanor. The counterfeit case lead to repeated trips to Evansville, giving Susan and Mike a chance to get to know one another. In time, Mike's visits to Evansville changed from professional to personal and became regular and often. Soon they started a romantic relationship.

When the call came in the two detectives were in bed, naked under the covers. A bottle of merlot and nearly empty wine glasses were perched on a bedside table. The TV was on but the sound was muted, allowing for after-the-fact romantic conversation. Strewn clothes on the carpet gave testament to the intense passion of moments earlier. Surprised to get a call this late in the evening, Susan looked at Mike, who gave a sympathetic nod. With an intrigued look on her face, Susan sat up in bed and picked up the phone.

"Susan?" exclaimed an excited woman's voice even before Susan could speak. Susan was a walker, which amused Mike. She would do the phone march, pacing back and forth, as she spoke. Susan was a plain looking woman without distinguishing features. She had short blonde hair and bright blue eyes.

"Yes, with whom am I speaking?" replied Susan in a tranquil tone, promenading around the room.

"This is Claire," continued the voice on the other side of the call.

"Yes. What can I do for you, Claire?" Susan said, a smidgeon of irritation barely noticeable in her voice.

"I received a call from Jack's phone. I think something awful has happened to him. I think he's hurt. I heard him grunt in pain; he couldn't talk—" said the increasingly excited and anxious woman.

"Okay, calm down. Let me see what I can find out and call you right back," vowed Susan, her interest piqued.

"Oh, and Susan, are you with Mike? Mike Ganz?" asked Claire, speaking softly.

After a few more exchanges between the two women, Susan hung up and called the Police Central Dispatch Station.

"Hey, Nicole, it's Susan Quentin. Anything exciting going on?"

"It must be a full moon. All the crazies are out this evening. What can I do you for, Suzy Q?" replied the police dispatcher with a grin on her face.

"I'm looking for a man, a doctor," answered the detective.

"So am I but I'd take a lawyer or engineer, or—" interrupted Nicole, smirking.

"Dr. Jack Norris. He's helping us with a case," continued Susan, refusing to acknowledge the joke. "Word is that he's been hurt. Have you had to dispatch EMS recently?" Nicole realized Susan was serious and not in the mood for jokes.

"Yes, I dispatched the ambulance to the scene of a fight with injuries, and to a man's house that was having a heart attack," she replied, a professional tone now in her voice.

"Hang on. Tell me more about the fight with injuries. How old a man?" interrupted the detective.

"Teenagers down by the train tracks, both taken to the hospital," answered Nicole, still consulting her logbook.

"That doesn't sound like the man I'm looking for. What about the heart attack? How old?"

"Seventies."

"That's not him either. The man I'm looking for is in his thirties. What else?"

"Car accident, but the only injury was a woman from Ohio. No locals hurt."

"Okay, what else, and more recently?" persisted Susan.

"That's it for this evening. Tell me more about what you're looking for. Maybe I can—" her voice was interrupted by a radio communication from the officers at the scene on Bell Road.

"Delta three-five to dispatch."

"Hang on a sec, Suzy," said Nicole when the voice on the

radio transmission stopped. "Delta three-five, go ahead," she spoke into the microphone in front of her.

"Yeah, Delta three-five. We're at the scene behind the address you gave. Delta two-four and Delta one-five are out here also; we have a male, white, appears to be drunk and on some kind of—" he searched momentarily for the right word—"super high. He's totally out of his mind and out of control. We're trying to place him in protective custody, but he's a fighter. Call an ambulance; he'll have to go to Memorial."

"Standby, Delta three-five, I will dispatch an ambulance to your location."

Nicole picked up the red phone on her desk. It was labeled "Evansville Rescue Squad—Emergencies Only." After a few seconds, a voice responded and she spoke.

"Rescue one, you have an emergency at 3076 Bell Road. Male apparently under the influence. Delta three-five at the scene requesting your presence." A moment later, she hung up the phone and made a quick entry into the logbook in front of her, noting the time and the type of the dispatch.

"Delta three-five, EMS on the way," she verbalized into the microphone.

"Ten-four, dispatch, Delta three-five," a reply echoed from the radio.

"Back at ya, Suzy Q," Nicole spoke into the phone receiver she had put aside momentarily.

"What was that all about?" asked Susan.

"A drunk on crack," replied Nicole.

"Did I hear Bell Road? Isn't that by Newton Memorial

Hospital? Find out his name, please. And get more info on the man," solicited Susan.

"Hang on," said Nicole as she again put the phone down and picked up the microphone, using her dispatcher voice once again.

"Delta three-five, I have a detective on the landline requesting a name on the subject."

"Negative on ID, dispatch," replied the cop at the scene. As the officer communicated with the dispatcher on the radio, the background was filled with a cacophony of loud babble of unintelligible words, as the confused and highly combative Jack fought the cops with all his might. The police officers ganged up on Jack and continued to endeavor to subdue him. In his furious insanity, Jack proved to be a challenge for the cops, who were attempting to place him in a protective vest that bound his four extremities. This continued to prove extremely difficult with a young, strong, aggressive and highly combative and confused villain.

"Ten-four, Delta three-five. Can you give a description of the man?" asked Nicole.

"This guy is in his mid-thirties, clean shaven, well-dressed, clean baby-smooth hands. He's stoned out of his mind on some super speed drug but he's not seen a minute of hard work all his life. He has a few fresh needle marks on his left arm; it looks like he's been shooting up," noted the police officer.

"Nicole, I heard all that. That's him. Tell them I'm on my way. Don't leave the scene until I get there. I only live a few minutes away," Susan spoke hurriedly. The phone line went dead.

9:04 PM

The trees, bushes and flowers around 3076 Bell Road glowed intermittently with the multiple blinking red, blue and white lights and strobes over the three police cars parked in disarray.

The assailant continued to wrestle with the officers. The two older policemen, sergeants Pedro Sanchez and Penny Newman, held up flashlights, provided radio communication as necessary and gave general directions to the other four cops. Among them was a rookie named Alfred Smyth, who had joined the force five weeks earlier. He was well built and quite capable of contributing to the might required to subdue the assailant. But Officer Smyth was nervous about the whole affair. This was his first real situation, as he would later call it. He had taken the time to release the safety strap holding his handgun in the holster. As he attempted to subdue the agitated man, Al mentally rehearsed the steps required to put two bullets between the perp's eyeballs, should the restraining process suddenly prove inadequate. For now, the crazed man was on his stomach, his movements restrained. He groaned like a furious animal. Three of the officers held him down while a fourth attempted to place a protective vest on him. An attempt to handcuff the man was unproductive, as the thug fought like a big fish out of water.

The goon could not be reasoned with by the police officers. No way, no how. He was fighting like his life depended on it. He wanted to kill or be killed. It didn't seem to matter to him.

As the ambulance sirens were heard over the dead of night, the aggressor suddenly hyped up, his energy unexpectedly heightened. This occurred at the unfortunate exact time that the officers let up for a split second, their attention drawn to the approaching EMS vehicle. This allowed Jack Norris to jerk free and get up on his feet. He groaned loudly and prepared to attack, a rush of madness entering his body out of nowhere.

As the others prepared to re-engage in the restraining process, Officer Alfred Smyth stood back straight, feet comfortably apart, his Smith & Wesson .357 Magnum drawn with the madman's forehead inside his front and rear sights, safety latch released. As he had done so often at the Police Academy only a few weeks earlier, Officer Smyth took a deep steadying breath and prepared to gently squeeze the trigger.

"No!" exclaimed Sergeant Newman loudly as she heard the hushed click, click, click of the retreating hammer and rotating cylinder. This yell alerted all the officers, who reflexively looked at Al. So did Jack. But unlike the others, Jack remained clueless to the grave peril ahead.

"Don't shoot," commanded Sergeant Sanchez, taking long steps towards the young police officer.

The ambulance arrived at the scene, while the evening stillness was suddenly assaulted by the deafening sound of a gunshot.

Over a year ago

July 8

10:14 AM

Dr. Ian Rupert entered the research laboratory. As the door closed behind him, the tension in the department became almost palpable. He strutted towards the animal laboratory. The workers smiled and greeted him politely as he strode by—some out of respect, most out of fear. Dr. Rupert was an influential man who was world-renowned in the field of research especially, that which involved cardiac investigation. He was a middle-aged, tall, lean, gray-haired, distinguished looking man, whose work had contributed significantly and often to the medical literature. He was in charge of the research department at the Medical School in Indianapolis. As such, he commanded a lot of respect. When Newton Memorial was designated as the major research hub of the medical school, Rupert moved his office to the hospital in Evansville, leaving behind the large campus of the mecca that was the great medical school in the capital. Besides a full complement of research PhDs, MDs, techs and assistants, Dr. Rupert had under him several research fellows, doctors-in-training that pursued the acknowledgment of having worked under the tutelage of the great professor. The research department cranked out multiple scientific papers, in many fields of medicine, giving the school a reputable name and recognition in the medical world.

With an air more fitting of a Roman emperor than that of a modern-day department head, Rupert sauntered toward the back of the laboratory passing by busy employees who took turns greeting the director. With every few steps, he would fake a smile and slightly nod his head, in response to the venerations.

The odor in the animal lab was distinct and unmistakable. It was a combination of animal urine and feces intertwined with the mixed scents of cedar chips, chlorine bleach, air deodorizer and God knows what else, used in a feeble attempt to mask the stench. Multiple small-animal cages were on display throughout the large room. Rupert entered a smaller area inside the animal lab, pushing past a door labeled Cardiovascular Research. Just beyond the door, a group of scientists in white lab coats gathered around several small cages. Each cage was marked with a sign, LFJ659, and contained four rats, one tagged with an ankle bracelet. Underneath the large print label, the signs also indicated, in smaller print, the dosage that had been administered to the marked rat in the cage. The research team was somberly discussing and documenting the results.

"How are these beauties doing today?" asked Dr. Rupert regally of no one in particular, as he approached. None uttered a word, but their body language spoke volumes, all eyes fixated on the contents of the cages in front of them. There was a sense of failure and sorrow for the animals. The initial smile on Rupert's face faded rapidly. The small creatures in the cages were all dead.

"Cut down the damned dose even more. It's still too high. Do you know how much damned money and time is invested in this drug? Right now, this stuff is nothing but rat poison. And find out why the damned control rats are dying. Let's get more rats in here and this time let's get some results," shouted Dr. Rupert angrily with obvious disappointment and annoyance in his voice.

"Clean up this mess," he commanded as he turned around, departing the area. The door slammed closed with a crash behind him.

Nine months ago

January 6

3:14 PM

Dr. Ian Rupert sprawled comfortably in his lazy chair, his feet up and his left hand around a snifter of warmed cognac, which he sipped occasionally. In his right hand, Dr. Rupert spoke calmly but confidently into a handheld recorder in between making expressive pantomimic faces after a sip of the exquisite spirits. His recorded voice would soon be plugged into his laptop and replayed, allowing for a computer-driven automatic transcription, which would be saved on a thumb-drive. Rupert would meticulously and obsessively document the progress of every research endeavor, the newest of which was a drug under development in the hopes of helping patients with congestive heart failure. After several months, the experimental potion he termed Rat Poison had started to show a glimmer of promise. His previous worries about the experimental drug LFJ659 were now behind him, with the promise of smooth sailing ahead.

"Research protocol LFJ659. January 6, 2006." Rupert would always start his dictations in this way. After a quick moment to gather his thoughts, he pressed the Record button again and continued to speak into the microphone:

> We have finally derived the appropriate dose. At a dose of 0.00025 micrograms per kilogram, the CHF rats given LFJ659 were able to exercise significantly longer than the control rats. Furthermore, as compared to the control animals, those given the experimental drug were able to exercise harder and experienced less heart rhythm disorders. These results have been consistently predictable over a period of up to two weeks. No death occurred at this dose. We will start a long-term experiment with LFJ659 looking at exercise tolerance, exercise capacity, arrhythmia burden and the incidence of sudden cardiac arrest. Once we evaluate the long-standing effects on the rodent CHF model, we will progress to the human phases. This is very exciting work with a lot of promise for the future management of the CHF patient.

Rupert paused and took another sip of cognac. One more

obligatory facial expression of pain, as the spirits slid down, flaming his esophagus. He got up slowly and walked toward his elegant desk.

"Donna, arrange a meeting for tomorrow morning at ten o'clock with Dr. John Connor and James Miller to discuss the next phase of Rat Poison. Have John begin to work on the IRB forms and process," commanded Rupert, authoritatively pressing the intercom button. Just outside the door, Donna, his secretary, quickly acknowledged the request. He sat back comfortably in his lazy chair.

"This drug is going to make me rich and famous," he said. This time he had not pushed the Record button. Instead, he put the Dictaphone down on the table next to his chair. He smiled and took the last particularly big gulp of cognac. The face again. This time, he ended it with an Aaaahhhh of contentment.

Eight weeks ago

August 3

7:59 AM

Dr. Jack Norris arrived at Meeting Room Three. He looked around the room and took his usual seat in the front. For a thirty-one-year-old doctor in his last year of training, Jack had accomplished quite a lot. His superior intellect had been obvious to those in charge, who bestowed upon him the title of Chief of Cardiology Fellows. His duties would consist of dealing with the everyday routine of supervising the training of young doctors and medical students.

This morning, like all others, Morning Report would start at eight o'clock in the morning. He would meet with all the resident doctors and medical students rotating through the cardiology service and discuss the cases admitted during the on call period, which began at five o'clock the evening before.

Meeting Room Three contained many seats, which gave it the appearance of a classroom. On display were several X-ray viewing boxes, a large blackboard and a retractable screen, which would be used to display images from an old-fashioned projector or PowerPoint presentations. A podium was to be used by the presenter.

The room was filled with eighteen young doctors in training, ranging from first-year interns to third-year medical residents. Also present were cardiology and electrophysiology fellows and twelve medical students, three of whom were complete newbies, today being their first day. They were the students assigned to Jack's group for the next two months on their cardiology and electrophysiology elective rotations.

"Let's see the list, George. How many hits did you get last night?" asked Jack.

"We admitted five patients. Here's the list," replied Dr. George Snyder, a second-year cardiology fellow who was in charge of the on call team the evening before. George was a short balding man who appeared much older than he really was, especially today with his unshaven face. His hair was short and dark. His eyes were brown and piercing.

As he perused the list of the five admitted patients, Jack announced, "Before we begin, let's welcome the three new med students. They will be with us for the next couple of months. Dr. Snyder, do you know the difference between medical students and a pile of dog shit?"

"Nobody goes out of their way to step on a pile of dog shit," answered all the residents monotonously, slowly and in unison. Their tone of voice indicated plainly that this joke was as old as dirt.

"No, no, no. Dog shit is crap. Medical students are invaluable members of our mean and lean team. They're here to help us and to learn under our tutelage; let's teach them," said Jack with jocularity.

After a few chuckles, everybody quieted down. On the viewing boxes hung X-rays showing two views of someone's chest, the most prominent shadow of which was the large cardiac silhouette.

Jack broke the silence. "Let's start this morning report." Jack scanned the list of admissions one last time. "Let us hear about Mrs. Lucille Hart. What is wrong with Mrs. Hart's heart?"

George Snyder was in charge of the presentation. He gathered his notes and walked to the podium. Another of the young resident doctors, Dr. Mary Taylor, a medical intern, got up and placed Mrs. Hart's X-rays on the view box then sat back down. By then, George was ready to start. As he spoke, Mary placed a copy of the presenting electrocardiogram on a projector displaying it on the screen, which another resident had lowered into position.

"Mrs. Hart is a sixty-one-year-old woman who has a history of heart disease with a known cardiomyopathy, an ejection fraction of thirty percent and recurrent admissions for congestive heart failure who presented with a tachycardia at a rate of 180 beats per minute. The EKG is shown here," George said, pointing to the large projection on the screen.

"Let's ask one of the medical students to decipher this mess for us. Who wants to go first? Start by telling us what a cardiomyopathy is, what the ejection fraction means, and what a tachycardia is?" interrupted Jack, as he looked about the room for volunteers.

"Cardiomyopathy is a general term indicating a dysfunctional heart. The ejection fraction is a measure of how well the ventricle pumps and the percentage of blood pumped out with each beat. Normal is fifty to sixty percent. Tachycardia is a rapid heartbeat disorder. This one is ventricular tachycardia," responded one of the students proudly.

"Very good," Jack said. "You are—" he asked, pausing for an answer.

"Peter Joseph, sir," answered the medical student nervously. He was one of the new arrivals.

"Okay, Mr. Peter Joseph Sir, why do you think the rhythm is ventricular tachycardia?" inquired Jack.

Peter smiled nervously, hardly aware that some of the others chortled from the way Jack called out his name teasingly. He was a young looking twenty-four-year-old, intelligent and highly motivated third-year medical student who had recently declared to all his classmates he was pursuing a career in cardiology. He loved to study the intricate workings of the heart and felt most comfortable with cardiac disorders. Before his arrival, Peter read many chapters in Braunwald's Heart Disease, Textbook of Cardiovascular Medicine, the bible of cardiology. He spent a great deal of time reading the chapter on myocardial infarctions, or MI, to review the mechanisms, physiology, and management strategies in the treatment of heart attack victims. During his reading, he came across the differential diagnoses of heartbeat disorders, including tachycardia, or rapid heartbeat disorders, some of which can be lethal. He wanted to shine during this month and since his mentor was an electrophysiologist, Peter wanted to know as much about arrhythmias as he could. He sought after excellent recommendation letters, a necessity if he was going to be accepted into a good cardiology program. Many had told him that he should not make this specific a decision so early in his career. After all, he still had to take many rotations and pass many exams in all the other disciplines of medicine, including pediatrics, surgery, psychiatry, and obstetrics and gynecology. He didn't care. His plan was to study it all just enough to pass the board exams and live through painfully long one-month rotations through the other services. These next two months were going to cover that which he loved most, cardiology and electrophysiology.

"Well, a previous heart attack would have provided Mrs. Hart with a heart muscle scar which is necessary for electrical reentry in the ventricle and to produce ventricular tachycardia. Other mechanisms of tachycardia would be rare given this presentation," answered Peter.

"Good job. You are absolutely right," said Jack. "Go on with the case, George."

"Mrs. Hart presented with severe shortness of breath, chest pains and dizziness. We were called stat to the emergency department and decided to cardiovert her to sinus rhythm, which we did successfully after intravenous Brevital for anesthesia," continued George.

"Pete, will you give us a 10 minute talk on Brevital anesthesia tomorrow?"

Peter nodded silently.

"Who wants to report on other therapies for the acute management of ventricular tachycardia?" Another student raised his hand and Jack nodded accordingly acknowledging the assignment. "What is your name?" he asked the student.

"I'm Christopher O'Neal, sir," answered the medical student. Just like Peter, Christopher was a third-year medical student of the same age, but unlike Peter, he detested cardiology. He thought it too cerebral. He preferred talking to people, instead of sticking tubes into their arteries and veins. He was considered the token psychiatrist of the bunch. He hadn't made up his mind yet about which branch of medicine he liked, but he knew he didn't want cardiology. As such, he dreamed of fast-forwarding through this rotation. Having met his mentor, Dr. Jack Norris, Christopher actually thought he was going to bear the cardiology cross relatively well. Christopher was plump and always happy with a big grin on his face that, at times, had gotten him in trouble.

"Oh, your last name is Sir, too. Are you twins?" asked Jack with a smirk. Jack gestured to the presenter to carry on.

"Her meds prior to admission were digoxin, one-fourth milligrams daily, and Lasix, forty milligrams twice daily," George said, continuing with the case presentation.

"Yikes, what's wrong with this picture? And tell us your name," asked Jack, of the third new medical student.

"I'm Taylor Twelly, sir. We're triplets." All laughed. "What's wrong with this picture?" repeated Taylor, pensively.

"Not fair. I asked you first," protested Jack.

"Not sure what the answer is," said Taylor. He was a tall and thin young man with a severe case of premature graying. This made him appear much older than his early twenties. He was in the do-not-like-cardiology-much camp with Christopher and sure was glad he was assigned to the cardiology rotations with Pete, who was likely to help him through what could be a painful couple of months.

"Peter or Christopher, let's play poll the audience. What's wrong with this picture?" continued Jack facing the new medical students.

"Well, with a known ischemic cardiomyopathy, low ejection fraction, previous MI and history of congestive heart failure, this patient should have been on—," Peter proudly piped in, before being interrupted.

"Okay, I got it now. Sorry. She should be on a beta blocker and ACE inhibitor," interrupted Taylor.

"Don't forget aspirin, Plavix, and a statin," added George.

"And what else?" asked Jack, looking at the audience in the room.

Dr. Mary Taylor, the on call intern, said, "Aldosterone antagonist. What do you make of her being on Lasix without potassium or magnesium supplementation?"

"Yes, I noticed that too. What were her admission electrolytes?" asked Jack.

"Very low. Potassium, 3.1 and magnesium, 1.5," answered George, picking up and reading from his piles of notes on the case.

"So, what's wrong with this picture?" reiterated Jack. No one answered. After a moment of silence, Jack continued.

"Bad doctor syndrome. This woman is lucky to be alive. Who's the attending on the case?"

"Dr. Skinner, the best cardiologist in Evansville," replied Mary, in a mocking voice recalling what a patient had said of Dr. Joel Skinner a few days earlier.

Dr. Skinner was a pleasant and calm man in his early fifties with graying temples, whom his patients absolutely adored. He would hold their hand at the bedside and listen to their many complaints. Unfortunately, like so many busy doctors in private practice, there was no time to keep up with the literature. Often his patients would not be on the appropriate, evidence-based medicines. He was treating them based on what he learned decades earlier in medical school. He bragged that he went to school at Yale, a great medical institution. Unfortunately, he never learned to teach himself. He had many patients and they all seemingly loved him. Because of insufficient medical therapy, his patients would have repeated admissions for the same problems. They were not appropriately referred to other specialists, as demanded by recent guidelines and management protocols. The only salvation these patients had was when they arrived in the emergency department late in the evening. The great Dr. Skinner would, in those circumstances, allow the hospital staff to manage the patient until he could make rounds the next day.

The young doctors would have to work fast. They would discuss the case in detail, formulate an appropriate plan and write their collective opinions in the chart, including necessary cardiac testing and prescribe the right medications. They would also educate the patient and family. The great Dr. Skinner would go along with the plan—another one saved. Fortunately, Skinner would not make his rounds today until early afternoon, so there was time.

"What do you have planned for Mrs. Hart's heart?" asked Jack.

"We should look for cardiac ischemia with a stress test. Start her on aspirin, Coreg, Altace, spironolactone and Lipitor and stop her Lasix and digoxin. Correct her potassium and magnesium," answered George.

"And—" Jack queried inquisitively with eyes wide open.

"Defibrillator," replied George and several other residents, almost in unison.

"Yes, if the heart doesn't improve on optimized medical therapy, she is at risk for sudden cardiac arrest and is a candidate for implantation of a defibrillator. Great job, people! Go write up the chart and talk to Mrs. Hart and her family about our recommendations. Remember to be kind to Dr. Skinner, but truthful. Be politically correct. I mean don't and I emphasize don't say: 'Your doctor hasn't read the literature in ten years and has you on all the wrong meds.' I'll go by and co-sign your orders and notes later." These issues with doctors not following appropriate guidelines really infuriated Jack.

One of the residents gave a review lecture on the use of Plavix in patients who undergo a coronary angioplasty with stent deployment. This was scheduled the day before, when the subject came up during morning report. By the time he was finished, it was nine o'clock in the morning and time to go make bedside rounds. The group discussed the steps to be taken the rest of the morning and plans to meet for lunch. The medical students followed Jack out of the classroom, like a group of ducklings following momma duck.

"Some doctors don't keep up with the literature?" asked Pete rhetorically, as they walked out.

"It's like if you go to an accountant to do your taxes, but he hasn't read about the recent loopholes and does your taxes with the information he learned in school twenty years ago. Can you imagine?" said Jack angrily, obviously irritated with the notion. "Don't get me started." He continued to walk toward the elevator, the students following in his wake.

"What do you call the guy who graduates last in his medical school class?" inquired Jack a few beats later, briefly looking back at the students who were walking slightly behind him. The three young men looked at each other puzzled. A slight grin on their faces suggested they understood a punch line was about to be delivered.

"Doctor," answered Jack, after a few seconds. The elevator arrived on their floor.

"Going up?" asked Jack holding the doors opened for the others to enter. He pushed the button with the number eight, illuminating it. Four older people stood quietly in the elevator staring up at the numbers over the door, seemingly unaware the others had entered. Number two was illuminated, announcing they were on the second floor. The complete silence inside the car was broken by the sound of the motor revving up. The car ascended slowly with an almost imperceptible jerk. Jack looked at the students then back at the numbers, imitating the others.

On the third floor, one older woman exited the elevator and an even older man entered. He pushed number six which then also became illuminated. On the fourth floor, a beautiful woman entered the elevator. No words were exchanged.

All stared at the numbers over the door, although they would much rather ogle at the lady. As the door opened on the sixth floor all exited except the medical team and the gorgeous woman. She was to die for. She was blonde with beautiful hazel eyes and long hair. She stood straight resembling a model about to strut down the runway of a fashion show. All her features were perfect. Her lips were just right, resembling a doll's. She wore a skirt and blouse that revealed close to nothing but concealed a world of sensuality, the likes of which the young men could only imagine. The elevator door closed and the car resumed its upward climb.

"The one of you that can tell me what number I'm thinking of gets to have an unforgettable evening with me," she said sexily, still looking up at the elevator numbers.

The medical students looked at each other in disbelief. The most beautiful woman each had ever seen just proposed to go on a date with the one guessing the right answer. Was she toying with them? Was this a dream?

"Zero?" exclaimed Jack, confidently.

"That's right," she answered excitedly. She turned to the medical students.

"Do you guys mind getting off at the next floor?" she asked in a very sensuous voice, slithering her elegant body towards Jack. Behind him, she massaged his shoulders and ran her hands down his chest and her right leg up Jack's thigh. Her skirt rose up her leg ever so slightly, exposing her knee and the lower portion of her shapely thigh.

The medical students were flabbergasted. Speechless. They could not believe their eyes; their hearts began skipping beats.

Suddenly the elevator door opened. It was the seventh floor. A well-dressed older man in his sixties walked into the elevator in front of the medical students. It was Dr. Thomas Lindsborg, Head of the Department of Medicine and, as such, he was Jack's boss. Dr. Lindsborg was a pleasant and kind man with a special knack to make those in his presence feel welcomed and at ease. Jack and the young woman stopped and stood up straight, as if the principal had just almost caught two mischievous teenagers engaged in a high school prank. As the medical students moved aside to give room for the older man in the car, Dr. Lindsborg glimpsed at Jack and the pretty woman.

"Hi Jack. Claire, good to see you. I wish my wife worked in the hospital, too. You are a very lucky man, Jack," said the distinguished older man.

"Good morning, Dr. Lindsborg," said the young woman. "Yes, I love to come and see my husband now and again. I want to make sure he doesn't stray with all the beautiful nurses on campus," she continued.

"Claire, Jack is so in love with you, you need not worry about such things. Isn't that right Jack? Oh, are these your medical students for the month?" asked Dr. Lindsborg, turning towards Jack.

"Yes, sir. This is Pete, Taylor and Chris. We just finished morning report and are about to start ward rounds," answered Jack.

"Okay, carry on, I'll meet up with you later," said Dr. Lindsborg, as the elevator door opened on the eighth floor and all got off, except the older physician who continued on to the tenth floor.

"Claire," said Jack sounding irritated. "What if I didn't get the number right this time and one of these guys guessed it?"

"Baby! Honey! Don't you know you and only you have my number? No one else." Claire answered using a sweet tone of voice. "Good to meet you guys. Did he tell you the one about the dog pile yet?"

Mesmerized and totally enthralled, the wide-eyed students nodded nervously, still unable to speak.

"Meet you later for lunch?" asked Jack.

"Sure, see you all later," answered Claire with a stunning smile. She walked in the opposite direction and turned the corner.

Practically paralyzed and dazed, the young medical students stood there speechless, silent and motionless, the events of the last few minutes still playing wildly in their heads.

"Wow," whispered Taylor softly, finally breaking the weary silence. Amused by it all, Jack walked ahead.

"Come on, knuckleheads! We're behind schedule already."

9:24 AM

Jack and his students walked briskly towards the nurses' station. Jack knew there was a lot of work to be done and he didn't want to take a chance of missing lunch with his lovely wife. They had to work fast.

"Code blue, CCU, bed five," repeatedly announced an excited voice over all the beepers in unison. The men made a beeline to the Coronary Care Unit. On their arrival, they saw many people inside the small cubicle that contained bed number five. A petite brunette nurse kneeled on the bed, her knees touching the seemingly lifeless body of the patient. She was performing chest compressions. Other nurses in the room performed the other duties necessary for a successful outcome in a case of cardiac arrest. Dr. John Connor was already in the room.

"What's the 411?" asked Jack calmly looking directly at John. Jack continued before Dr. Connor could say a word. "Can we get whoever is not directly involved in the code to step outside? We got too many people in here."

Some people turned and backed out of the cubicle giving Jack room next to the bed of the motionless body. CPR was ongoing with a distant cadence: "one-one thousand, two-one thousand, three-one thousand, four." At each count of five, a respiratory therapist would squeeze a bag that was both hooked up to the oxygen outlet on the wall as well as a tube coming out of the patient's mouth, which had previously been inserted into the windpipe.

As words were exchanged, Jack automatically and almost unconsciously eyed the chest excursion when the bag was squeezed. Jack compared the patient's chest movements to that of the stomach area, which was minimal. The patient's color was generally pink. With this rapid visual assessment, Jack was confident that the tube was properly inserted into the airway and that oxygenation was being performed adequately.

"This is a fifty-seven-year-old man who presented with chest pains. Cardiac markers negative times two. He just arrived a few hours ago. Sudden arrest with v-fib, shocked times three; we're on our second atropine and second epi. No results. Asystole on the monitor," verbalized John.

"Okay, John, you go ahead and run the code. Students stay here and watch a pro at work. Do not try this at home, kids. Leave it to the professionals," ordered Jack as he winked at John. Jack exited the cubicle to find the patient's chart. He wanted to assess all the lab data for this case.

"Where's bed five's, Bessie?" asked Jack of the ward clerk who anticipated the request and immediately handed the chart to the young doctor. As he sat down at the nurses' station with the chart in front of him, in the background the telltale escalating hum indicated that the external defibrillator was charging up to deliver another shock.

"Clear," then a thump was heard coming from the cubicle.

"No pulse. Again at 360. Continue CPR until ready to shock," requested John in a firm but calm voice. The process was repeated.

"No pulse," assessed John a few seconds after the shock. He continued: "What's the down time, Heather?"

"Thirty-two minutes, Dr. Connor," answered a woman's voice from within the room.

"Okay, let's call it; note the time of death," ordered John. Soon afterwards, one by one, the rescuers exited the room, a look of failure and sadness on their faces.

"Is this a coroner's case?" asked Jack, as John and the medical students joined him at the nurses' station.

"No," answered John quickly. "This is a clear cut cardiac event."

"Well, the guy just came in less than twenty-four hours ago, he ruled out, I think we need to call the coroners' office," disagreed Jack.

"Okay, I'll call them in a bit; first, I want to call the family," said John.

"What are you doing here, John?" asked Jack.

"I was here trying to recruit the patient into one of the research studies," answered John sitting down.

"Guys, this is John Connor. John, these are the guys."

The three medical students and John shook hands, each stating their name. As this was being orderly carried out, Jack continued: "John is one of our research fellows. He'll tell you what types of patients he needs so you can scout for him."

"I'll give each of you the inclusion and exclusion criteria for what I need. I'll have my beeper number on there so you can contact me ASAP if you find a potential candidate," stated John in a professional voice. With a complete change of demeanor, John playfully and excitedly turned to Jack.

"Hey Jack, what time's the game on Sunday?" Then turning to the students he asked, "Any of you bozos play soccer? We need a goalie on Sunday."

The students shook their heads.

"You gotta stop taking on students that don't play soccer, Jack."

"Well, to pass this rotation, they have to learn soccer. If we have time, we'll teach them a little cardiology," Jack continued. "Are you coming over Saturday for the Chelsea versus Major League Soccer all-star game? Plenty of beer and pretzels."

"Sorry, I forgot to tell you. The head coach for the MLS all-star team called and wants me on the team. Can't say that I blame him," said John.

"Oh, why, do they need a water boy?" stated Jack, smirking.

"I don't know, but since I'm on the team, I'll put in a good word for you, Jack," said John.

"Are you coming over to watch the game?" inquired Jack once again.

"I'll come. I want to hang out with your wife. I have to try to talk her into leaving you and marrying me. The game's at five, when should I show up?"

"Come at eight. If the door is locked and nobody answers, go back home."

"Very funny," said John sarcastically. "Good to meet you, boys; I hope you can be a good role model and provide adult supervision for Dr. Jack Norris these two months. Gotta make a phone call and get back to the laboratory," said John, pronouncing the last few words in a Transylvanian vampire accent, mockingly, as he left the nurses' station.

Heather McCormick and Julie Gerharp entered the room and sank down onto a large couch, expelling deep breaths as they did, sounding exhausted. They were both young but dedicated nurses that had worked in CCU for a couple of years. They were bright and thorough, qualities Jack really admired. He felt very confident in their patient assessments. Julie had been in charge of doing CPR. Heather took notes and gave the intravenous medications ordered by the code leader. Here and there, Heather would give a suggestion that was usually respected. She would say: "It's been five minutes since the last epi." This would be a clue that it was time for the doctor in charge to re-order the administration of epinephrine in the resuscitative efforts of the dying patient. Instead of saying: "Don't stop CPR for so long," she would ask: "Doctor, do you want us to continue CPR?" She knew very well that the answer was yes, but she had mastered the way to contribute positively to the situation and yet give the appearance that the mighty doctor was really making all the decisions. Julie was totally devoid of this quality. She called it like it was. If something was being done incorrectly, she would simply point out the facts and demand an explanation for the deviation from protocol.

"Dr. Norris," started Heather. There was something bothering the two nurses.

"What's up?" answered Jack with a concerned tone. The students remained quiet.

"Why do you think Mr. Roper died?" asked Heather.

"Well, because rule number one: patients die; rule number two: doctors and nurses can't always change rule number one."

"Come on, we're serious," interjected Julie, getting the notion that Jack was teasing.

"We've noticed a few patients, usually pretty young, in their forties or fifties, who come in with chest pains, rule out for a heart attack, but die for no apparent reason. Like Mr. Roper," continued Heather.

"We've had three between the two of us over the last couple of months. Roper is number four," interjected Julie.

"Weird, huh? Get me their charts; I'll see if there are any common denominators," dismissed Jack.

"They all become agitated; the monitors suddenly show tachycardias, for no good reason," continued Julie not wishing to be dismissed so easily. Heather remained silent with a concerned look on her face.

"This may be nothing or just a coincidence, Dr. Norris. But there seems to be an epidemic of cardiac arrests in otherwise healthy relatively young male patients," said Heather.

"Okay, I promise to look into this. Get me the charts. Put them on my desk," Jack remarked in a fatherly, calming and soothing voice trying to reassure the women.

"Thanks," they said as they prepared to leave the room.

"Ladies, before you go. These are the medical students for the month, Pete, Taylor and Chris. This is Julie and that's Heather. They are the best nurses in the world," said Jack making the introductions.

"Good to meet you, guys. Welcome to Memorial. Dr. Norris, I bet you say those nice things about all the nurses in the hospital," said Heather. The nurses exited the small room, smiling.

"These gals are like mother hens." Jack turned to the medical students. "That's a good thing. They really watch over their patients. Nurses like this are to be respected. They will save your ass many times throughout your career. Oh, and they like chocolate. They all love chocolate. Are you taking notes? These are great clinical pearls."

The four men rose and walked out of the nurse's station. Rounds continued uneventfully afterwards. Jack assigned each student a patient to review and discuss the next day.

"Read up on your patient, boys. I'm starting each of you with only one patient, so no excuses. Read up on their problems and be ready to talk about differential diagnoses, pathophysiology, clinical findings, and management options and so on. Okay?"

Six weeks ago

August 16

1:20 PM

The ambulance drove rapidly, slowing down at red lights, but not stopping completely. The emergency lights and siren signaled something dreadful was going on inside the emergency vehicle. Mr. Floyd Sullivan had called 911 when he developed pain in the middle of his chest while at work. He was only thirty-nine, although he looked much older. There was no history of heart trouble in his family and Floyd stopped smoking three years earlier. The paramedics had started an intravenous line and a bag of five percent dextrose in water was hanging, slowly dripping into his vein. A clear plastic cannula delivered two liters per minute of oxygen into his nostrils, the tubing hanging over his ears. The cardiac monitor indicated a steady heart rhythm at eighty-two beats per minute. Occasionally, a skipped beat, referred to as premature ventricular contraction or PVC, disrupted the steady and regular beeping sounds. The patient seemed stable but a rapid transfer to the hospital was nonetheless customary. No words were spoken during the twelve-minute ride to Newton Memorial Hospital.

"What ya got?" asked a nurse as they arrived at the emergency department's ambulance bay.

"Chest pains, gone after two sublingual nitros. IV with D5W. Monitor with normal sinus rhythm and frequent PVCs," answered the paramedic, giving a brief report as the team rushed the stretcher with the scared patient into the depths of the emergency department.

"Okay, put him in room three," commanded the nurse, totally disregarding the patient who quietly listened to the entire conversation of medical lingo, clearly not understanding much of it.

With this, the paramedics wheeled the stretcher to the appropriate room where another nurse and technician greeted the team.

"This is Sully. His full name is Floyd Sullivan. He had chest pain relieved by nitro. Monitor shows frequent unifocal PVCs." The paramedic repeated the report to the receiving nurse while the team slid the patient from the stretcher to the hospital bed. The heart monitor leads were exchanged, replacing the ambulance gear with like hospital equipment. These multiple steps were accomplished in less than fifteen seconds, as if by a well-oiled machine. It was easy to imagine that this process was skillfully repeated numerous times each shift and was now attained without conscious effort by the emergency workers.

The paramedics said goodbye to the patient, wished him well and left.

"How are you feeling now, Sully?" asked the nurse.

"The chest pain is back a little bit. It's not as bad as it was at work," answered the patient. The technician started to hook the patient up to an EKG machine in order to produce the required electrocardiogram.

"Hold still while I do this. If you move, the signal doesn't come out right and the doctors make me do this all over again," said the technician. Sully complied.

"Dr. Norris," yelled the nurse to the passing young doctor. He was leading the group of medical students and young doctors in training back upstairs having been summoned earlier to render an opinion about a rhythm strip that turned out to be artifact and harmless. The team was eager to return and finish rounds on the fifth floor before Grand Rounds, a weekly conference at the hospital delivered by an outside guest speaker. Today's topic, Sudden Cardiac Arrest in Patients with No Structural Heart Disease, to be delivered by Dr. Anton Damato, a famous electrophysiologist, promised to be a great learning opportunity.

"What's up Lorrie?" answer Jack making a sudden stop and entering room three. The others followed him into the small room.

"This is Mr. Floyd Sullivan. He goes by Sully. He had some chest pains, which were relieved by nitro, but returned. He is having frequent PVCs. Can you look at him for me?" inquired Lorrie Nunez, the head nurse in the emergency department.

"For you, anything," smiled Jack as he took the chart. He shook the patient's hand. "I'm Dr. Norris. What does the pain feel like?" he asked spying the electrocardiogram on the bedside table. A few seconds later, he picked up the EKG printout and handed it to Dr. Kathryn Mansfield, a first year cardiology fellow. Kathy accepted the tracing and stared at it inquisitively.

"It's like a fire on the inside of my chest, doc," answered the patient calmly.

"What does the EKG show, Kathy?" asked Jack turning to the young doctor.

"Lots of PVCs, otherwise normal," answered the cardiology fellow who, by now, had passed the electrocardiogram to one of the students. The three medical students now analyzed the tracing, as they listened to the exchange.

"Can you say anything else about the PVCs?" persisted Jack looking directly at Kathy.

"Remember, I'm just a plumber; I'm not an electrician," she replied, indicating she was much more comfortable dealing with issues involving the coronary arterial blood flow than with electrical matters, such as PVCs.

"Fair enough. But I want you to be able to recognize this pattern. The PVC has a tall R-wave in lead two and left bundle branch type morphology. This means it's coming from the front of the heart, the area called the right ventricular outflow tract or RVOT. The prognosis with these is excellent; they tend to occur with stress," said Jack confidently.

Turning to the patient who had a worried look on his face, Jack continued: "The skipped beats you may be feeling are not worrisome and your pain does not sound like it is from your heart. We're going to do some tests to be sure, but I'm not too worried at this point, okay? We'll give you some medicines to help your pain go away."

Jack smiled, as he looked Sully in the eyes, providing him with much needed reassurance. Placing his hand on Taylor's shoulder, Jack continued: "This doctor is going to stay with you and get you admitted to the hospital for observation. We'll know more by tomorrow morning. This is Dr. Taylor Twelly." This said, Jack turned to Taylor: "Do your thing and call me when you're done so we can go over the orders. The rest of us will go finish rounds upstairs." Both men nodded. As Taylor grabbed all the paperwork and sat on a chair right next to the patient's bed, the others exited the room.

Six weeks ago

August 17

10:42 AM

The doctors entered Sully's room, smiling as they did.

"How was your night, Mr. Sullivan?" asked Taylor.

"Not bad. No more pain. That medication you gave me really worked." Sully seemed happy and satisfied. "Am I going home today, doc? Please say yes."

Giving the impression that he disregarded the patient's question, Taylor turned to the group of doctors.

"His cardiac markers were negative times three. His

stress test was negative for cardiac ischemia or infarction and his LV function is normal. Protonix stopped his chest pain completely. I think he can go home," said Taylor feeling confident, but awaiting for approval from Jack nonetheless.

Jack turned to the patient.

"Your pain was not due to your heart, as we suspected. Your cardiac markers were normal. These blood tests tell us you did not have any heart injury. You had indigestion. Take the Protonix and follow up with your regular doctor." Sully gave thumbs up and an even bigger smile than he had mustered before.

"Thanks, doctors. You people are great. I'll call my wife to come pick me up," replied Sully still smiling.

Taylor and Sully shook hands. As the group exited the patient's room, Taylor stayed behind and said: "Give me a few minutes to do the paperwork and write you up a prescription. We may have some Protonix samples to give you." He left the room.

The team continued with rounds. The morning routine remained without incident. A few patients were discharged and as many admitted, each assigned to a medical student and a resident doctor.

After rounds were over, it was 12:34 p.m. Stomachs growling, it was lunchtime. The team walked downstairs to the cafeteria.

"Who's going to make Starbucks rounds today? It's on me," asked Jack looking for volunteers. Before one came forward, the pagers beeped rapidly and in unity, followed by an excited voice: "Code Blue, emergency department; Code Blue, emergency department." The young doctors proceeded to the location of the cardiac arrest immediately.

To their dismay, they saw that the man receiving CPR by the emergency department staff was Mr. Floyd Sullivan, whom they had just discharged in great condition just a few hours before. Disheartened, the cardiology team added their services to the ongoing efforts. The patient was intubated and ventilation was attained via a bag, which was being squeezed periodically, delivering oxygen through a tube directly into the dying man's lungs. Chest compressions were rhythmically delivered to the singsong: "One-one thousand, two-one thousand, three—"

None of them asked the question they all had on their mind: What the hell just happened? This guy was well a couple of hours ago. Despite all efforts, the code was unsuccessful and Sully was pronounced dead.

Nothing was said. The team would discuss the case later, entertaining different theories about what might have happened. For now, they all stood at the bedside, in silence, flabbergasted, defeated and sad. The worse was yet to come—to explain all this to Mrs. Sullivan.

An autopsy would later reveal that the patient died from an acute aortic dissection. This is an emergency condition that can lead to a quick demise due to intra-abdominal internal hemorrhage. The second the walls of Sully's main artery split apart then burst, he was a dead man. How he died was easy to explain. What remained mysterious was why this would happen to a healthy man like Mr. Sullivan. He had none of the risk factors associated with this clinical entity.

Five weeks ago

August 26

12:28 PM

Joe McIntyre was happy to be out. The last five days had been frightful, but now that he was leaving the hospital, he could breathe a sigh of relief. In fact, as he exited the front door, he did.

"I'm too young for this shit," he thought, still in disbelief that at age forty-two he had a heart attack. His father had his at fifty-four but unfortunately, the heart attack had suddenly stolen his life. Joe still remembered how his dad dropped to the floor, lifeless, like a sack of potatoes, while scolding him about smoking. Though Joe's father smoked for years, he had always forbidden Joe and his brother to take up the nasty habit. He sometimes would go on a rampage about how bad smoking was while puffing on a cigarette. The advice had been mostly fruitless and in vain. The warnings had been ignored.

The guilt was inevitable. Joe had been told many times that his father's demise was not his fault. He was not responsible in any way. Nevertheless, he had never forgiven himself. Yet, despite it all, Joe had taken up smoking having succumbed to peer pressure. Joe smoked one and a half to two packs of cigarettes a day. Despite nicotine being a stimulant, smoking gave him the feeling of calmness he had grown to enjoy and require. The nicotine abuse had been the major factor predisposing Joe to coronary artery disease. The arteries that feed his heart muscle had clogged up with plaque to about half the vessel's diameter. The blood could still flow unimpeded through the blockage and gave him no symptoms whatsoever. No symptoms until the morning of his heart attack.

He had gotten up at a quarter to six to the alarm clock, as he had done for the last eight years since he started working at the plant. Soon after getting up from bed, Joe started to feel a squeezing sensation in the middle of his chest, like a vice becoming ever so tight. He also noticed a cold sweat and a bit of nausea. One of his coronary arteries had become occluded by an expanding mass of clot a few seconds earlier, preventing all downstream blood flow. At that occlusion site, the plaque had suddenly cracked, exposing its inner materials to the streaming blood cells. Without blood flow, the front portion of his heart muscle would start to suffer irreparable damage.

He took an antacid to no avail. By then, his wife, Sheila, noticed his obvious discomfort as he paced the bedroom floor. Joe looked ghastly. She couldn't say why or how, but he didn't look like the man she knew for the last twenty-seven years.

Sheila knew about heart attacks. Her father had one a few years before. In a few seconds, she relived the pain and agony of the moments spent with her father at the time of his event. She knew Joe was having a heart attack. She dialed 911, gave details of the situation, answered some questions and an ambulance was dispatched. Fortunately, Joe had reached Newton Memorial within thirty minutes of chest pain onset, so the degree of heart muscle damage was still insignificant. As the ambulance arrived in the emergency department, he was rushed to the cardiac catheterization laboratory where doctors used a wire to disrupt the clot that had formed in the coronary artery. This was followed by a balloon, which stretched the blockage in the artery allowing normalization of blood flow. This angioplasty procedure was concluded by placing a metal mesh tube, or stent, that would stay in place, forever scaffolding the area, hoping to minimize the risk of re-occlusion. Thanks to the rapid actions by the whole team—from the paramedics at the home to the emergency department staff, cardiologists and catheterization lab personnel—blood flow was restored quickly and cardiac markers would later indicate only a small amount of heart damage. Because of some short episodes of rapid heart beating emanating from the site of the small heart attack, the cardiologists had sought an electrophysiology consultation. Jack and his team had evaluated this and opined that the arrhythmia would not require further specific treatment, other than the usual post heart attack management, which was already in place.

"If you smoke, you pay the piper in the end. On average, smokers live seven to ten years less and with reduced quality of life. Alternatively, you can decide to quit now and enjoy more years of productive life. Your choice! I can't do it for you, but I will meet you halfway, if you are interested."

Dr. Norris was all business, straight and to the point. Joe had only met him five days before but had an instantaneous connection to the young doctor. He appreciated his directness. Joe vowed to quit, even if it killed him.

Armed with a handful of pills and educational booklets on Percutaneous Coronary Interventions, Coronary Risk Factor Modification and How to Live after a Heart Attack, Joe left his hospital room determined to live.

9:12 PM

Joe and Sheila finally sat down to relax. They had supper, consisting of a meal low in sodium, fat and cholesterol. To drink, they had water. Despite the horror of the last few days, the couple had learned many important facts about heart disease and its prevention. Newton Memorial Hospital offered patient and family education for those admitted with heart disease. Joe participated in all the available exercise classes and smoking cessation programs and met with a nutritionist, who provided guidance in what to eat and drink. Sheila was supportive and attended the classes, whenever possible. Today's evening meal was their first solo attempt to follow the lessons. They were both experiencing feelings of accomplishment. It felt good.

The dishes were washed and put away. The kitchen table was cleaned and set for the next day. A vase with beautiful fresh flowers in the middle of the table provided balance and esthetics.

Joe and Sheila curled up on the couch in front of the TV.

"What do you want to watch? Law and Order, reruns of ER, CSI or—"

"Hey, let's look for some health-related educational program," recommended Joe, interrupting Sheila.

"Great idea. I'm tired of the same old shows. Here's the TV Guide," she replied, handing the small table booklet to Joe.

Outside, the air was warm. The small winding road in front of the McIntyre residence was silent and empty. The subdivision was either already asleep or getting ready to go to bed.

A large dark luxury sedan drove by slowly. The car stopped in front of the McIntyre's residence for a few seconds. Then, it drove on. Slowly. Observing. Stealthily searching. It would go around the block then stop short of the house. In the dark, quiet and still, like a jungle predator waiting for the right time to pounce on its prey, the car and driver would remain unnoticed.

Back inside the home, Sheila lay on Joe's right shoulder gently, as if she could break him if she pressed with the full weight of her head. The TV was on.

Suddenly, Joe stood up shaking Sheila off him. He was profusely sweaty and his pupils shrunk to the size of a pinpoint. He became progressively agitated and began pacing back and forth through the small family room. Sheila stood and watched for a moment, unclear as to what she was witnessing.

"What's wrong, honey?" she asked, her concern increasing.

"What? What d'ya say? Who's there?" Joe said, breathing a mile a minute. He looked confused and upset. But at what? Why? Joe continued to pace, with increasing speed and vigor. He looked wild eyed. Sheila tried in vain to calm him. The more she persisted, the worse he got. He seemed to have forgotten who she was.

She dialed 911. By the time Sheila got off the phone with the EMS operator, Joe was climbing on and off the couch. He rumbled on about strangers watching him from here and there. He pointed wildly to the TV, a window and the hall leading upstairs. He searched around the room, first behind the TV, then under the pillows. Then he grabbed a vase.

"Who are you? Stay back," Joe yelled. He then murmured something else, God knows what. Something Sheila could not make out.

"What baby? Tell me what's bothering you?" Sheila questioned, tears now flowing down her face.

"Go away!" she heard him say, in between other incomprehensible phrases. He used the vase like a shield and weapon, whenever Sheila attempted to come closer. For a short period, she was able to touch him. His heart thumped hard and fast inside his chest.

"Sweetheart, your heart is pounding fast. Let me take you to the hospital," she pleaded.

He turned to get away stumbling onto the ground. The vase broke in his hand, cutting him. Blood ran down his arm. Joe looked at his bleeding hand with confusion. A deep gash was visible from which crimson pulsated profusely with each heartbeat. This appeared to make him even more like a dangerous wounded animal, if that was possible. Not at all the calm, cool and collected man Sheila fell in love with many years before. Why was this happening?

Joe ran around the room aimlessly. Then, he paced frantically like a caged beast. He erratically looked around as he exited the family room stumbling towards the kitchen. As he entered the breakfast nook, he gave the appearance of a wild creature in unfamiliar surroundings cornered by perilous foes. He walked into the table scattering the plates they had just neatly arranged in the proper places earlier that evening. The pain caused Joe to stop and flinch. For a split second, Sheila connected with Joe, looking into his eyes. All she could see in those eyes was rage. By now, Joe's speech was an incomprehensible jabber. He was pale with rivulets of sweat streaming down his face. His chest wall overlying his heart was visibly thumping, even through his shirt.

Sheila tried again to approach him using loving and soothing words. Wildly and with furious madness, Joe opened cabinet doors and pushed appliances off the kitchen counter, becoming increasingly startled as these items hit the tile floor. He then pulled out the drawers causing them to fall on the floor noisily. This exacerbated his fury and anger. The next thing Sheila saw was a large butcher knife, which sliced her face from her left temple to the lower portions of her neck. She suddenly stopped moving and took her last normal breath. Joe had plunged the huge knife deep into her thorax, causing a sucking chest wound and lacerating her right ventricle. Blood and air gushed out of the wound as he removed the bloodied blade.

Joe looked at her dying face and paused. As her brain function hastily dissipated into nothingness, Sheila's last coherent thought was that she departed this world by the hand of the love of her life. She would never understand why. For a split second, Joe seemed to comprehend the gravity of the situation. He, too, met his demise, first dropping to his knees then falling flat on the kitchen tile floor smashing his face hard, the knife still in his hand. The impact caused a deep laceration on Joe's chin. Sheila's blood flowed and mixed with his, an expanding pool of blood surrounding both bodies.

Just outside the house, a mysterious well-dressed stranger peeped inside through a side window. He had made sure the sedan was hidden on a side street. It was dark out, the sky increasingly fuliginous with the advancing nightfall. As the sirens approached, the visitor swiftly departed, making certain he continued to remain unnoticed.

It would be later determined at autopsy that Joseph Matthew McIntyre died of a massive brain hemorrhage, the cause of which remained unidentifiable.

Four weeks ago

September 2

11:32 AM

It was almost lunchtime. The medical team took the elevator to the basement and the group walked toward the employee cafeteria. Jack and the students were going to meet Claire and John for lunch.

They went through the cafeteria line and each made their food selections.

"Do you need adult supervision here?" asked Jack as he approached the table where the students, John and Claire were sitting with their food trays. They had started to eat without him. Jack had stopped momentarily to talk to one of the medical attendings.

"Very funny, ha, ha, ha," mocked Claire, continuing to eat.

"Are we flying to the game this Saturday?" asked John with his mouth still full.

"Oh yeah," answered Jack. He turned to the students. "The three of us are flying to Columbus, Ohio to see the Crew play D.C. United. Any of you want to come along? We have room on the airplane." Jack paused waiting for a reply.

"I didn't know you were a pilot, Dr. Norris," said Peter.

"Oh, yes. He's a great pilot," answered John. "He says any landing he can walk away from is a great landing. Right, Jack?"

"Sure, so the propeller got stuck on the tree top. Big deal, we got to the ground, right?" Jack persisted with the joke.

"What are you saying?" asked Claire concerned.

"He's just kidding, honey," Jack interjected. "You know I am a good pilot. I make those soft landings you like. Unless the wind blows us off the runway onto the grass." Claire did not look amused. Deep inside her, there were still small butterflies about flying, though she would not admit it. She would fly when Jack asked her. But mostly, she did it for him, to be with him and go places with him.

"Jocularity—I recognize the style," interrupted Claire mockingly with a serious tone of voice. She didn't mind Jack's usual jestful mannerisms, however, certain topics were off limits. Flying jokes were definitely one of them.

"I forgot, no joking about flying. Claire does not like flying jokes," said Jack, facing all but Claire.

"So, what kind of plane do you fly?" asked Chris.

"Beechcraft Bonanza, A-36, the best single-engine airplane in the world. I love it," answered Jack.

"I love flying. I can't believe you fly and have your own plane. How cool is that?" said Chris enviously.

"You should come fly with me. Let me know when you want to go up. All I need to go flying is an excuse. Hey, want to come to the game this weekend?" asked Jack.

"I can't. I promised my parents I would visit this weekend. It's my little sister's birthday," answered Chris.

"So, what's up in research, John?" asked Claire hoping to change the subject. She knew Jack could go on talking about flying and airplanes for hours.

"We're doing some pretty neat research. I could tell you, but then—" John was rudely interrupted first by Claire, and then all the others joined in, "you'd have to kill us!"

"Seriously, you can tell us some stuff. What are we going to do, sell your trade secrets to the Russians?" continued Claire.

"Nowadays, it's not the Russians you have to worry about. It's the terrorists," said Peter.

"You guys cooking up weapons of mass destruction in the lab, these days?" asked Jack with a smirk on his face.

"Yeah, if you're a rat," said John. The whole group grinned. After a small pause John continued. "We're working on a new drug for patients with congestive heart failure. It stimulates the cardiovascular system and we hope will improve heart function, reduce cardiac mortality and improve quality of life. Do you know how many rats we have killed just trying to figure out the proper dose? For a while, we called the stuff Rat Poison. It took us several months just to get in the ballpark. We'll be starting human trials soon. I'm working on the IRB protocol right now."

"What's an IRB?" asked Peter.

"Institutional Review Board," answered John. "It's a committee that reviews and approves all research. It's made up of doctors, lawyers, clergymen, businesspersons and so on. All research has to be approved to make sure it's ethical and subjects are duly informed of their participation in the study, risks, that sort of thing. Once I have the protocol written up, we'll go before this board and get approval for human research with the drug. For now, the drug seems to be doing some good on rats, at least. If the dose is right. If we give too high a dose, the poor little creatures maul each other to death. Horrible stuff."

"How do you research congestive heart failure in rats? Do you have a CHF rat model?" asked Peter.

"Yes, we create the model by ligating the LAD and causing an anterior infarct," answered John.

"Doing what?" interrupted Claire looking at John, eyes petitioning for an explanation.

"We do open heart surgery on the rat and tie off the major artery that feeds the heart muscle, the LAD, or left anterior descending coronary artery. This causes a large heart attack in the front portion of the heart. The rats, subsequently, develop congestive heart failure. Then we can test our new drug."

"Poor little things," she returned, gloomily.

"Well, it's better them than me. I know one day, I'll be old and I'll get congestive heart failure. I want doctors to know how to treat me and help me live better and longer," said John.

“Have you seen some of these CHF patients? They really need help,” interjected Jack. The doctors and medical students nodded approvingly, all eyes on Claire.

“We also have this new gadget to study the heart muscle. It helps visualize the walls and see if there is infarcted or ischemic tissue there.” He then turned to Claire to define these terms for her benefit and continue with his explanation. “We are administering tiny air bubbles into the rats which allow us to improve visualization of the heart muscle. This permits determination of whether the muscle consists of healthy cells or cells about to die due to oxygen starvation or dead cells,” he paused to allow questions. Scanning the group for body language, John continued, “You should see the difference this stuff makes in helping us see what’s going on.”

“What type of imaging are you doing?” asked Jack.

“Ultrasound,” answered John.

“Neat,” exclaimed Peter. “Can we come down to the lab and see it?”

“Sure, come down today. Are you guys finished with rounds?” asked John.

“Almost,” answered Jack. “We’ll stop in later, if we have time.”

“I have a slow afternoon. I would love to see the lab, too, if it’s okay,” said Claire.

“Of course. I’ll see you later. I’m late for a meeting.” John got up and left at a fast pace.

Lunch over, the group dispersed. The medical team returned to rounds and Claire returned to the psychology department, where she had a patient to see in twenty minutes.

3:12 PM

There was one more patient to see. The team gathered around the bed of the elderly woman, Pete's patient. He began the bedside comments.

"This is Mrs. Joy Nathan. She is eighty-six and presented with an acute coronary syndrome three days ago. She had coronary angiography, which showed an occluded right coronary artery. This was angioplastied and stented two days ago. That was followed by atrial fibrillation. We were called on consult."

"Doctor, what is arterial fibula?" asked the patient, her face showing signs of concern.

"Atrial fibrillation," corrected Pete finishing the sentence for her. "It's an electrical problem in your heart affecting the top two chambers. Instead of beating, they are quivering fast.

That makes the bottom two chambers of your heart go fast and out of rhythm. It also puts you at risk for clots which can cause strokes."

"Oh, I don't want a stroke. My mother died of a stroke. My father lived with a stroke and I think my mother was better off than my poor father," said Mrs. Nathan.

"We've started you on Coumadin and Lovenox. These are blood thinner medications that prevent clots from forming so you won't have a stroke," continued Pete.

"I noticed that you gave me a few new medicines," she said.

"Yes, the other is a beta-blocker to lower your heart rate," said Pete. "If your blood is thinned enough and your pulse is slower by tomorrow, we'll give our okay for you to be discharged."

The other doctors had been standing back listening to the exchange between the elderly woman and the medical student. Then, the group left the room giving the patient reassuring smiles.

"How have her numbers been? Is she fully anticoagulated?" asked Jack as they reached the hall outside room 817, where a cart with many patient charts was waiting.

"I have them right here," said Pete. He proceeded to dig into his pockets. First, his lab coat pockets, then he put down his clipboard to facilitate the process and dug deep into his front pant pockets, then the shirt pocket and finally the pockets in the back of his trousers. All grinned at this amusing display of disorganization. Finally, Pete returned to the clipboard he had put down over the chart-rack.

"Hah, here they are." Pete removed several papers, which

he spread out on display over the chart stand in front of them. Several fell off on the floor. Pete bent down to pick them up causing more to fly off. The other two medical students joined the process. As this scene, befitting a Three Stooges episode, was unfolding, Jack looked up the lab values on his handheld Palm Pilot.

"Hey, Larry, Curly, and Moe," interrupted Jack shaking his head. "Here's the INR. It's one-point-four-seven today. What do you want to do, Pete?" he asked.

"I'll give her five of Coumadin, today," he answered with authority.

"Okay, write the order so we can get out of here," said Jack, as he dialed a number on the phone at the nurses' station.

"I'd like to make an appointment, please," he said in a serious voice a few seconds after dialing. "When's the next available appointment for Dr. Claire Norris? I have a patient for her; a med student with an aversion to orderliness." By then they could all see that he was playing a joke. He forced a smirk. "Are you ready to meet us downstairs?" he asked. "Okay, we'll be there in a few."

Pete had written his order and placed the chart in one of the appropriate slots for charts with orders. Chris pushed the rack with all the other charts and, with Peter's help, in no time, all the charts were where they belonged. The group walked towards the stairs. On the way down, they discussed the clinical issues relating to Coumadin therapy and the need for frequent monitoring using INRs—International Normalized Ratios.

"Perfect timing," said Chris as he opened the door for Claire and all others to enter the research laboratory. Having walked a few feet into the lab, they were spied by John Connor who strolled towards them greeting them.

"Welcome to my home away from home. I just purchased a new scent spray. I hope you like it," said John taking in a big breath through his nostrils. All imitated him and in doing so, experienced the typical odor that was the animal lab. They walked toward the ultrasound room, first passing through the animal lab where the smell intensified significantly. As they passed by the rat cages, John spoke more about the CHF experimental drug. A sign indicating the purpose of the work in this area was on display: Experimental Drug LFJ659.

"This is Rat Poison, the drug I was telling you about at lunch," said John continuing to walk. The others followed him. "LFJ659 is being tested to try to improve the quality of life in patients with CHF. It stimulates heart contractions and improves blood flow through the circulation. The mechanism of action remains unknown but it is different than any other known cardiovascular treatment. The drug seems to improve CHF in the rat model. We'll see what it does in humans when we get that phase started. I will need your help to recruit patients for this study, okay?" asked John looking back at the students who nodded. They entered the ultrasound room.

"Here we have an echocardiogram of a rat. This is not too different structurally from that of a human. Just smaller." As he talked, John touched the appropriate buttons on the ultrasound machine and the screen came alive, revealing a little rat heart beating rapidly.

"This is faster than I'm used to seeing," said Peter. Jack nodded agreeingly.

"The normal heart rate of a small mammal is much faster than an adult human," explained John. Despite being faster, Jack was confident he could read the rat's echocardiogram. The ultrasound on the screen showed the heart chambers allowing visualization of the heart valves and major blood vessels entering and leaving the heart.

For the benefit of the students and Claire, John pointed out the structures visualized on the screen.

"This is the left ventricle," he said using a pen as a pointer. "This is the left atrium and this the right side of the heart." After a short pause to allow the information to sink in, he continued: "Who can name this valve?"

"Mitral valve," answered Peter rapidly with an air of confidence.

"Correct. What does this blue color represent?" asked John of the students as he turned on the color Doppler. No one answered, the students' eyes burning an impression on the ultrasound screen with their intense analysis of the images.

After a pause, John came to the rescue. "Blue color represents blood flow away from the transducer, whereas red indicates blood flow towards it. The blue jet you see here is showing blood flowing from where to where?" asked John again demonstrating his point using his pen.

"That blood is flowing from the left ventricle to the left atrium. That's the wrong way," said Chris pensively, not knowing exactly what to say next.

"That must be mitral valve incompetence," said Peter.

"Right," said John. "Indeed that is mitral regurgitation. This is caused by the heart attack we gave the little guy. In a few days he'll have florid CHF," said John.

"CHF?" Claire appeared confused.

"Congestive heart failure," said John. He pushed another button and a new image appeared, this one brighter and with much more detail.

"As you can see, this wall is much less bright than the others. This is the area of the heart attack. These images were obtained after we injected the bubbles. Aren't the pictures better?" asked John.

"It's like HD-TV," remarked Taylor in admiration. "Even I can read this study. It's so much clearer."

As John continued to ooh and ah the visitors with the ongoing research efforts, an older man peered through a glass window. His eyes met John's and the young doctor paused, his muscles tensing. Suddenly and briskly, the door to the lab opened and Dr. Rupert entered.

"What are you doing here?" demanded the director with an air of arrogance and irritation.

"I was just showing Dr. Norris and his students—" John started to speak, timidly explaining his behavior as if he was just caught with his hand in the cookie jar.

He was rudely interrupted by the commanding voice of Dr. Rupert.

"I can see that. I need you to finish your work and I do not appreciate interruptions and delays."

Caught totally by surprise, Claire, Jack and the medical students retreated leaving John to receive the tongue lashing alone.

Even as the door to the research lab closed, Rupert's voice could still be heard.

A man passed them on the way out. He stopped, noticing the situation.

"Oh my. Dr. Rupert is on a rampage again. I am so sorry. I'm James Miller. I'm the chief technician here in the lab. I'm sorry about the yelling. Dr. Rupert is under a lot of pressure and gets disturbed easily," said the older man noticing the facial expressions of disgust on the lab visitors. James Miller was a portly man in his sixties, with scant gray hair and a protruding belly. His attempts to put the retreating group at ease, by explaining the poor behavior demonstrated by his boss, was admirable.

"He yells a lot, but he doesn't mean anything by it. He'll be okay. Don't any of you worry about it," continued James in a soothing fatherly voice. "Let me go in there and rescue poor Dr. Connor." With this, James smiled and disappeared behind the lab door.

"Thank you, Mr. Miller," said Claire, not sure if he had heard her at all. "What a nice man. He reminds of my grandfather, so kind and attentive," she said to the group as they walked away.

"What an idiot, that Rupert," said Jack. All remained silent, not sure what to say.

5:04 PM

Jack and Claire were happy to be home. Rupert's angry words were still bothering Jack. In the shower, Jack's thoughts were of the outburst displayed in the research lab.

"Just like a child, having a temper tantrum. He has no right to behave like that," he contemplated to himself. "I don't care if he is the research director. What an asshole." Deep down Jack was furious. The longer he thought about the events in the lab, the worse he felt.

After his shower, Jack put on comfortable clothes and joined Claire, who was cooking supper, in the kitchen. On his arrival, she was singing.

Jack sat down in front of the TV.

"Hey, what did you do with the money?" he asked her.

"What money?"

"The money your mother gave you for singing lessons." A kitchen towel hit him on the head.

"I used it for throwing lessons," she replied.

"I'm still fuming about Rupert—"

"Can we please stop thinking about him? Let go of it. He's a man under a lot of stress and—"

"Okay, let's drop it. Your psych analysis, too."

"Fair enough. We are creating a new section within the Department of Psychology at the hospital. Cardiac Psychology. I'm thinking of taking the position. I would work solely with the psychological issues and problems of cardiac patients. I'll need your help in learning about cardiac problems. What do you think?" asked Claire after an uncomfortable long moment.

"If you think that would make you happy, I think you should do it. Of course, I'll help you with whatever you need. I do think cardiac patients are complex and unique and having someone that would deal only with cardiac patients would seem beneficial. I love the idea." A smile appeared on Jack's face. He would love to be able to work more closely with Claire.

After a short silence, Claire continued, a dreamy look in her eyes: "After I get this new program started and you finish your fellowship, we can—"

"Here we go again," interrupted Jack.

"Well, what do you think? Won't it be time to add to our little family?" asked Claire, with a smile.

"Yes, you're right. We'll get a puppy. A Vizsla puppy." Jack's enthusiastic words were suddenly cut short. Claire had thrown a small couch pillow that hit him squarely in the head. She had walked over to the couch where Jack was sitting. They wrestled playfully and laughed for several seconds ending up with a long amorous kiss.

Fourteen days ago

September 17

7:44 PM

The score was two goals to one. The Old & Arthritic, a team consisting mostly of physical therapists, had been the only team to beat the Heartbeats the previous three seasons of the coed indoor soccer league. As such, the Heartbeats, a team captained by doctors Jack Norris and John Connor, remained in second place. Jack hoped that bringing up these facts right before the game, would give his teammates the burning fire necessary to get the win.

The Old & Arthritic had proven to be formidable opponents as they scored two well-orchestrated goals. Right before the half, a questionable handball inside the box by one of the Old & Arthritic defenders had led to a penalty-kick, which resulted in a goal for the Heartbeats.

The time clock ticked downwards. It was now a minute and a half before the end of the match and the Heartbeats knew it was now or never. Vera and Jennifer were playing midfield. Jack, playing right fullback, had passed the ball to the women advancing the point of attack to the middle of the field. Seeing the right corner of the pitch unattended, Jack ran up the field. A relatively inexperienced Old & Arthritic left defender had come up to defend the midfield. Vera saw the possibilities unfold, even before the ball was played. Jennifer had passed her the ball. With a precise one-touch pass, Vera placed the ball in front of Jack, now in full gallop. John Connor saw it, too. From his left forward position, John tracked to the middle of the field, anticipating a pass from Jack to quickly change the point of attack with a shot on goal.

Jack collected the ball near the corner and had a quick decision to make. He could either kick the ball on goal or pass the ball to John, now positioned a few feet in front of the goalkeeper but well guarded by the left fullback.

Jack kicked the ball on goal. The Old & Arthritic goalkeeper dove to her left and smothered the ball, yet again denying the Heartbeats from scoring. Several more seconds later, a loud buzzer resonated, proclaiming the end of the game.

"We'll get them next time," said Jack to Vera and Jennifer with a wink. The Old & Arthritic troupe shook the hands of the Heartbeats players, repeating the usual rhetoric.

"Good game."

"Good game," came the reply.

"Jack, I need to talk to you," said John with a serious look.

"I know I should have passed that ball to you; I thought I could—" John interrupted Jack.

"No, not that. I really need to talk to you. I have been trying to decide if and how to tell you this. I need your help." John's face was serious.

"Yeah, sure. What's up?" asked Jack.

"Great game, guys. See you next week," said Vera, going by the two doctors walking in her socks, her indoor soccer shoes in her hands.

"Yeah, you too, Vera. You were great today. Good game. We'll get 'em next time," said Jack who then turned to John with a look of concern. John had remained still and quiet.

"Jack, I think there's something wrong at the Research Lab. I need to talk—" John was interrupted again.

"Hey, Jack, what's the league fee? I forgot to pay last week. I'll do it right now," said one of the team members.

"Sixty dollars, Brooke." Jack looked back at John.

"Jack, I can't be here next week. We're going to Atlanta," said another member of the team who was passing by.

"Okay, Brad. Can your brother cover for you?" asked Jack

"No, he's going, too," answered Brad.

"Don't worry. I'll get somebody to play for you. Have fun. Come back safely." It became clear that Jack and John could not have a serious conversation—not here, not now.

"Jack, can we talk tomorrow? There is something bothering me and I need to discuss it with you. Claire, too."

"Come over tomorrow for dinner, after work. Can you?" asked Jack, worried about his friend.

"Yeah. That's great. Let's talk tomorrow." John walked away. Jack tried to follow him but before he could, he was mobbed again.

"Good game, Jack." It was Fred, the best player on the Old & Arthritic. They touched knuckles. Five of his players accompanied Fred.

"Yeah, yeah, yeah. We may never be able to beat you guys. But, we'll keep trying."

"It's just our luck. We always have a close game against you," interjected one of the opposing players.

"You guys have an awesome goalkeeper. What's her name?" inquired Jack.

"Anna Diaz. She is pretty good," answered Fred.

"Your team has a wonderful defense line. Are you playing outdoor at all?" asked one of the players.

"No, I'm getting too old for outdoor," said Jack.

"Listen to you, too old! If you change your mind, let me know. I'm getting an outdoor team together and could use you," solicited Fred.

"Okay, I'll ask my people if any of them are interested," offered Jack.

"Want to go get a beer?" asked another man in the group.

"I can't. Gotta get up early tomorrow." Jack raised his hand to signal he was leaving and walked fast to the parking lot. His feet and thighs ached as he rushed but he hoped he could see John. He did not. The space where John parked his car was now empty.

Thirteen days ago

September 18

6:02 AM

The air was cool, increasing the airplane's lift characteristics. The takeoff had been accomplished with textbook precision and the aircraft climbed effortlessly at a thousand feet per minute to seven thousand feet. Jack scanned the airspeed indicator to ascertain that the pull on the yoke was just right. It was. Once at six thousand feet, the warning buzzer alerted him that the time to discontinue the climb was near. He had filed this flight to seven thousand feet; seven thousand

and one would be legal but in bad form, if you asked Jack. He made all the necessary yoke and trim changes and soon the airplane stopped climbing. He leaned the fuel and air mixture and positioned the prop lever at its correct setting. Immediately beneath him, he could see the fluffy material of a large cloud being overtaken by the speeding aircraft.

Being the senior cardiac electrophysiology fellow caused Dr. Jack Norris' already busy daily schedule to become even more hectic and sometimes unbearably so. The time he could devote to fly the Beechcraft Bonanza became ever so scarce. His Bonanza was to him as a pacifier to a baby. The airplane had belonged to his dad, from whom Jack had acquired the love of flying and aircrafts. He would make every effort possible to get up at five o'clock in the morning at least every other week so that he could take her for a flight into the clouds. He loved that best. To direct the Bonanza into the fluffy whiteness of a calm cloud relaxed Jack to the point where the expected troubles of the rest of the day would become meaningless. He would fly just above the clouds until it was time to return home. A plunge into the white swirls of cotton-like mass would make instrument flying necessary. He felt challenged but in control.

His beeper vibrated alerting him of an incoming message. Jack knew he had to return to the airport. He had flown for forty-five minutes though it seemed like only forty-five seconds had passed. Evidence of a busy day ahead was mounting as his cell phone quivered.

"Evansville Tower, niner-eight-gulf-kilo ready to return home," he requested of the bored airport tower controller who sipped black coffee. Niner-eight-gulf-kilo were the call letters identifying his aircraft. The Beechcraft Bonanza was a six-seater, three hundred horsepower beautiful machine fully equipped with instruments for all meteorological flying conditions and autopilot. Today, like so many others, had been a training sortie. He would not engage the autopilot, although it was set and ready to take over with a touch of a button, should it become necessary to do so. It had not. He wanted to hand fly the airplane and fly it as well, or better, than the autopilot. The airplane was beige and brown and the envy of all the general aviation pilots in the hangar of the small airport of Evansville.

"Roger, niner-eight-gulf-kilo, any special requests this time, doc? Nobody in the pattern, so you can approach however you'd like. State intentions," replied the man on the other side of the microphone.

"Yeah, niner-eight-gulf-kilo, ILS-36 approach with vectors. This will be a full stop," Jack returned in a commanding reassured voice. The ILS, or instrument landing system, is an aviation process that facilitates landings, especially crucial in conditions of poor visibility. Using this would expedite his arrival on the ground and hasten his ability to answer his pages and return the phone calls. By now, the pager and phone had vibrated yet again.

"Roger, niner-eight-gulf-kilo, fly one-nine-zero and descend at pilot's discretion to three thousand feet," commanded the controller. Jack repeated the instructions to announce he had understood and would comply.

By the time the Bonanza came to an almost complete halt at the second intersection of the runway, Jack had received two more pages and another phone call. Although not atypical for a busy doctor to be summoned so often during the workday, it seemed unusual for this to happen before eight o'clock in the morning. This piqued his curiosity. He had not had a chance to see who was trying so persistently to contact him. He would wait until the airplane was parked and secured on the tarmac before examining his pager and cell phone.

Jack checked his beeper's numerical display first. Four pages from the same extension at the hospital appeared. His cell phone's Missed Calls display indicated the same number had tried him three times. One of the numbers was from the cardiology department office. He dialed it. An excited Dr. Stanley Mansfield answered on the first ring. Stan was a young looking, thin junior cardiology fellow who Jack tolerated despite his constant nervous demeanor and obvious lack of confidence.

"What's up Stan?" said Jack into the receiver.

"Where the hell are you, Jack? This place is going to hell in a hand-basket. That patient we admitted yesterday, what's his name, Butterfield or Butterhands or—"

"Butterworth," interjected Jack in a composed controlled voice in an attempt to calm down the nervous young doctor on the other side of the phone call.

"Yeah, that's it. He just shot John Connor dead, and a whole bunch of people at the hospital. Right here in our CCU. Oh, my God! There's blood all over the place," continued Stan, obviously distraught.

"What? John's dead?" Jack was devastated. He felt like his heart had just dropped to his feet. He couldn't believe what he had just heard. "I'm on my way. Calm down, Stan, and give me the details," continued Jack as he hurried to his car, cell phone to ear.

7:38 AM

The trip to the hospital seemed longer than ever. Stan was of no help. He was too disturbed and troubled to give any useful accounts of what had happened. Jack decided it was best to hang up and concentrate on the drive. In the distance, he could hear sirens blaring. He was in shock, barely able to grasp what he had just been told.

It can't be John that was murdered! Who would want to do that, anyhow? He just talked to me last night. Actually, he tried to talk to me last night. He couldn't, I didn't make time for him. With this last thought came a river of tears. Jack recalled the events of the previous evening at the soccer game. John attempted, without success, to discuss something with him.

I was not there for him when he needed me. What if what

was troubling him was what got him killed? Oh my God, what have I done? Jack wept, as he dialed Claire's cell phone.

"Honey, something terrible has happened," he said when his wife answered the call. He took a deep breath and continued, "John Connor has been shot at the hospital. I received a call while I was flying. Stan said John's dead, Claire. Also one of the CCU nurses, Heather. I'm on my way to the hospital now. Please call your supervisor at Newton Memorial and see if they want you to come in. They may want to keep as many people away from campus as possible. If you do come in, call me before. And please be careful." A pause. A sniffle. Claire's words were comforting.

"Yes, I will be careful, too." Another moment of silence as Claire continued to talk.

"Not too well. My stomach is in a knot. I have a sinking feeling in my chest. What about you? How do you feel?" Jack listened as he drove.

"This is terrible. I can't believe this sort of thing happened here. In our hospital. In our town," exclaimed Jack despondently, when it was his turn to speak again. Then, he listened again.

"I love you, too. I'll call you later, as soon as I know more." Jack hung up. More tears. In anger, Jack slapped the steering wheel with a closed fist. Hard. He wept and drove on. Approaching the medical facility, he used a tissue to wipe his tearful eyes and blow his nose.

As he entered the Newton Memorial Hospital campus, Jack realized that Stan was not exaggerating. This was big. There were police cars, trucks and vans all over, all flashing red and white lights.

Jack stopped at the Doctor's Parking Area gate and removed his wallet from his back pocket. In it, a keycard would automatically signal the electrical clearance that would allow the computerized gate to permit entrance. Just like every other morning for the last five years, the gate opened and he drove in. Unlike every other morning, however, two cops waited at the entry into the garage.

"Hang on, sir. We're checking ID for all people coming in and out," ordered the younger of the two police officers.

"Sure," replied Jack showing his hospital badge. "What happened?" he continued, mystified.

"Don't know much yet, doc. We're still assessing the crime scene."

Jack parked his car. The general parking garage was nearly full. The police had prevented the night shift personnel from leaving and the morning shift employees were arriving. Jack saw multiple people in groups, no doubt discussing the morning's events.

The doctor's parking area, however, was still deserted. The residents and doctors in fellowship training that were not on call were not expected to arrive until around eight o'clock in the morning. It was early. Jack was surprised to see Dr. Rupert's car in its usual parking stall. "LAB RAT," read the license plate of the black 745 Li BMW, which was impeccably clean. Reading the license plate, Jack could not help but smirk.

"Geek," he said softly under his breath shaking his head nonchalantly to no one in particular. The roomy interior with its elegant leather gave the Beamer the feel and comfort of a couch. Not that Jack had ever sat in it.

"When you are as all-mighty important as the great Dr. Rupert, you simply don't have to get out of bed early. You have people working for you that are willing to do the early chores," mused Jack. Dr. John Connor was one of the blessed to work under the great research guru. Dr. Connor was also one of the dead.

Never before had he noticed Rupert's car in the parking lot so early. He had many people doing the grunt work so he could drive his 7-series BMW and wear expensive suits. Dr. Rupert did the thinking and got the research grants. He was known for his political shrewdness and prowess.

As a powerhouse of a man, everybody knew the infamous Dr. Ian Rupert. Jack knew him well and he felt some degree of pity for him. Despite all that power and money, Rupert had never married. Jack's thought reverted momentarily to his wife and how much he loved her.

"Too busy for a family. Who would want to marry him, anyhow?" guessed Jack. "Why is he here so early today?" he whispered to no one. "Did Rupert get John killed?" Jack was in the throes of denial and rage. He needed someone to blame. More importantly, he needed someone to tell him that John Connor was not dead.

As a cardiac electrophysiologist, Jack didn't work closely with Dr. Rupert. Thank God for small favors. On a rare occasion, Jack had requested an appointment with the great Dr. Rupert to discuss a research patient on his service. Going to see Rupert, Jack had thought, was like petitioning an appointment with the pope. It was a complex and nerve-wracking task to accomplish. However, to Jack's surprise, despite his air of arrogance and brilliance, Dr. Ian Rupert had been helpful and kind during the discussions. Jack understood why the man had acquired the power and importance he achieved. Maybe he deserved some of it. However, Jack's last encounter with Rupert, that abominable man, was forever etched in his memory. The laboratory scene when Rupert literally and rudely kicked Jack and his entourage out continued to play and re-play widely in his mind.

So, what's the bastard doing here so early? The same thought returned. Jack remained pensive as he hurriedly headed to the cardiology department office on the third floor. To get there quicker, he took the stairs two by two. By the time he reached the first landing, his thoughts shifted to the horror he was about to face.

"I paged you several times as soon as I heard about the shooting," offered Beverly, the cardiology department secretary.

"I was out flying. I couldn't answer when you paged. What do you know, Bev?"

Beverly was an older, proper woman who Jack thought was the most organized and sensible person on earth. She had worked at Newton Memorial for thirty-eight years in many different departments. She had gotten to know everyone. Everyone knew her well. Everyone admired her.

"One of the cardiac patients in CCU shot Heather and Dr. Connor. Do you know Heather McCormick? She is—" Beverly paused and sighed deeply. "She was a nurse. She was such a beautiful and nice person. Very hard worker." Beverly stopped and wept for a short moment, tears flowing down her cheeks. Jack had slowly approached the older woman. He gestured for a hug and she got up from her chair. The two embraced for a long moment in silence, all eyes tearing.

"Yes, I knew Heather. She was a great nurse." Jack paused. "Do you know of any other details?" asked the young doctor, barely able to talk, the emotions choking him at the throat.

"He also killed Mike Huber. He was a nightshift security officer," she continued, when she was able to speak again. Jack removed two tissues from a box nearby and handed Beverly one. He used the other to wipe his tears. She imitated Jack, sobbing.

"That's all I can tell you. I only know what people who stopped in the office have told me. And what I gathered from a few phone calls. Sorry," apologized Beverly.

"No, no need to apologize. I'm going to see if I can find out more. Page me if you need to talk, okay?" Jack forced a smile. Beverly dabbed her teary eyes again.

Jack hurriedly exited the cardiology office and walked to the Coronary Care Unit on the second floor. Jack didn't feel it was appropriate to press Beverly for any more information. She was obviously very upset. As was he.

As he approached the Coronary Care Unit, he saw a huge commotion. The unit and the surrounding waiting room area were crowded with wall-to-wall cops. The entrance was roped off with a familiar yellow police tape. He had seen that sort of tape on TV cop shows but never before in real life. At every several feet stood a police sentinel, making sure those who entered the area had proper clearance. Jack couldn't see inside the CCU. He noticed there were people taking pictures, observing occasional bursts of flashing lights coming from inside the unit, now turned into a crime scene.

7:42 AM

The older detective, Lieutenant Herbert Fuller, arrived at the scene later than the others. As the senior detective on the force, Herb would be in charge of the investigation. His partner, Detective Sergeant Susan Quentin, was busy snooping around looking for evidence and clues. White sheets covered the four lifeless bodies, two on the floor next to the bed, one on the hospital bed and a fourth farther away closer to the door into the room. Blood spatter was visible on the walls near the bodies. The pattern of spatter, or lack thereof, would surely mean something to Susan, Herb and the other criminologists. Evansville was a small community and Newton Memorial Hospital was a small community hospital. The four murders at the facility would cause quite a stir in the district. A swift resolution to the carnage was necessary.

"Good morning, Suzy. What do we have here?" inquired Herb as he approached her.

"Hey, Herb. A man was admitted yesterday. This morning, for no apparent reason, while everything appeared to be going well, he suddenly became confused and combative. The nurses say this is very unusual, to this degree anyhow. The man pulls out a gun and starts to shoot. No one knows where he got the gun. He killed Dr. John Connor." She paused to point to one of the bodies on the ground covered with a blood-soaked white sheet. She lifted up the sheet, allowing Herb to inspect underneath. Herb bent down to take a closer look and make mental notes regarding the position of the body. Susan stayed on her feet holding up the corner of the sheet. The dead man was young and handsome. He was pale from the fatal bloodshed. A bullet wound had ceased spewing blood from the center of his chest, the obvious mode of death. Herb picked up the deceased's hand to check for rigidity. None was present, the telltale sign of a recent kill. Herb stood up and Susan allowed the white sheet to drop and again cover the body.

She continued as she slowly made her way towards the other remains on the floor: "He also shot and killed Heather McCormick, a nurse on the unit. She was caring for him." She paused once again, bent at the waist and picked up the sheet. Herb repeated the previous steps, coming to similar conclusions. Her fatal wound was to the head, the bullet disfiguring her face. Both detectives stood as the white sheet fell on the nurse's corpse.

"After these two went down, there was exchange of gunfire between this man, Mike Huber, a security guard here at Memorial, and the shooter." By the time she murmured these words they had circled around the small area stopping by the third covered bloodied body. Herb picked up a corner of the sheet as he had done before. He studied the remains making mental notes.

"The shooter is the late Mr. Arthur Butterworth." Susan made her way to the hospital bed in the center of the small room, followed by Herb. She once again lifted the blood-soaked white sheet covering the deceased patient. Herb eyed the body. Multiple gunshot wounds were visible on the man's torso, dressed in a typical hospital gown, now soaked with bloodstains. Herb grabbed the corner of the linen to pick up the proverbial smoking gun, located next to the body. This would allow inspection of the revolver without placing unwanted fingerprints on the weapon. The typical smell of a recently fired revolver permeated the air, reaching the detective's nostrils. Herb's eyes connected with Susan's. Herb gave a silent nod. Both detectives slowly backed away from the bed.

"I checked earlier. The gun was fired six times," added Susan unsolicited. Herb nodded in silence, taking it all in, in a thinking mode.

"We know who shot whom. We have plenty of witnesses. What we need now is to find out why. We need to establish the routine around here. We should get someone from the hospital to help us with that part of the investigation," said Herb, pensively. "Someone who knows medicine, who knows the routine here at the hospital, who knows which records we need to see, who knows—"

"I agree. But who?" interrupted Susan. "What if we ask someone that is involved with the killings to help us?" she continued after a short pause.

"We'll pick somebody who seems right; we'll watch him or her closely until we're sure we're not getting a wolf to help us shepherd our sheep. What's the new kid's name?" Herb looked at Susan and touched his right index finger to the right corner of his mouth, as if this would allow him to recollect a name he had obviously forgotten. This was a typical Herb-ism.

"Jim Franklin?" answered Susan recalling the name of the young man that had joined the detective force only a few days before.

With this Herb continued, "Yes, we'll have him follow our medical helper."

This said, both detectives turned to the crowd of medical personnel just outside CCU. Young and old doctors, nurses, technicians and secretaries loitered in the area with curiosity. They had been asked by the cops to wait until they could be interviewed and released to go home. The detectives joined the other detectives already interrogating the witnesses to the killings. Before so doing, Herb asked all detectives to give him a review of what had been learned already. They would compare notes later.

8:17 AM

"And you are?" asked a female voice coming from behind Jack as he approached the scene of the crime. Jack turned to face the woman.

"I'm Jack Norris. I'm one of the doctors here," he replied.

"I'm Detective Susan Quentin of the Evansville Police Department." A police badge and a photo ID over her left breast corroborated her story. The two shook hands firmly.

"What happened in there?" asked Jack hoping to gain more insight from the woman.

"Four people died. One of the patients became agitated and started shooting," she said.

"Where did he get the gun?" asked the young doctor.

"We don't know. I have been looking for you. We'd like to ask you some questions," she persisted.

"I just got here. I don't know anything about what happened," said Jack almost apologetically.

"Yes, I know. You were flying your airplane." Jack looked puzzled, amazed and intrigued by her words. Noticing his astonishment, she continued, "I'm a detective, that's what I do."

"I was at 7,000 feet when the killings took place. But two of the people killed were my close friends. I'll do anything I can to help you. What do you want to know?" asked Jack.

"We need to know about usual routines, who is expected where and when, what happens when a patient is admitted, who sees the patient. That sort of thing. We also need to know what you know about the patient, Arthur Butterworth."

"Sure, not a problem. I'm glad to help any way I can."

"Where can we go to have some privacy?" she asked.

"How about my office?" he replied.

"Sounds good. Let me get my partner." The woman entered the yellow-taped Do Not Cross area and disappeared into the crowd of law enforcement agents.

Jack noticed the busy officers walking in and out of the area, the professionally sounding walkie-talkie lingo emanating from multiple belts, all in unison. Two men, jackets labeled Coroner, came across Jack's area guiding an empty stretcher.

"Excuse me, please," they murmured repeatedly, walking towards the entrance into CCU. Jack helped the men by lifting the yellow tape so the two could pass. He found himself on the other side of the tape and slowly walked into CCU, unnoticed by the busy sentinels. Knowing he shouldn't and that he would later be sorry, Jack became overwhelmed by curiosity and walked towards the crime scene. As he entered the unit, his eyes first focused on the two bodies on the ground, both of which had been uncovered to allow pictures to be taken. For a split second, Jack fixated his gaze on the empty, lifeless eyes of his best friend, John Connor. He didn't tolerate this long, bothered mostly by the blood-drained pastiness of his face. He had to look away. His eyes unconsciously moved to John's chest, now completely covered in blood, an obvious bullet hole right in the middle. The nightmarish scene only worsened, when Jack's gaze unintentionally shifted to the young woman. Though in his mind he could still see her beautiful, youthful face, his vision returned a head with a faceless expression, the bullet having disfigured grotesquely all the elements of Heather's previous attractive features. Instead, a large hole in what used to be her forehead and nose was now surrounded by blood and what appeared to be brain matter. A sense of fear and disgust overcame Jack and he hurriedly retreated to the waiting room right outside the CCU entrance door. Jack found a chair and sat down, his whole body trembling like it had never done before. It took several minutes for him to even begin to feel a little better. He walked slowly to a nearby cooler and had a big gulp of cold water. Then another. This soothed the intense fire inside but only infinitesimally. Susan emerged with her partner, an older man, also dressed impeccably with every hair in place.

"This is my partner, Detective Herb Fuller," introduced Susan. Herb extended his hand and shook Jack's forcibly, looking him squarely in the eye. In all his years as a detective, he had learned to look people in the eye. He knew the eyes were the windows into the soul, heart and brain. Herb made a vocation out of interpreting eye contact. Looking into Jack's eyes, he saw concern, kindness, gentleness and strength. A little bit of horror, too. Just like that, he knew he could count on this young man for help.

"How are you, doctor?" asked Herb.

"Not too well," answered Jack with tearful eyes.

"I am sorry for the loss of your friends and all of this mess. Detective Quentin told me you were willing to talk in your office. We can step away from here right now, while the crime lab people take their photos and collect their specimens. If it's okay with you, can we go now? We'd really welcome your input," said the older detective appreciatively.

"No problem. Follow me to my office." The three walked in silence toward the cardiology office, Jack leading the group. They excused themselves as they wound in and out past many groups of people, mostly hospital staff and police personnel. Susan held a small notebook where she had written several bullet points. Herb had no such notebook.

When they arrived at the staircase, reassured that they were no longer around people that might overhear their conversation, Detective Fuller resumed the exchange.

"What we have here is Arthur Butterworth, a man in his sixties," he said in a soft voice.

"Sixty-three," corrected Jack. "I admitted him yesterday."

The cops nodded, Susan wrote something on her notebook and Herb continued his narrative.

"As I understand it, Butterworth was admitted routinely yesterday. This morning, and without provocation, he went berserk. Somehow, he managed to find a small-caliber revolver and took a nurse hostage in his CCU room;

the other staff summoned hospital security and the police. When the security officer arrived, the man was described as wild and paranoid. The result was that the nurse and one of the doctors were shot and killed as they were retreating from the bedside. They had tried in vain to persuade the patient to give himself up. The man did not appear to understand and pulled the trigger. Shots were exchanged with the guard culminating in the perp's death as well as the security officer."

They arrived at Jack's office. Jack nodded at Beverly who was on the phone. She remained motionless with mouth agape and watched in disbelief as the three walked by and entered Jack's office.

"Please make yourselves comfortable. Will either of you take some coffee, soft drink, water?" Jack asked politely, as he took his chair behind his desk. This was a small table almost completely buried with papers, electrocardiographs, large X-ray envelopes, and stacks and stacks of medical records. In the midst of all that, like two tiny islands about to be swallowed by the immenseness of the vast sea of paperwork, there was a mug and a name-sign afloat. It read, Jack Norris, MD, Chief of Fellows, Department of Cardiology, Section of Electrophysiology.

"Nothing for me," answered the older detective, as he sat and looked over at his partner as if to solicit her reaction to the same question.

"No, I'm fine, thanks," replied Susan.

They all sat down. Susan had the notebook on her lap and a pen ready to take notes.

Herb began. "Dr. Norris," he paused as if to choose his words just right. "We have a lot of witnesses as to who pulled the trigger and caused all these deaths. What we need to do now is try to understand why. We need to find out where the gun came from. We'd like to start by gathering some information about routines here at Newton Memorial and about this patient."

"Sure, I can help you with that," volunteered Jack.

"What time did you last see the deceased patient?" asked Herb.

"I was with him at around five; I helped with the admission process before I went home."

"Did he have a gun on him?" continued Herb.

"Not that I noticed, but I didn't go through his personal things. The nurses do that when patients are admitted. They take a complete inventory of all the possessions. Did you review that document?"

"Yes, we did look at the paperwork and no mention of any weapons. We didn't talk to the nurse that admitted him, since she ended her shift at seven o'clock yesterday evening. We'll talk to her later today."

"Do you own a gun, doctor?" asked Susan suddenly.

"Oh, no, not me. Why? Do you think I gave him a gun?" Jack appeared uncomfortable with the question.

"It's just a question. We have asked it of everybody we talked to this morning," she explained putting Jack a bit more at ease.

"Do you know anybody that owns a gun? Can you think of anyone that works here that might have brought in a gun for any reason? Any reason at all?" asked Herb.

"No, not really. I'm just not a gun person."

"Did you have any arguments or issues with the people killed today?" asked Herb.

"No, John and Heather were my friends. I've seen the security guard around campus, but didn't know him at all. And the patient, I met him for the first time yesterday evening," answered Jack. Susan wrote on her notebook.

"What about the medical issues? Could the patient have been faking his symptoms?" asked Herb.

"I don't think so. His EKG was abnormal and he had runs of tachycardia." Jack studied the expression on the faces of the detectives and suddenly realized he needed to explain in layman's terms. He continued: "His electrocardiogram showed abnormalities suggesting a heart attack and a heart rhythm disorder that cannot be faked."

"Is there any way at all that he could have fooled you?" asked Susan.

Jack paused for a beat. "There may be drugs that mimic the EKG changes we saw, but—" He paused again, pensively.

"Like what? What kind of drugs?" persisted Herb, intrigued with the possibility.

"I don't know. Let me research that and get back to you."

"The other thing bothering us is why he became agitated and paranoid. The nurses say this is unusual for somebody to do this when they had no psych history. Is it?" asked Susan.

"Yes, in my entire career dealing with cardiac patients, I never experienced anything close to this. Sure, people get scared and sad, some may cry, some become a bit agitated. But not enough to shoot people," confessed Jack.

"As far as the typical routine around here, did anything seem out of place or unusual this morning?" asked Susan.

"No, but I just got here. I don't know that I can say yet," answered Jack.

"Tell us what a typical day is like for the doctors," asked Herb.

"Well, let's see," began Jack, "everything starts with morning reports at eight in the morning. That goes for an hour. All the medical students, interns, residents and fellows—"

"Interns, residents and fellows? Help us out with the jargon, doctor," interrupted Susan politely and inquisitively.

"Sorry." Jack paused for a few seconds to gather his thoughts, then continued: "These are doctors in training at different levels. The first year of training after med school, they are called interns, then two years of being a resident in the Department of Internal Medicine. Those that don't want to specialize are done; they become internists. For those of us that want to specialize, then we do a fellowship. In my case, I did a fellowship in cardiology for three years and I am now doing a fellowship in electrophysiology." Before Susan had a chance to interrupt for clarification, Jack smiled and explained: "Electrophysiology is the field within cardiology that deals with heart rhythm disorders."

"We appreciate your explanations. Please continue," interceded Susan.

"So all the med students and doctors in training rotating through the department of cardiology come to a session every morning at eight to discuss the cases that were admitted the night before by the on call team. I oversee that meeting. Medical rounds start around nine to nine-thirty in the morning. The trainees are grouped and assigned a certain ward to round on. Each group has a few students, an intern, a resident and a fellow. So at the time the murders occurred—" Jack paused. "What time did the murders occur?"

"Around six-fifteen," answered Susan.

"That early in the morning, there is nothing going on. The nurses don't change shift until seven. There are people in the unit drawing blood, setting up portable X-rays machines, and getting EKGs on patients," responded Jack.

"Do you know if the patient had any visitors?" asked Herb.

"Yes, his wife and daughter were with him yesterday. They were with him when I left him. They seemed concerned and close to the patient," answered Jack.

"Do you know if the patient had any visitors this morning?" inquired Herb.

"I don't know about this morning."

"Do you know if anyone unusual came to see him since his arrival in the hospital?" asked Susan.

"I really don't know."

"Do you have any theories or thoughts about why this man might have wanted to commit these murders?" questioned Herb.

"Dr. John Connor was a research fellow. I know they use and sacrifice many animals down in the research lab. My first thought was some animal activist group, but that seems far-fetched," answered Jack.

"Okay, Dr. Norris. We appreciate your time and if you could let us know later about any possible drugs that could have been used to fake the patient's medical condition, that might be helpful," said Herb.

The detectives got up, shook Jack's hand and left the small office, having made plans to meet again at four o'clock that same afternoon.

As he watched them depart, Jack remained standing by his desk, motionless and in silence, his eyes gathering moistness again.

"The bastard murdered John. He killed my best friend. May that son-of-a-bitch killer rot in hell forever and a day." Jack wept once again, tears flowing down both cheeks. Once the sobbing ceased, he would compose himself and call Claire. More than anything right now he needed to hear her voice. She would provide comfort, strength and much needed direction.

9:05 AM

"So, what do you think about young Dr. Jack Norris?" asked Herb, when he and Susan were no longer within an earshot of Beverly, who sat at her desk talking on the phone taking notes. The detectives walked by slowly towards the elevator, gesturing goodbye as they briefly made eye contact with the busy secretary.

"He seems sharp and trustworthy enough. I don't think he had anything to do with the murders, do you?" she replied.

"No, I don't think he's involved. He seems to be honest. I think he can be helpful to us. Let's see what he comes up with," continued Herb.

"He was flying at the time of the murders. At least we know he didn't give the perp the gun this morning," she said.

"Unless he gave it to him yesterday during the admission process. But I don't think so," said Herb wisely. Susan nodded.

"I'll research as much as I can about him and I'll assign Jim Franklin to follow him for a while. I'll find out if he owns a gun and if he had any reason to dislike those murdered," said Susan.

"These early cases always disrupt my morning routine. I need coffee and food. Have you had breakfast, Suzy?"

3:42 PM

Jack spent three hours in his office. He read textbooks and used the PC. He accessed all the medical websites he could think of for answers to the question: How does one fake the abnormalities on the electrocardiogram he witnessed the day before? A list of drugs that could have affected the EKG changes was predictably and repeatedly shown in every source he examined. Jack knew damn well that if one of these had been ingested, there would have been other signs.

He worked through lunch.

At two o'clock, he realized there were several in-patients on whom he had to round. He knew the medical students and residents had been sent home at the recommendation of the police as the murder scene was probed and inspected.

But, there were patients to be seen. He would do that quickly without students to teach and residents and junior fellows to guide. The last thing he wanted to do was to be late for his meeting with detectives Fuller and Quentin.

It was 3:58 p.m. exactly when the two cops arrived.

"Come in, please and make yourselves comfortable," remarked Jack to the cops gesturing for them to come in and pointing at the empty chairs in the small room.

"Well, what did you come up with?" began Detective Quentin.

"I came up with nothing. There is no known drug anyone can take to fake the objective cardiac signs displayed by this patient without having other overt signs of toxicity. The only explanation is that this man really did come in with an acute coronary syndrome." Jack paused, suddenly realizing he was going to be interrupted by the detectives for using medical jargon. He forced a smile. "Sorry, but this guy really did come in with a serious bona fide heart problem. He did not fake it. I also checked on his cardiac markers; uh, blood tests we order routinely to check for heart damage and his were slightly positive. Therefore, he did have a heart attack. This was for real."

"Okay, that settles that issue," stated Susan.

"No, not yet. He might have been given an experimental drug. I want to continue to search but I need more time. I need to visit the medical school library and do a more extensive search of the literature," interjected Jack.

"Okay, for now it doesn't appear that he got himself admitted just to kill someone. The next question is where he got the gun. Why the bizarre psychiatric behavior," inquired Detective Fuller, who had remained silent.

"Sometimes people with heart attacks have anxiety and panic attacks. But to the degree of murdering doctors and nurses," replied Jack pausing briefly, clearly puzzled with the notion. "It's strange. I'll review the medical record closely and search for drugs that may cause these symptoms," he continued.

"I think these are all the questions we have for you, at this time. Please get back to us when you complete your research. We will have a meeting every morning at eight-thirty at the police station. You are welcome to come, anytime you have some information, doctor," stated Herb.

"You can call me Jack."

"Fair enough. I'm Herb and this is Susan. Our cell numbers are on the card, if you come up with something," said the older gumshoe, giving Jack his business card. Susan mimicked the gesture giving Jack her card. Jack reciprocated.

"Incidentally, Jack, we need you to keep the details of our conversations private," said Susan as they exited the room.

5:12 PM

Jack was thrilled to be involved in the investigation, but at the same time, being involved provided a continuous reminder of his loss. It would keep the wound open. But he would do it. He would be strong and get the job done. He owed this to his best friend. He would find out what happened and why John was killed. Only then could the wound begin to really heal.

Before leaving the hospital, Jack swung by Dr. Thomas Lindsborg's office. If he were going to take time to help the police, first he would have to get permission from his boss.

Arriving on the eighth floor, Jack first noticed that the beautifully decorated door to Lindsborg's office was closed. An extravagant and overstated sign on the door read: "Dr.

Thomas Lindsborg, Medical Director, Head of Department of Internal Medicine & Cardiology."

Gina, Lindsborg's secretary, had already left. Her desk was positioned gracefully to the left of the director's elegant dark mahogany door. Jack approached her desk and sat down. The desk was impeccably clean and organized. Not a thing out of place. He took out his pen from his breast pocket and started to write a note for her requesting a meeting with Dr. Lindsborg for the morning. As he began writing the words, he realized there was a conversation between two men in the director's office. One was definitely Dr. Lindsborg. The other voice sounded vaguely familiar. Straining to make out the words, Jack realized the second man was Rupert. He was speaking.

"Of course, this is stressful. For everyone. For you, too."

"How can we help the staff? Besides psychological assistance, of course? I already spoke to Joel Garrison. He will make all his psychiatry residents and psychologists available as necessary to help our staff."

"Give them some time off. I gave my research staff two weeks off. They will want to be with their families and friends and process this. Some may want to transfer to another facility. I told them I would support their decision. Of course, the research lab can stop for a while. In the hospital, with sick patients, the show must go on." There was a pause.

"You know the offer stands. Anytime. Just let me know. The place is very relaxing and soothing. I, myself, spend a lot of time there," offered Rupert after a moment of silence.

"I may take you up on that. Let me talk to my wife and see what she says. I will let you know. A weekend up at your cabin in the mountains may be exactly what we need."

There was a short pause as the door to the director's office slowly opened. Jack didn't notice at first but as the conversation continued, the louder tone of the voices made this obvious. He was still writing the note.

"What about this weekend? The cabin's all yours, if you want to go up there," insisted Dr. Rupert.

"Jack," said the familiar voice of Dr. Lindsborg.

"Good afternoon. I was just leaving a note for Gina to arrange a meeting with you tomorrow morning. I didn't know you were still here."

"I am so sorry about John. And Heather. Come in, let's talk." Jack walked into the ostentatious office guided by Dr. Lindsborg. As he was entering the office, Dr. Lindsborg turned to Dr. Rupert behind him.

"We'll probably take you up on your offer to use your cabin. I'll give you a call later this evening. I really appreciate it. Thanks." The two men shook hands and said goodbye. By then, Jack was inside the office. Dr. Lindsborg closed the door, entered the spacious room and sat at his captain's chair behind his desk gesturing for Jack to sit. Jack picked one of several elegant and comfortable chairs and sat down.

"I told Gina to go home early. I saw no reason to have her stay here given today's events. What a mess, huh? Are you doing okay? I know you were close with John Connor," asked Dr. Lindsborg in his concerned and customary fatherly manner.

"Thanks for your concern. I'm doing okay. I'm angry about his senseless death, but I'm coping all right."

"Give yourself time to heal. I'd like you to see a psychologist and talk this through."

"I'll see Claire tonight and—"

"You should see a different psychologist, Jack. I'm serious about this. I know Claire will tell you the same thing. She can help you, too, but I want you to know that there are mental health personnel available to help you. Please avail yourself of their services. Don't take this for granted. I'm having all the students, residents, and fellows do this." Dr. Lindsborg's face was serious and exuded concern.

"Okay, I'll do it. The police asked for my help with the case. They asked me to do some medical research for them. This may be the best therapy for me. If I'm helping with the investigation, I'll feel better about the whole thing."

"The police asked me that earlier today. They interviewed me at length this morning. One of the things they felt was important to their investigation was to have someone from the hospital helping them. I thought of you and told them so. I do agree that could be therapeutic for you. Are you willing to do it? And more importantly, are you up for it?"

"I think so."

"Okay, then do it. Keep me informed and let me know how I can help. Meanwhile, I'm giving most of the staff two weeks off. I will ask the attendings to do all the rounds. We will hold off on all elective procedures and surgeries until the smoke clears."

"I appreciate that. Thank you." Jack sat up paralleling the director's movements.

"One of the early theories is that the patient faked a heart attack to come into the hospital purposefully to kill someone, possibly John, Heather, or both. The patient's EKG showed significant changes and he did rule in for a small heart attack. Can you think of a way to fake this? " asked Jack with a pensive gesticulation.

"Faking a heart attack? I don't think so," answered Dr. Lindsborg.

"I'll search the medical literature for drugs that may fake EKG signs of heart attacks. What about a research drug? Are you aware of any research drugs being investigated here at Newton that may fit the bill?" Jack finally got himself to ask the question.

"No. Do you think our research department is out killing people?" said Dr. Lindsborg, walking slowly towards the door signifying that the meeting was over.

"No, of course not. I think I'm tired and not thinking straight." Jack returned the grin.

"I understand. We all have had a tiresome day."

As he drove off the hospital campus, Jack attempted to reflect on all possibilities, especially those that involve thinking outside the box. He was emotionally spent and physically exhausted. Any fruitful speculation would have to wait until he had a good night's sleep and some food. His thoughts went back to John Connor and Heather McCormick. Jack wept silently and drove on.

6:17 PM

Jack couldn't wait to get home and hug Claire. He entered the house quietly and searched for her. She heard him come in and approached him. They embraced for a long moment. In silence, Jack felt some relief in Claire's arms; he felt anchored.

"I'm so sorry about John," Claire started, her eyes tearful, her tone serious. Jack remained quiet, tears flowing down his cheeks.

Claire took his hand and guided him into the living room. They sat comfortably on the large couch, silent, wordlessly commiserating their loss.

"Tell me what you know," asked Claire, breaking the stillness after a long moment.

"It's just crazy. I admitted a man yesterday with a heart

attack. He was doing well and stable. His heart attack was relatively minor. He was polite and calm. This morning, for no apparent reason he became agitated and confused, pulled out a gun from God knows where, and shot John and Heather, one of the CCU nurses. Security came in and exchanged shots with the patient. They both died. Four people dead and why?"

"Where did he get the gun?" asked Claire intrigued.

"No one knows. Nobody saw the gun until he used it this morning."

"And why did he become agitated and paranoid? Did he have a history of psych disorders?"

"No. No history of any disturbances. Everything appeared normal until he started shooting."

"How strange. How senseless."

"The cops want my help. I'm researching the possibility that the man used a drug that gave him paranoia. Maybe the same drug that may have mimicked a heart attack and arrhythmias."

"Is that possible?"

"I spent all day today researching and came up empty handed. I'll go to the medical school library and do a more extensive search there. There is a meeting tomorrow morning at the police station. I'm going to go and see if I can help out with anything else."

"Jack, I'm not supposed to tell you about my patients. But, I'm seeing a woman in therapy that lost her parents and brother about three months ago. The father was healthy, physically and psychologically. He was admitted at Newton Memorial overnight with chest pains. A heart catheterization showed his heart was normal. He was discharged in great condition. Twenty-four hours later, he suddenly became agitated and confused and shot his wife and son, then dropped dead of a heart attack. The daughter was not home at the time, but found them later. All of them dead. She has been in therapy ever since. She told me her father was a stable man. Never had any psychiatric problems. Very calm man. They believe the stress of being in the hospital caused his psychiatric disturbance, but it seemed odd to me. It sounds like your patient that murdered John and the others today."

"It does seem odd. Do you think there's a connection?"

"I don't know. Maybe."

"What's that patient's name?"

"I don't know. The daughter is Peggy Snyder. I'll find out what his name was and let you know tomorrow."

The possibility was intriguing. But what would that mean? If these events were connected, these men were assassination puppets? If so, who was the marionette master? And how was he pulling the strings?

This type of voodoo was implausible. A more probable explanation for it all would likely be forthcoming. Jack was anxious to learn more about the homicides and what the cops had uncovered. He looked forward to the morning meeting at police headquarters.

Twelve days ago

September 19

8:27 AM

Jack arrived at the Evansville Police Department Headquarters. The old ornate building also served as Evansville's municipal building, containing all city functions including courthouse and the mayor's office. In front of the magnificent art-deco edifice, there were several marble steps. To the sides, there were tall beautifully sculptured columns, giving the structure a façade of stylish sophistication and elegance. Walking up the front stairs, Jack could not help feeling both insignificant and important. He kept his head high and pushed through the main door.

Inside there was a large foyer, highlighting an elegant marble stairway leading upstairs. A graceful chandelier hung high overhead. To the left, another door was labeled: Evansville Police Headquarters. Jack pushed the door open and entered. There were several people, some sitting, others standing in line, waiting to see an older police officer with gray hair sitting behind a tall countertop. Multiple conversations among many people echoed loudly in Jack's ears.

Jack looked behind the counter, hoping to see a familiar face.

"Good morning, Jack," said a woman's voice. It was detective Susan Quentin, who had spotted him entering the building from the office she shared with the other detectives. She shook his hand and led him to the conference room.

When the door opened, Jack could see several people inside, some dressed in police blue uniforms and others well dressed in plain clothes. The room itself was much like the conference room where Jack and the others met every day for morning report. A podium and blackboard were positioned in front of the large room. There were several chairs, each with a small desktop just large enough for a note pad.

"I think we're all here now. Please have a seat," said Detective Herbert Fuller taking control of the pandemonium in the room. All sat down including the newly arrived Jack and Susan. Quickly, silence reigned.

"First, some introductions are in order," continued Herb after a few seconds of complete stillness. "We have with us as part of this investigative team, Sergeant Mike Ganz from the FBI. He has been here before to help us with a few of our big cases. Most of you know him. He's here to help us out with this one." Mike stood up and waved hello to all, a grin on his face. As he sat back down, he winked at Susan. Jack noticed the gesture. Herb continued to speak.

"Also Dr. Jack Norris from Newton Memorial has agreed to assist in the investigation. Suzy and I felt an inside source was necessary to expedite our data gathering as far as the hospital is concerned. Welcome, Dr. Norris and thank you for coming." Herb pointed and gestured at Jack. Jack stood and looked all around the room. People gave him silent nods and grins. Jack sat down again as Herb continued.

"I will summarize the case, as we know it. Arthur Butterworth was a sixty-three-year-old man admitted to the hospital with a heart attack. Dr. Norris tells us he was a legitimate cardiac patient. Dr. Norris, would you mind reviewing for us the information you have on his medical condition?"

Shyly, Jack stood up slowly. As he spoke, he sounded professional and concerned.

"I believe this man came into the hospital with real problems. It's hard to fathom that he came in or was planted purposefully to make a kill."

"Doctor, is there any question about that?" asked Mike inquisitively.

"There were changes on the electrocardiogram when he first arrived at the hospital, highly suggestive of a heart attack. There are poisons and drugs that can be taken to mimic those changes, but the man subsequently had blood tests showing heart damage."

"Are there poisons or drugs that can fool doctors with the blood test results?" persisted Susan.

"None of which I'm aware, but I'm doing a full literature search to confirm that. I'll let you know what I come up with, but I'd be surprised if this is anything but a guy that came in with a heart attack." Mike and all others looked at Jack intensely as he spoke. All nodded in acknowledgement.

After a short moment, Herb continued.

"We appreciate your help with that, doctor. The way I figure it, if Butterworth was acting alone, he either came in to kill somebody or decided to kill somebody after being in the hospital. If he really had a heart attack, the latter is more probable. Then the question is, why would he want to kill those people? I have interviewed the family and friends and I can't get any prior connection to any of the people murdered. No one in the hospital at all. We'll need to find out where he got the gun. It seems he didn't arrive in the hospital with a gun."

"Who brought the patient to the hospital? Did he have any visitors after his arrival?" interrupted another detective Jack didn't know.

"He came in by ambulance," interjected Susan. "Mrs. Butterworth and his daughter visited him in the hospital for an hour. They say he never had a gun. He was totally opposed to guns. The wife told me a story about the time his father took him hunting when he was a little boy. The father shot a rabbit. The sight of this bunny shot to death created a psychological issue with guns. All his life the man detested anything to do with weapons. The family assured me that the patient would never have anything to do with any killing or guns. Jim is checking into that, but I believe the family. I don't think we'll find any reason why this guy would want to kill anybody. So why did he? There is no question of that. He had a smoking gun in his hand." Susan was confused. Even angry. What was missing here?

"The witnesses at the scene say the man was oriented, calm and amicable the whole time," continued Herb. "He was very appreciative of their help. He said, 'yes please and thank you.' The man suddenly became very agitated and paranoid. What is it you doctors call it—?" Herb looked at Jack and paused inquisitively.

"Freakin' crazy?" deadpanned Jack. All laughed, much-needed relief from the wretchedness of the moment. Jack continued after a moment. "I think you mean acute dissociative delusional disorder."

"That's it. Anyhow, the nursing staff couldn't calm down Butterworth. He became even more agitated. He took out a gun from somewhere and pointed it at the staff. The staff backed off immediately and retreated to a safe place. All except the nurse taking care of him, who got trapped in the room at gunpoint. He didn't permit her to leave. One of the doctors went into the room to talk the man down and get the nurse out of there. Butterworth shot the nurse then the doctor. The man shot twice more but hit no one. The bullets were recovered from the wall in the adjoining cubicle. Meanwhile, the hospital security had been called. A security guard was nearby. He had a gun and pulled it out. The guard and Butterworth exchanged shots, both being fatally wounded." Herb paused a moment for all to digest the information. Exteriorly, Jack appeared composed. Inwardly, he was mortified and overwhelmed by the factual description of how the life of his best friend was coldly and abruptly terminated.

"So, the number one question is where he got the gun," continued the lead detective.

"Did the gun come back registered?" asked Mike.

"Nah, no registration. The serial number was destroyed and ballistic reports are pending," said another detective.

"Keep at it, Jimmy. Let me know when you have something. I think the gun is the key to solving this case," said Herb.

"I can search the FBI database and cast a wider net. I'll talk to you after the meeting and coordinate with you, Jimmy," said Mike assertively looking at the young Evansville detective, then Herb. Jimmy and Herb nodded silently.

"Dr. Norris, will you let us know if you come up with any drugs that may be involved? We'll send a full drug screen on the perp. It'll take a while to come back. The routine drug test should be available today," said Susan. Jack nodded.

After this, several other people had a chance to speak. Some were part of the Crime Scene Unit and spoke about their findings. Much minutia was brought up about the microscopic materials found at the scene, the victims' cars, the perp's clothing and belongings, but the gist of it all was that nothing helpful was found. The detectives interviewed all the witnesses, family members, relatives of relatives, friends and their cousins. Nothing. Nothing important was uncovered. The murders continued to appear unprovoked and senseless.

Several detectives had interrogated all the people that had been in the hospital. This included patients that had been in the CCU cubicle turned murder scene, before the killer patient. All these detectives and cops had a chance to talk about what they had learned. After endless dissertations by numerous people, the bottom line was the same—no helpful hints or clues. In the midst of the lengthy discussion, someone reported that Dr. Rupert had been seen in CCU about an hour before the murders. That bit sparked Jack's interest.

"Rupert up and about at five o'clock in the morning? No way," thought the young doctor. Jack found that incredibly unusual but he didn't say a word. He had never seen Rupert in the hospital before ten in the morning. One of the detectives added that Dr. Connor entered the unit a few minutes before the whole thing went sour.

"Another humongous coincidence," thought Jack, the biggest skeptic about coincidences in the world.

John would not be in the hospital that early either, thought Jack to himself as others spoke. Jack's mind wandered. He didn't like Rupert, but him being at the hospital so early had to mean something. It had to mean Rupert was involved. What if his feelings towards the man were biasing his reflections? Was he being fair and impartial? At that moment, Jack vowed to let the evidence lead him where it may.

"We'll meet again every morning to gather our thoughts and get marching orders for the day. Any information you discover let me know right away. I will coordinate the data," said Herb authoritatively disrupting Jack's meditative state, jerking him back into reality. "Jack, see what you can find out and let me know if something useful comes up."

Jack nodded agreeingly. "I should have some information for you in two or three days. If a drug was involved, I'll find it," he added confidently.

4:50 PM

"Lucy, I'm home!" exclaimed Jack, trying to put on a happy face. This was the worst ever imitation of a Cuban accent. Claire was busy in the kitchen. Jack approached her and they kissed.

"How was your day, Dick Tracy?" inquired Claire, completely aware of his tactics to convince her he was coping well.

"You'll be surprised to know, it was a bit intimidating. We had a meeting for several hours going over all the evidence." Jack's initial smile faded as he continued. "Claire, I've been thinking about this all day. I think Rupert has something to do with the murders."

"Rupert? Why do you think that?" This received Claire's full attention.

"I have worked at Newton Memorial for how many years

now? Rupert has been there almost as long. Every morning I drive in to the doctor's lot and drive by his parking stall. I always read his name on the placard posted on the wall. Do you know why? It's always empty." Jack put emphasis on the word always. "The day of the murders his car was in there when I got in at 7:30 for the first time ever. I hear he was in around five o'clock. Why? Is it a coincidence?'

"Hmmm, I see what you're saying, Jack. But what motive could Rupert possibly have? And how did he do it? He didn't pull the trigger. How could he influence that man to kill John, Heather, and the guard?"

"Those are the real questions. Let's think outside the box. The man had to be put under some hypnotic state. Drugged, perhaps?"

"What kind of drug could do this? Have they done a drug screen on the murderer?"

"Yes, and preliminarily it was negative. You know, in real life the process is much slower than on TV. Law and Order detective's Logan or Boren or CSI Grisham would have the whole case solved in one-hour and that includes commercials. They get lab results pronto. Here in the real world these things take time. Lots of time. They have sent blood, urine, hair and God knows what else to be tested for drugs. We'll see what that full report adds to the case."

"What about hypnosis? Could Rupert, or anyone else for that matter, put somebody under hypnosis to such a degree that he would perform these heinous acts?"

"I don't know. Rupert had been in the unit an hour or so beforehand. He apparently was not present at the time. If it was hypnosis, wouldn't he have to be present at the onset of the delusional state?"

"I think you're probably right. I don't know much about hypnosis." Claire paused for a moment. "Did you talk to the police about your suspicions of Rupert?"

"Not yet. It would be premature. I hate the son of a bitch, but I want to be fair. I don't want to be like those doctors that fall in love with their diagnosis too early then pursue data in support of their biased first impression and neglect the truth and facts. I'll do my own investigation into Rupert and keep my mind open."

"Your own investigation? Listen to you, Detective Norris," exclaimed Claire facetiously.

"While the cops do their thing, I will do my parallel investigation from the medical and hospital point of view. I know I can add to the search for the truth. I want you to help me."

"Okay, sure. What about motive? That's what I can't figure out," said Claire after a short moment of silence.

"Another million dollar question."

"What about the patient I was telling you about last night? Did you tell the cops?" inquired Claire.

"No. Get me more information. Did you find out the name?"

"No, not yet. I want to get permission from my patient. I need to be ethical. I already divulged too much to you. Give me a bit more time."

"A few days ago, Heather and Julie came up to me in CCU after a code and told me they thought there was a cardiac arrest epidemic at Memorial. I sort of blew them off.

Next thing you know, Heather is shot." Tears appeared in Jack's lower eyelids. He paused. More tears appeared when he continued, "John, too, tried to talk to me about something that was bothering him at work. I didn't pay much attention at the time and then—"

"Jack, you don't think it's your fault, do you?" interjected Claire, dabbing Jack's eyes with a tissue.

"No, I don't think it was my fault," lied Jack. "But what if I had paid more attention to them? What if I looked at the patient records with cardiac arrests and found something obvious? Some connection to this madness! What if—"

Claire clutched Jack's hands and held them tightly. "Jack, don't 'What if—' yourself, this is not on you," Claire paused, looking into Jack's eyes.

"I know. I know. My resolve to help solve this is strong, Claire. Maybe, I should have done more before, but I will give it all I got now," Jack said. Claire gave a faint accepting smile.

In better spirits, Jack stood up straight. "Heather and Julie were going to pull out the medical records for the cardiac arrests at Memorial over the last year, so I can see if there was anything unusual. I'll see if Julie has them."

With renewed interest, Jack gave a fake smile and walked to the small decorative table in the kitchen on which his cell phone rested. He removed the mobile device from its charging perch and prepared to dial the CCU at Newton Memorial Hospital.

As Jack waited for the call to go through, Claire said softly: "Be gentle with her. Just like you, Julie has lost her best friend in a terrible tragedy. She may not be ready to deal with this yet."

"I know Julie pretty well. Believe you me she is ready to kick some ass. And so am I."

Eleven days ago

September 20

6:07 AM

"Evansville departure, niner-eight-gulf-kilo with you, three thousand going to four thousand," said Jack into the microphone in front of his lips. The headset was securely and comfortably positioned around his head and covered both ears, facilitating radio communications. Moments earlier, the Evansville Tower air traffic controller had commanded instructions for Jack to switch frequencies to the departure controller. Jack had done this routine numerous times before during his many flights. Like all others, the take-off had been precise. As expected, the departure controller's voice returned an acknowledgement.

"Gulf-kilo, radar contact; climb to nine thousand feet direct to Indianapolis."

"Nine thousand, direct to Indianapolis," repeated Jack cryptically, as mandated by FAA regulations and protocol.

Even as he spoke, Jack directed the Bonanza to fly a direct route to his destination. His GPS had been programmed before departure to allow this maneuver at this time with only minimal effort and little more input. In no time, the aircraft was climbing and on the proper course. The purpose of this trip was twofold. Most importantly, Jack wanted to clear his mind and think. The calming properties of flight were therapeutic for Jack, which was what the doctor ordered. For this effect to be maximal, Jack engaged the autopilot, which would reduce his need to concentrate on flying. The second reason for the trip was to visit the medical school library to continue his research endeavors for a drug that could have caused the effects observed on the man turned delusional killer.

Almost reaching an altitude of nine thousand feet, the autopilot signaled and automatically made the appropriate changes in the trim settings to allow for leveled flight. Jack merely supervised in his continuing contemplative state.

Where did the gun come from? Who could gain from these catastrophes? What could Rupert's involvement be? These questions tumbled inside Jack's brain.

"We will find the son of a bitch responsible for all this," resolved Jack in deep thought.

Time flew by and before Jack knew it, the airplane

approached its destination airport, now seven miles from touch down.

"Bonanza niner-eight-gulf-kilo, descend to three thousand and join the localizer; cleared for the ILS-2–3-right approach." The approach controller spoke in a matter of fact manner, conveying a sense of calmness and professionalism. Jack repeated the instructions acknowledging them.

A long moment later, now with the runway in sight, Jack received further instructions.

"Niner-eight-gulf-kilo contact Indianapolis Tower at 120.9."

"Tower, 120.9 for niner-eight-gulf-kilo." Jack changed frequencies and spoke again. "Tower, niner-eight-gulf-kilo, ILS-2–3-right."

"Niner-eight-gulf-kilo cleared to land 2–3-right, wind 190 at five knots."

"Clear to land, 2–3-right, niner-eight-gulf-kilo."

The landing on the runway lined up at 230 degrees was impeccable and soon the plane was parked at the ramp in front of the Indianapolis Signature FBO, the local business that provided services for general aviators. They would be requested to fuel the airplane and keep it safe until Jack's return later in the day. Jack had called ahead and requested a rental car, which was ready to go. Very familiar with the city from his days as a medical student, Jack drove to the medical school library. He detoured briefly from his journey to stop at Starbucks for a grande, dry, one-extra-shot cappuccino. Caffeine ammunition was a necessary ingredient for this mission.

The library was almost a home away from home. Having been in school before the Internet explosion, Jack had spent a lot of time at the library. He was familiar with the place and it was like coming home to Mama. He placed his coffee cup on an out of sight table in the back of the cavernous room and went about procuring books. The search itself took almost two hours. Several books of different size, age and repair were strewn on the table. Jack's hunt for information was long and lasted way past lunch. It had also been fruitless and unrewarding. Beginning to be aware of hunger pains, he stopped to take a sip of coffee. This was the third time in the last hour he tried to drink out of an empty cup.

"It can't be a drug. There is no known drug that could do all this to a man, without other manifestations. This has to be the wrong angle. Unless it is an unknown experimental agent; maybe one Rupert is—"

Jack's thoughts were brusquely interrupted by an earsplitting familiar ring tone from the cellular phone on the table. The loud sound jerked Jack into the here-and-now. The caller ID indicated the caller was from Newton Memorial Hospital. He put the Bluetooth receiver in his ear and answered.

"Hello."

"Dr. Norris, it's Julie. I have all the charts for you."

"How could you have had time to—"

"I stayed up all night," interrupted the nurse. "I put the charts on your desk. Somebody killed my best friend and I will do what it takes to see justice served." Jack could tell in her voice she was determined, but emotionally devastated.

"Thank you, Julie. I will look at the charts and see if that takes us anywhere. Hang in there, okay? We'll get to the bottom of this."

"Please let me know if I can be of any other help."

After exchanging a few pleasantries, they hung up. Jack sat for a long moment, numb, unmoving, unthinking. Then, he got up, drove back to the airport and flew home.

Ten days ago

September 21

8:30 AM

"We are gathered here today to pay our last respects to our dear friends and colleagues, John Connor and Heather McCormick." The priest spoke slowly, clearly, and solemnly into the microphone amplifying his voice. As he spoke, Father Daniel looked at the people filling all the available pews. It was standing room only at Holy Rosary Catholic Church. On this sorrowful morning, the ceremonial acknowledgement of these lives lost, heralded the burial of two young and dedicated souls. All eyes were moist, most pockets and purses equipped with the necessary tissues. Soft whimpers could be heard in the background here and there, as the words echoed throughout the large room.

"John and Heather will be missed dearly. They were devoted to their profession and—"

The words were difficult to utter; the brain wants to say, but the emotions choke the sound. Many well-dressed young professionals took turns speaking at the microphone, sharing their sincere tender sentiments about John and Heather. The sadness in the room expressed the poignancy in their hearts.

A long line walked slowly from the back of the church to the altar, in front of which were the two coffins, where the two lifeless bodies laid in their final resting position. Each visitor glanced at John, who rested peacefully in an open casket, his clothes concealing the wound that ended it all. Heather's coffin was closed. A picture of her young beautiful person was perched nearby, a sorrowful reminder of what once was. An overwhelming feeling of disgust and grief was palpable. Two people destined for greatness now lay lifeless.

The families were sitting in the front. They were hugged lovingly by those passing, mostly in silence, as there were no fitting words to be murmured. No words that could possibly soften the blow that was the loss of a child. Of a sibling. Of a friend. A best friend.

When the procession was over, the coffins were transported with much ceremony to the awaiting limousines outside Holy Rosary Catholic Church. These hearses would guide a long motorcade of vehicles with headlights on, to the cemetery. It was all so sad. Disheartening.

The burials proceeded as usual. The overcast gloomy day's misty rain added unnecessary melancholy to the event.

1:30 PM

Jack returned to his office after the funeral. More than ever, the fire raged inside, heightening his resolve. He sat at his desk in his office at Newton Memorial with the door closed. Beverley had knocked twice, once to bring him a cup of her famous coffee and another to remind him it was lunchtime. She offered to bring him a sandwich from the cafeteria and, after some persuasion, he agreed. The short pause to eat actually did Jack more good than he bargained for. More relaxed and clear-headed, he continued to work. A knock on the door interrupted the silence.

"Come in."

"Hi, Dr. Norris." It was Julie.

"You can call me Jack, Julie. I'm making some progress.

How are you holding up?" He stopped what he was doing, pausing to attend to the young nurse.

"It's quiet in CCU. The hospital is on diversion and the patients in the unit are just the ones we had from before. They are all doing okay. I asked permission to come see if you needed my help."

Jack realized that, just like him, Julie needed to do something constructive to calm the fire inside. A fire created by the loss of a best friend.

She brought coffee. Jack realized the secret was out.

"Does everybody in the whole hospital know of my coffee addiction? I vehemently deny it, you know."

"Your secret is safe with me, if mine is safe with you." She lifted her other hand, showing a cup. "It's an iced white chocolate mocha," she said after a short pause. She smiled.

"Here's what I have so far. First, I did a computer search to determine the number of in-hospital cardiac arrests. I didn't count those occurring in the catheterization laboratory. From 2000 until 2004, there were about fifty cases per year." Jack suspended his conversation for a few seconds as he searched for a particular file on his laptop, where he had tabulated the data.

"Ah, here it is. Fifty-two in 2000, fifty-five in 2001, forty-nine in 2002, fifty-three in 2003 and fifty-two in 2004. Last year, the number was forty-six. This year, if the numbers continue to rise at the present rate, we'll have sixty-one."

"It looks like something happened starting earlier in 2006 and continues until now. But, Jack, what does this have to do with Heather and John's murders?"

"I'm not sure yet but this is either a huge coincidence, or there is some connection."

"I know what you always say to the students and residents about coincidences. You don't believe in them. I don't either." There was a pause. Then she continued.

"I want you to count on me for any help I can give."

"Thanks, Julie. I appreciate that."

"What else have you found out?"

"I went back to when the number of cardiac arrests sharply increased and looked through all the charts, including those you had given me. So far, I intensely reviewed five charts belonging to patients who arrested with no good cause. I still have many more to go through. Are you sure you want to help?"

"I need to. Tell me what to do."

Jack explained to the determined nurse to look for age, presence of known heart disease in the past medical history, whether the patient had a heart attack during the index admission, look at the lab data for cardiac marker elevation, potassium levels, EKG abnormalities, test results, especially those that determined the overall heart function and so on. He helped create a chart on a blank piece of paper for information gathering.

"As you go through the charts, if you have questions, let me know, okay?" asked Jack. She nodded already working on the top chart of the To Do pile.

The therapeutic benefit of doing something constructive was priceless to the two friends. They spoke to each other infrequently and when words were exchanged, it was Julie asking a specific question about an EKG or laboratory result.

They worked until five, though much more needed to be done. Jack thanked Julie for all her help as she left. He continued to work until six. At that time, prompted by a text message from Claire, Jack gathered several charts and, loaded to the gills, walked to the parking lot.

Nine days ago

September 22

2:02 AM

Jack fought nodding off to sleep. He had continued to work for hours on the large kitchen table. Data gathering and tabulation was tedious but Jack's obsessive qualities did not permit him to stop until it was all done. Stacks of charts loomed in front of him. Jack finished his evaluation of another patient's chart. He picked it up and placed it on the Done mountain of records. This proved to be the straw that broke the proverbial camel's back. The center of gravity of this stack changed sufficiently off axis that the whole heap spilled on the tile floor with a thunderous racket. The clatter woke Claire up, who had previously been sound asleep in the bedroom. She put on her robe and walked to the kitchen. As she approached, Jack was kneeling on the floor picking up the charts.

"Sorry, I woke you up, honey."

"That's okay. I hate to spend a third of my life sleeping. What a waste," she said with a sleepy smile.

"I've done a lot of work. I'm almost done."

"You should come to bed. You do need to get some shut-eye so you can think straight tomorrow. Actually, today."

"You're right. But I can't stop now. I need to go through all this information so I have time to analyze it before our next meeting."

"In that case, how about some coffee?"

"Oh, my angel of mercy. Yes. Please."

Claire made a pot of coffee as they continued to speak.

"So, what have you found so far, Jack? Use this as a practice session for the meeting with the cops."

"Great idea. Well, several men were admitted to Newton Memorial with chest pains. Most of them ruled out for acute coronary syndrome—"

"Which means the pain was non-cardiac, right?"

"Right, pain from other causes; some had chest wall pain, others had stomach upsets, and so on."

"All those things can cause chest pains but the heart checked out okay; is that what you're saying?"

"Exactly. A few had minor heart attacks, but all were stable. All were relatively young." Jack paused to look at his report in progress. "From thirty-two to fifty-one years old.

All the patients then had a cardiac arrest for no good reason. The code team responded."

"Hang on, slow down a bit. Remember, when you talk to the cops, they will require you to speak in non-technical language. What's a code team? They need to understand the usual routine at the hospital."

"I know. I appreciate you stopping me to correct me. The code team is the pre-appointed team of nurses and doctors that responds to the bedside of a patient in case of a dire emergency, such as a cardiac arrest."

"What exactly is a cardiac arrest? Will you explain that a bit?"

"An arrhythmia causes the heart, all of a sudden, to go into a rapid tremble. The heart muscle quivers so fast, that there is no effective pumping and the blood flow stops." Jack stopped for a moment to demonstrate a quivering heart with his cupped hands. "The patient drops dead and will die unless an immediate shock, or defibrillation, is delivered across the chest. The monitors at the nurse's station pick up the rapid heart rhythm disorder and alert the techs to call a code. The code team responds."

"Why do you feel these patients should not have had a cardiac arrest?"

"There are certain factors that most patients who eventually suffer a sudden cardiac arrest display, such as a large heart attack, weak heart muscle with congestive heart failure—"

"What's congestive heart failure?"

"Water accumulation in the lungs from ineffective heart contractions. The fluid floods the airspaces and the patient becomes short of breath, weak, fatigued and so on."

"What other factors are there for sudden cardiac arrest?"

"Very thick heart muscles, changes on the electrocardiogram indicating problems with how the electrical impulses recover after normal stimulation."

"How do you assess that?"

"We look at the QT interval." Before she could ask, Jack explained further. "The QT interval is a part of the EKG that measures electrical recovery. When this is either too long or too short, cardiac arrests can occur. None of these were found." After a short moment, Jack continued. "There are conditions that can cause problems with very low or very high potassium levels in the blood, or very low magnesium levels. These can cause cardiac arrest."

"Let me guess. You found none of these. What about that nurse several years ago that was killing his patients with potassium injections? Did you look for that?"

"Yes, there are specific EKG changes. The T-waves become peaked. I didn't find any of these types of T waves."

"What about that movie—what was the name." Claire paused pensively. "Coma, young people were being killed to harvest organs for transplantation. How were they killing those patients?"

"They were given carbon monoxide instead of oxygen during minor surgery."

"Did you look for that?"

"No, not really," said Jack slowly and hesitatingly.

"Should you?" she asked.

"Well, carbon monoxide causes minor cardiac arrhythmias or skipped beats. And headaches and confusion. And disorientation. Come to think of it, we should really look into that. The perp at the hospital was said to have become confused." Jack stopped, noticing a smirk on Claire's face.

"Listen to you. The perp. You're talking like a cop already. How can you rule that in or out?"

"Tissue samples to measure carboxyhemoglobin levels. I will have the cops look to see if the oxygen bottles had been switched for either carbon monoxide or carbon dioxide. Thanks, Claire. You're a great help." That said, Jack yawned and put his head on Claire's chest. She caressed his head and face approvingly.

"Let's get a few hours of sleep. What do you say?"

"Yeah, lets." They turned off the coffee machine and walked to the bedroom hand in hand. Soon they were both deep asleep.

8:12 AM

Jack arrived at the police station and walked to the front desk. He was eager to share his investigative work of the last three days with the detectives.

"May I help you," asked the sergeant behind the counter. She was heavyset and dressed in a blue police uniform.

"I'm here for the detective meeting this morning," said Jack.

"Meeting? What meeting? Who are you meeting with?" she inquired.

"Detectives Fuller and Quentin," he answered.

"I don't know of any meetings. Let me find out for you," she whispered. She dialed a number and waited for a connection. Her eyes wandered to avoid contact with Jack's.

"Are the detectives having a meeting this morning?" she finally spoke. She listened then hung up the phone.

"There are no scheduled meetings this morning, sir," she alleged.

"No meeting?" Jack said, surprised.

Jack thanked her and left. He walked to his car and looked up Herb's cell number. He dialed it and waited.

"Good morning, Herb. It's Jack Norris. I thought you were having a meeting this morning." Jack waited for a reply.

"We have worked on this case for the last three days and came up with nothing. We've looked at every angle imaginable. We don't need any more meetings. We're ready to close the case."

"Close the case?" asked Jack, perplexedly.

"Yes, we came to the conclusion that Butterworth must have had a gun when he was admitted and—"

"What about my research?"

"What did you find? Any drug that could have caused him to kill those people?"

"Well, uh, no, not really."

"Okay, then. I don't see any other possible explanation. The man was witnessed to have pulled the trigger. There was nobody else there with him. We're putting the case on hold for now."

"I have some possible related cases. Can I—"

"What cases?" interrupted Herb.

Jack was flabbergasted. He was speechless. He wanted to scream aloud, but he was tongue-tied. He needed time to gather his thoughts.

"Never mind. Can I meet with you sometime today?"

"I don't think we have anything to talk about, Jack. The case is closed; at least for now. Have a nice day."

The phone line was disconnected.

"The case is closed?" whispered Jack to himself in astonishment.

Jack drove around town aimlessly for an hour. When he stopped the car, he dialed Susan's cell number.

"Susan, we need to meet," he proposed.

"About what?"

"The murders at Newton Memorial. Are you really giving up on the case already?"

"Jack, we considered all the possibilities. Even Mike Ganz, our FBI liaison, agrees this case should be closed. Jack, we agree that the case was bizarre and unusual, but some people have weird responses to stress. We can't find any connection to anyone other than the perp. We believe Arthur Butterworth was acting alone. We're still searching for the gun. The FBI is helping us with that. They have an extensive database. So far, they have found nothing."

"I have some data to show you." Jack paused for a second. "Some stuff I found."

"Herb told me you couldn't find any drug," said Susan.

"No, not drugs. Other people that were killed, possibly in connection to this case."

"You think this guy had killed other people? We don't have any other opened murder cases."

"Just hear me out. Can we meet? Please," solicited Jack insistently.

"Okay. Meet me at the station in thirty minutes. I'll see if I can talk Herb and Mike into coming, too."

Jack sighed. He drove towards the police station. He called Claire. He updated her on all the frustrations of the day. In turn, she gave him the name of the patient whose unexpected, mysterious and bizarre actions left a grieving daughter without parents or brother.

Susan and Mike were waiting for Jack on the front steps to the enormous edifice. Together they walked into the police station and headed for the conference room.

"Okay, what do you have that is so compelling, we should reopen this case?" asked Susan, calmly.

"Two things," answered Jack. "There is a man by the name of Jeff Snyder that you should look into. He was admitted at Newton Memorial with chest pains. Everything checked out okay. His heart was normal. He went home and suddenly developed confusion and paranoia, just like Butterworth. He killed his wife and son, had a heart attack and died."

"Where did this happen? It wasn't in Evansville," said Susan.

"And you think these cases are related? How?" inquired Mike, looking intently at Jack.

"I don't know yet, but don't you agree that it sounds similar to our case?" asked Jack.

"Sure it sounds similar, Jack; we see cases like this all the time. They sound alike, but it doesn't mean they are linked." Mike spoke confidently.

"You said you had two things," interjected Susan.

"There has been a slew of cardiac arrests at Newton Memorial over the last several months. I'd like to present the data to you," proposed Jack.

"I doubt the hospital or any of its staff had anything to do with these murders. Do you think there is a ring of murderers working at Newton Memorial? That's a bit far-fetched." Mike spoke authoritatively, as only an agent of the FBI would dare, during such great uncertainty.

"I'd like to see what you have, Jack, but it does sound far-fetched to have doctors or nurses responsible for these atrocities," interrupted Susan. Mike turned to face Jack, his arms folded as he waited for a reply. Jack had learned from Claire to notice body language. She claimed he would learn a lot from it about the patient's demeanor and feelings. She taught Jack that the body posture of folding one's arms was a sign of non-acceptance. For some reason, Mike Ganz could not bear the notion that the professionals at Newton Memorial Hospital could engage in such foul play. For that matter, neither could anyone else.

"Interesting," Jack thought to himself. "What happened to keeping an open mind?" As these thoughts emerged in his mind, Jack said aloud facing the inquiring eyes now turned toward him, "I get bad vibes from one of the doctors: a Dr. Ian Rupert. He is in charge of the research laboratory. I had noticed he arrived at the hospital much earlier than usual the day of the murders. He was seen in CCU around five o'clock in the morning the day of the murders. Previous to that, I had never seen him at the hospital before ten o'clock."

Mike interrupted Jack rudely. "We must be careful. You are talking about a powerful man who is known for his work in research. Isn't he?"

"Undoubtedly; I'm just saying—"

"What would his motive be?" Another discourteous interruption followed by an awkward moment of silence.

"I don't know. But I think you should investigate further," responded Jack sternly.

After a long moment of silence, Herb and Susan agreed to consider the information Jack had gathered. Overwhelmed, Mike remained skeptically unspoken, his body language speaking volumes.

Jack went out to his car and brought back his laptop. The three detectives sat in the conference room, quietly waiting Jack's return. Having delivered many lectures using PowerPoint, Jack felt back in his element. As he entered, they remained seated, motionless and in silence.

Jack set up his computer and began his presentation, describing his research findings. He started by describing the patient characteristics of those who are known to be at risk for cardiac arrests. He then described two groups of individuals: those that had cardiac arrests with these features and the group of patients that had cardiac arrests unexpectedly.

He first depicted the great increase in total numbers in cardiac arrests with a graph he titled "Cardiac Arrest Epidemic at Newton Memorial Hospital." A clear-cut spike could be seen in the last six months, as compared to the previous sixty. As far as the etiology leading to the deaths, Jack admitted to being befuddled. He enlightened the detectives about his theory that the patients may have been poisoned. The type of agent used was not known but it may be useful to obtain appropriate tissue from all the bodies looking for something in common. The agent might have been carbon monoxide or carbon dioxide. This should be discussed with the medical examiners. They could entertain these diagnoses in their post-mortem search for clues and the truth. The cops ought to look to see if the oxygen tanks could have been switched with one of these or other poisonous gases. Susan looked intrigued and little by little started to write notes on her notebook. The detectives remained silent, even when Jack finished his presentation.

"This seems too far-fetched." Mike spoke first breaking the uncomfortable silence.

"Are there any other reasons to explain this spike in cardiac arrests? Anything at all?" inquired Herb.

"And how do you tie these cardiac arrests to our murders?" asked Susan.

"I can't, except that this is an unusual discovery. The murders, we have all agreed, were extremely odd. To have two extraordinary events occur at the same time, it would be unlikely these events are unconnected. It is more likely that one single causative factor is at play leading to both peculiar circumstances. It is just playing the odds. We do this in medicine all the time. Two weird symptoms at the same time in an otherwise healthy patient, it is most likely that both symptoms are connected than unrelated and appearing out of the blue," explained Jack persistently.

The detectives once again considered the implications of the information in silence.

"I'm sold," said Susan looking at Herb and Mike. Herb took a deep breath but did not speak for a beat.

"I imagine it's worth a fresh look. What do you think, Mike?" asked Herb.

"I think there's a good medical reason for the increased numbers of cardiac arrests at Newton Memorial that is unrelated to the murders. I think Jack is biased to the connection and is missing something. Probably something simple. No offense, Jack," said Mike calmly and reassuringly.

"None taken, but Mike, prove me wrong." Jack knew he made a compelling argument and his point was gathering momentum. Silence reigned again.

"Okay, we'll reopen the case." Herb spoke authoritatively, convinced of Jack's assertions. Susan nodded then stared at Mike.

"Okay, fine," Mike said reluctantly, finally agreeing with the others.

"Suzy, talk to the medical examiners and ask them to specifically look into the possibility of poisoning with gases," said Herb.

The truth, the detectives would soon learn, was that Butterworth's erratic and bizarre behavior was likely to have been induced by some sort of chemical poisoning. As such, the medical examiner had already been keen on the possibility and had spent a great deal of time and money gathering data to prove or disprove this hypothesis. The results from all the specimens collected for chemical analysis were pending. Unfortunately, the most commonly sought drugs had not been found. A more thorough search for unusual chemicals would take a long time.

With the case back on the front burner, attention was turned to the weapon once again. The questions were again delineated and entertained: Where did the gun come from? How did it get to the patient? It didn't seem that the patient brought the revolver to the hospital with him, although that remained the most likely possibility. If someone else provided the weapon, he or she would be the most culpable person and the real killer, most especially, if Butterworth was found to have been poisoned. Theories were re-entertained about the nursing staff, the cleaning crew, and the previous patient in that room possibly leaving it there and so on. No speculation made sense.

The detectives agreed that they would find and interview the previous patient to occupy the bed and whoever cleaned the room and made the bed before it became Mr. Butterworth's. They would speak to the nursing staff again, although the first go-around, on the day of the murders, had proven fruitless. One of the strategies of proper police interviewing is to go over details repeatedly. What once remained locked and hidden by the mysterious neural connections of the shocked and stressed brain would sometimes later surface and become quite clear, once the dust settled.

The ongoing endeavor to find the gun's previous owner had remained fruitless. According to Mike Ganz, the great FBI detective, despite all the tricks of the trade used, the serial number continued to resist identification. Whoever destroyed this information really knew what he or she was doing. When ballistic analysis was conducted, there was no record of this gun being utilized in a crime beforehand, according to the vast FBI database. The search for the gun connection continued. Mike discussed the details of his diligent pursuit for the gun's owner.

The group also discussed Jeff Snyder. During a short lunch break, Herb and Susan consulted their police computer and made several phone calls. Snyder's case occurred in a small rural town several counties away, the reason the Evansville Police was unaware of it. Although likewise bizarre, the Snyder case was hard to tie into the hospital murders. The question arose about the possibility that there were cases like it in other townships, a question worthy of investigation.

After three hours of discussion, it felt like there was no forward progress at all except, of course, that Jack was able to spark up interest in the case. The truth remained undiscovered with no end in sight. At the conclusion of the meeting, Jack felt a twinge of hopelessness. The miracle of television had distorted his reality about detective and police work. In the real world, the process was slow, tedious and methodic. There was a lot of painstaking theorizing and diligent assessment and re-examination of that which was known and unknown. It was going to take a long time to get to the truth. Nevertheless, the truth would become known. Jack just knew it.

Herb Fuller, who was turning out to be first-class at quarterback, gave each participant marching orders. With renewed interest, Herb was once again calling all the right plays and doing it in such a way that engendered all team members to work hard towards the common goal.

Jack's assignment was to return to his office. At the behest of the detective, Jack requested Jeff Snyder's hospital chart for his review. Susan and Mike would search for unusual homicide or suicide cases throughout surrounding counties, especially those typically obtaining medical care from Newton Memorial. On the hunch that the patient in CCU was drugged, since no drugs were known to cause those effects, Jack considered a research agent. He asked the cops to call Rupert and get him to disclose all the research drugs he was using. They would call the hospital's attorney and get the ball rolling.

Jack sat at his desk going through the medical records tabulating his results and writing comments as he went.

The door to his office suddenly opened.

"Why are you sticking your nose into my business?"

Jack recognized the voice, even before he looked up to see who had spoken.

"Dr. Rupert, what makes you think I'm doing that?" This time Jack would not be intimidated.

"You're checking up on my research protocols, aren't you?"

"Yes, I am. I am interested in finding out what sorts of experiments are being done at Newton. Is that wrong of me?"

"You're damn right, it's wrong! It's none of your business."

"Why is it a secret?"

"It's just none of your business, young man. You are in deep trouble. I will see to it that you never practice medicine in this state or in this country." Dr. Rupert angrily stomped out of the room.

"Asshole," whispered Jack to no one in particular.

Jack called Susan's cell phone.

"I just received a visit from Rupert. He is angry that we are looking into his research. This much opposition must mean he has something to hide, don't you think?" asked Jack.

"I don't know. People sometimes overreact to simple requests by the police."

"So, are we getting the research records?"

"They have to give them to us, but it looks like they will drag their feet. We've contacted the district attorney to subpoena the files from Rupert. It'll have to go to court and it will take forever. But we'll get them," reassured Susan.

"Susan, thanks for talking to me and reopening the case. I know there's something going on; much more than meets the eye."

"Thanks, Jack. We'll keep investigating. We'll do the best we can to get to the bottom of all this."

They hung up.

5:06 PM

Clutching Mexican carryout, Jack opened the door leading from the garage to the kitchen. Claire met Jack at the door. With a kiss and embrace, she hung herself on his neck. The aroma of nachos al carbon emanated appetizingly from the bag. Claire directed Jack to the kitchen table and together they dished out supper as they conversed.

"Claire, I really believe Rupert is responsible for all this mess."

"I know you do. How do we prove it?"

"We?" emphasized Jack.

"Sure, I'd like to help."

"Claire, there is one thing I can't shake off my mind.

The night before John and the others were killed, we had an indoor soccer game."

"Yes, I remember."

"John tried to talk to me after the game about something that was bothering him. Something about work. The hospital. But we never actually talked. There was too much going on. Too many interruptions. So, John and I planned on talking the next day. The day he was—." A long pause. A sad face. A sob. A single tear escaped and made its way down his left cheek. Jack sniffled as Claire gave his right hand a sympathetic squeeze. With his left hand, he wiped the fallen drop.

"What exactly did John tell you?" asked Claire.

"Not much. He tried to tell me there was something going on at work. I could see it was bothering him a lot. At the end of the game, normally he'd joke around and point out all my soccer blunders. That day, he was serious and quiet. I wish I had taken the time to talk to him longer."

"It wasn't your fault. But whatever was bothering John was probably related to his death, don't you think?"

"I'm sure of it. But what?" inquired Jack.

"Have you brought it up at the meetings with the cops?"

"No. To tell you the truth, I forgot all about it until now. Not sure why. I'll discuss it with them at our next meeting."

"For now, what can I do to help you?" Claire volunteered.

"Help me think through this. How can we begin to tie Rupert to the murders?"

"Motive and opportunity; why and how would he do it?"

"I don't know yet. I do know he was at the crime scene before the murder and him being at the hospital that early is very unusual. It cannot be a coincidence. How would he … how would anyone make a killer out of a God-fearing, law-abiding man?"

"I just thought about something when you said Rupert was at the hospital much earlier than usual the day of the murders. There have been other incidents; what do you call it, an epidemic of cardiac arrests. Was Rupert in early all those days too? Let's look for a pattern," proposed Claire enthusiastically.

"That's a great idea. We'll need to get into his office, somehow. We'll need to trick his secretary. Are you in on this with me?"

"Of course. Till the end, my love," she said, dramatically.

"The other thing I'd love to get my hands on is the research files. The police asked Rupert for them. According to Susan, he has to produce the records, but he got a hold of his lawyers and they'll drag their feet. They'll bury us in legal paperwork for months."

"That one is even easier. All research protocols have to be approved by the IRB committee. Get the records from them." As Claire said these words, Jack's demeanor changed. The previously ever-present grim look that had overwhelmed him earlier began to fade.

"You know, I would have married you just for your titanic sex-appeal. But you're pretty darn smart, too. And you can cook." A cheesy shrimp from Claire's plate suddenly became a projectile. With precise bulls-eye accuracy, the slug whacked Jack squarely on the tip of his nose. With catlike reflexes, he caught the piece of fish in the air and stuck it in his mouth.

"Food fight," he yelled picking up a soggy nacho.

"You mess it up, you clean it up." Jack reconsidered the throw. Instead, he placed the nacho in his mouth. He was a strong, well-built man, who could bench-press well over three times his own body weight. But, like most men, he hated the prospect of being defeated by a woman barely one hundred and twenty pounds soaking wet. Again.

"That is a great idea. Rupert is out of town for meetings and conferences more often than he is in town. Will you help me figure out if he is in town and at the hospital every time someone prematurely goes to meet his maker?"

"Sure. How do we do it?" she asked.

"I have an idea." For a moment, Claire faced her plate and took a bite of lettuce. Suddenly, her face was struck by a piece of chicken.

"You asked for it, buddy. I warned you." A tickling session ensued, one that would shortly make Jack beg for forgiveness and compassion. Claire was a world-class tickler.

She knew exactly where all the hot buttons were. It was not long until Jack was on the floor on his knees cowardly pleading for mercy. If he promised to clear the table, do the dishes and give Claire a long massage, without asking for sex, she might just consider leniency. Then again, she might not. For now, the barrage of tickles poured on incessantly at an alarming and indefensible pace.

Eight days ago

September 23

7:50 AM

"Good morning, Janet," said Jack as he entered the administration office area. Janet Boyer was a beautiful short brunette, who loved the attention she received from wearing tight-fitting clothes. Today, she was sporting tight black pants and an over-stretched red blouse buttoned-up only to mid bosom, almost revealing more than it concealed. Despite leaving little to the imagination, she managed to give the appearance of being professional and proficient at her job.

"Hello, Dr. Norris. May I get you a cup of coffee?"

"Oh, no, thanks. I just finished a cappuccino. I am interested in research. I know this office coordinates all the research projects here at Newton Memorial—"

"Here and all the affiliated facilities. Dr. Shuman is in charge of the department. He coordinates the Institutional Review Board for the entire system; there are five sister hospitals including the medical school. Newton is the largest research facility and does require most of our attention," interrupted Janet proudly.

"I would like to research, well, medical research. What we know, what we are studying, what we need to study, and so on."

Jack stopped for a moment hoping Janet would pipe in. She did not. She returned a look of confusion, remaining intrigued and silent.

"So, I'd like to know, if I need IRB consent for that sort of study," continued Jack trying hard not to chuckle. This was more difficult than he anticipated. Bullshit can only get you part way into the IRB files; for the rest, you need a strategy with abundant cunning and sneakiness. However, so far, the bullshit part was not going well. Right outside the main door, Jack thought he could hear Claire's intense but silent laughter. On the other hand, maybe what he thought he was hearing was his nerves of steel melting with his sudden lack of bravado.

"Let me get this straight, Dr. Norris. You want to know if you need IRB permission to look over the files for all the ongoing research efforts so that you can study their content?" asked Janet, still perplexed.

"Yeah, that's it. I want to study the studies going on and

on-going here and everywhere, too." Boy, this was tougher than he thought. Could he end up in jail for this?

A short pause later, Janet smiled, as if something clicked inside her head. Jack could almost swear, he briefly saw a light bulb over her head. On the other hand, maybe it was just the light reflection from the window behind her, announcing the beginning of a gorgeous sunny day ahead.

"No, IRB files are not confidential. Anyone can look at them anytime. Would you like to look at them here or should I make you copies?"

"Copies. Yeah, copies. Copies would be great. Wow, yeah, definitely copies. I can look at them later. After rounds. I'm pretty busy. Lots of patients to see. Yeah, copies. Please. That'd be great."

"Okay, give me a couple of hours and I'll have all the IRB summaries for you. And let me know if you need anything else." Janet stood up. With a smile, Jack got up, shook her hand and turned to leave the room. Unfortunately, he tripped on a large chair and almost fell. Gathering his composure, he straightened up his lab coat and tie and gracefully walked out of the room.

"Did you hear all that?" he finally asked his wife, once out of earshot from the secretary.

"Every word." Claire chortled. "You are some clever detective. Don't give up your day job."

"Was it that bad?"

"I want to study the studies you got going for my study of the studies," imitated Claire mockingly.

"Well, who knew those things were open for anyone to see. I figured I had to outsmart her to let me have the files."

They walked to the main elevators. Jack tried to regain his dignity, but Claire continued to tease him about his encounter with the ditsy secretary.

"Okay. Can we continue with our plan? What time is it?" asked Jack.

"It's 8:05. She should be there by now."

"Okay, make the call. We have to get serious. This part is even more involved and potentially dangerous." Jack's demeanor became stern. They walked to a phone on a desk right outside the research lab. The area was deserted. Claire dialed. Jack kissed her and left.

"This is Ruth down in the mail room. There's a package here for one Ian Rupert. Does he work up there?" Claire tried to sound unpolished and unsophisticated. She even gave it a bit of a drawl. After a few moments, she hung up the phone and hurried to the previously agreed area.

Jack waited until Donna, Rupert's secretary, left her desk. There was no one else around. It certainly was too early for Rupert to be in. When he was sure the coast was clear, Jack approached and sat at her desk. All items were meticulously arranged and organized. He first looked at the appointment book. Rupert was in Michigan giving a lecture. Jack took the appointment book and photocopied all the pages going back twelve months. He returned the appointment book to Donna's desk, ascertaining that it was placed exactly as he found it.

Jack then entered Rupert's office. The lights were off. He turned them on and closed the door behind him.

"Excuse me, but are you Donna?" asked Claire who had positioned herself as a sentinel nearby the main elevators.

"Yes. Have we met?" answered Donna inquisitively.

"No, but I have heard about you. You are Dr. Rupert's secretary, aren't you?"

"Yes, I am."

"I just think the world of him. I am highly interested in research. My focus is mindfulness meditation and how it can help the healing process. You know, so many people do not care about mindfulness meditation and the existential being that is the soul. Nevertheless, if all is not properly aligned, how can we expect the sick body to repair and restore health and well-being? I believe we need to study how the soul and body interact to make us whole."

"Let me interrupt you. Dr. Rupert is out of town today and tomorrow. If you would like to make an appointment, I would be more than happy to arrange one for you. What did you say your name was?" Donna asked. Despite the body language and feeble attempts Claire made not to allow Donna to get near the elevators, Donna slowly crept up and approached the buttons. She pushed the Up button causing the light to illuminate.

"Yes, I would love to share my ideas with Dr. Rupert. I will be back in town in two or three weeks. I will contact you then and arrange for an appointment. Can I buy you a cup of coffee? I'd love to chat with you and find out more about Dr. Rupert and his work here at Newton Memorial."

"No, thanks. I have a lot of work to do. I must return to my office," persisted Rupert's assistant.

Feeling defeated and unable to delay the secretary further, Claire stopped trying.

"Well, good to talk to you. We'll talk again soon." Claire walked off. Soon the elevator door opened and Donna entered the car. The doors closed. Claire quickly fished out her cell phone from her purse and speed-dialed Jack's number.

"She's on the way up. I couldn't stall her any longer. Sorry."

12:06 PM

Jack and Claire went out to eat at their favorite restaurant. They were excited about their recent finds and couldn't wait to discuss them.

Jack's cell phone rang. It was detective Susan Quentin.

"Hi Jack. I searched the county for unusual murders or homicides over the last six months. I found two other bizarre circumstances that resemble our case and the one you discovered. Then, I searched surrounding counties. Six more cases. Some committed suicide under suspicious and bizarre situations; others had murdered loved ones before dying of odd medical conditions. All these cases occurred out of town. Interestingly, none took place in the same police jurisdiction. Is this a coincidence or is it the strategy of a deranged assassin picking and choosing victims to purposefully avoid suspicion by the separate authorities?"

"Wow, this goes deeper than we thought," exclaimed Jack. Claire looked on, puzzled.

"We contacted the families and obtained proper legal permission for review of their medical charts. Will you check these out for us? I'll have the files delivered to you in a few hours. Will you report on your preliminary findings tomorrow morning?" implored Susan.

"Sure, I will. You can count on me."

They hung up the phone. Jack filled Claire in on the phone discussion.

3:46 PM

Jack and Claire rushed home hoping to start on the investigation right away. They were eager to analyze their ill-gotten goods.

"Let's put everything we collected today on the kitchen table. Here is the list of all the dates of homicides and suicides we just got from Susan. Let's compare that to Rupert's appointment book." Jack arranged the paperwork on the table. In silence, the couple compared the dates.

"You were right." Claire spoke first. "Rupert spends more time out of town than in town."

"Every time someone offs themself or others, he happens to be in Evansville. Coincidence?" volunteered Jack.

"That's true. This is not proof positive that he is involved, but it is intriguing. What about timing? Was he in the hospital early in the day?" said Claire.

"For some of these dates, he has appointments as early as eight o'clock. I arrive at the hospital at that time every morning and I have never seen his car there that early." Jack remained puzzled.

"But some of these cases happened in other counties many miles from here. How would he be involved? What times are these murders taking place?"

"The times vary from early morning to late evening," answered Jack reading quickly through several pages where he had summarized the information.

"Okay, this doesn't tell us a whole lot. He is in town, but we can't put him at the scene of the crime. And no smoking gun in his hand. We still don't have a motive. We may just have established opportunity," reiterated Claire smartly.

"This all suggests to me, he may not be working alone. Let's review the IRB research files. That may give us some clues," said Jack.

"Go through all these research projects and explain them to me, one by one," suggested Claire.

And so he did. The first three folders reflected on-going trials involving gene manipulation in the pig model, in the unrelenting fight against different cancers. Jack made extensive notes about each study, including lab personnel involved, equipment required, and anticipated costs. At each turn, Jack explained to Claire the intricate workings of the particular protocol.

The next three folders consisted of studies involving human research with a novel drug for angina, JAC272. This agent had shown significant promise in earlier short-term investigations, allowing patients to be able to perform more physical activities despite their atherosclerosis. Men with known coronary artery disease and exertional chest pains would undergo treadmill stress testing at baseline. They would then use JAC272 orally and return every six months for a repeat stress test. Each individual would serve as his own control. Jack explained that a novel therapy for angina patients would be very welcomed, especially in individuals with severe limitations who had exhausted other medical and surgical interventions.

There was an ongoing trial in humans assessing the utility of cardiac magnetic resonance and computerized tomography imaging to evaluate patients with different types of chest discomfort.

The next five folders involved different aspects of a novel agent, LFJ659, to treat heart failure. This drug offered hope for the symptomatic relief of these patients by stimulating the strength of heart contractions in the hopes that the heart would become more efficient. The folder contained information about how to surgically manipulate the rats to create a heart failure model. This would be done by dissecting the left anterior descending coronary artery, the main arterial supply to the front of the heart. This vessel would be tied off causing the rodents to have a large heart attack. With the heart muscle thusly weakened, the rats would subsequently and predictably develop signs and symptoms of heart failure, unless of course, the operation proved fatal. The surviving animals would then be randomized to receive an intravenous dose of placebo or LFJ659. The dose-determining initial research efforts had been difficult. Initial cost estimates for this phase had been underestimated and petitions were made for additional capital. Many more rats than initially estimated were necessary to complete this phase. The reason for this remained ambiguously unstated. Different protocols were now on-going to fully evaluate the effects of the drug. Rats treated with this agent over two to three weeks fared better than the control counterparts; they could walk longer distances, for longer periods, have less fatigue, and less incidence of sudden cardiac arrest. The early human phases of experimentation with LFJ659 were just about to begin.

CMC1224 was a new drug being tested in humans in the hopes of curtailing the frequency of an arrhythmia termed atrial fibrillation. Jack explained that this rhythm disorder was the most common of all; in the United States, one out of ten Americans in their seventies and eighties are burdened by this problem. The atria, the top two chambers of the heart, quiver rapidly making the ventricles beat fast and irregularly. As such, atrial fibrillation places individuals at risk for developing clots, which can cause strokes and disability.

Research efforts also included a new mode of delivering drugs into the body. Jack took a long time reviewing this folder. The concept was new to him. As he did so, Claire left to go make coffee. By the time she returned with two large mugs of Mr. Coffee-dripped medium boldness House Blend Starbucks, Jack had completed his review of the contents in the folder.

"Wow, Claire, this is really cool. They have come up with a way to insert medications into tiny bubbles. This one experiment in pigs with liver cancer is delivering chemotherapy right to the site of the malignancy. Nuclear-tagged molecules in the bubbles allow tracking throughout the body. When the bubbles reach the site of the cancer in the liver, they use ultrasonic waves, at a pre-specified frequency, to burst the bubbles allowing release of high concentration of the chemotherapeutic drug right where they want it. They dial in the correct frequency and bang. This is expected to cut down significantly on systemic side effects. They are putting the medication right where it is needed, so it doesn't affect other organs. Very neat, huh?" Jack had a look of excitement and enthusiasm.

"That is pretty cool. Is it working? Are they getting results?" she asked.

"I think so. They are comparing medication delivery by bubbles to the site of the malignancy versus giving the medication intravenously. The response rates are much higher with significantly less side effects."

"Are they using this technology with other medications? Targeting other organs?"

"Not yet, but there are plans to use this technology in the heart, brain and—"

"Yes, I can see how it would deliver medications to the brain for seizures, brain cancer, Parkinson's, et cetera," interrupted Claire.

"Exactly. This is exciting stuff. This is also the bubble study John was trying to show us when we visited him in the research lab with the medical students. Using these bubbles filled with air, ultrasound visualization of the heart structures is enhanced marvelously. I was very impressed with the images when Rupert kicked us all out, that son of a bitch."

"Now, now, Jack. Let it go with Rupert, already. So what else is there?"

Jack moved on to the last couple of folders and read their

contents. After a moment, he announced to Claire this was a study of congestive heart failure fluid-overloaded patients resistant to medications. The research involved an apparatus resembling a kidney dialysis machine that ultra-filtrates blood and removes excess water. Jack gave testament to the utility and importance of this tool. He had seen it work wonders in some of his sicker heart patients in whom nothing else had made a difference.

The last folder was the most interesting yet. Jack studied it intensely, each moment more enthusiastically than before. After a long period of silence, Jack looked at Claire:

"Wow. No, double wow!" exclaimed Jack.

"What, what?" Claire could feel the fervor and exhilaration in Jack's voice. She craned her neck to see the papers in the folder.

"Biological pacemakers. Wow! They are using mesenchymal pacing cells—"

"What kind of cells?" interrupted Claire.

"Mesenchymal cells are early cells in differentiation taken from bone marrow, capable of developing into any type of tissue. The researchers have found the gene that codes the cells into becoming cardiac pacing tissue. If this work is successful, in the future, instead of surgically inserting pacemaker devices in the hearts of patients with slow heartbeat disorders, I will be implanting these types of cells. The early research in dogs seems promising. They are using the canine model to induce sinus node dysfunction. The sinus node is the area that produces the heartbeat. The dog undergoes a procedure to destroy the node and develops a slow heart rate. Before implanting the biologic pacemaker cells, they document that the heart beats at twenty to thirty beats per minute, even when they make the dog exercise on a treadmill. The mesenchymal cells with rearranged genes geared to make them like sinus nodes are deployed and they take over the heartbeat. Voila! As good as new. Treadmill testing then confirms the dog's heart responds appropriately to exercise. The pulse goes up appropriately. This is so neat."

"That is neat. I suppose inserting these cells into the heart would be much easier on the patient than undergoing a pacemaker implantation?" asked Claire.

"I imagine," Jack said, taking a few seconds to ponder the realm of possibilities, a smile on his face.

"So where does all this take us?" asked Claire, breaking the silence and jerking Jack into the reality of the moment. "Are we any closer to understanding why or how the murders took place?" she continued.

"No, not really. Let's look at Rupert's calendar entries. I saw some unusual entries." While speaking, Jack looked through several pages of the copies he had made of the calendar. Then he continued, "Rupert wrote down two names on the edge of the calendar. One is a Major Wayne Rooner. Who could he be? A cop? A soldier? Boy scout troop leader?"

Claire smiled. "Maybe he's an airline pilot? Why don't you ask the cops?" she said.

"I will. The other name written on the side is Muhammad Akrim."

"Did they have meetings? And when, and why?"

"Couldn't tell you." Jack walked to his computer, hit the Esc button to wake it up and Googled the names Major Wayne Rooner and Muhammad Akrim. Claire followed him and watched in anticipation. They were not rewarded with any returns from the information highway.

"I will have the cops investigate these names," said Jack with a tired tone in his voice. He pulled out his Treo from his left pocket and found the phone number for Detective Herb Fuller in his Contact database.

Seven days ago

September 24

8:10 AM

"I reviewed the medical records in detail. I also looked into the ongoing research projects at Newton Memorial over the last year. The whole thing starts with different trials whereby the number of rats being purchased for experimentation skyrockets for about three months. As this starts to taper off, the money required to purchase rats decreases to its usual baseline. Soon afterwards, we start to see a spike in the number of in-patients dying of unusual causes at Newton

Memorial. After the in-patients start dying, we see the out-of-hospital casualties of equally bizarre circumstances. It is noteworthy that these were all men of similar age group and previously in good health. Deaths were premature, freakish, unexplained and marked by confusion, paranoia and bizarre behavior. The causes of death have been acute heart attack, intra-cranial bleeding, acute aortic dissection and cardiac arrest occurring in patients who had just been studied in the hospital and discharged with markers of a good prognosis. The tests are not one hundred percent foolproof, but for so many patients to have tested normal and go on to die so soon afterwards is implausible. These circumstances have all the ingredients of a research study. It is methodical and systematic." After speaking these words, Jack sat down and waited for comments from the agents, detectives and other police officers in the meeting room.

"Good work, Jack. This does seem to provide some pretty convincing evidence that the hospital is the source of the crimes. It seems to be related to the research laboratory," said Herb agreeingly.

"I don't think we have proof that the research lab is involved. It could be that an employee anywhere in the hospital is scoping out the patients," interjected Mike.

"True, but I think that's where we must concentrate our efforts first. We have to start somewhere. Thanks for such a thorough and insightful analysis, Jack," added Herb appreciatively.

"What about motive?" asked Susan.

"Until proved otherwise, motive is almost always money. Who would gain financially?" asked Herb.

"The head of the department, Dr. Ian Rupert. Have you interrogated him yet?" asked Jack.

"No, but I think we need to," answered Herb.

"We don't have enough to compel him to talk. We should wait and get more information," said Mike.

"I think we have enough to ask him to come in for a brief discussion," disagreed Herb.

"You will be tipping him off to our strategy and investigative direction. I would wait," rebutted Mike.

"Okay, I will bow to your learned opinion, Mike. You have more experience than we do here in Evansville." Herb looked at Susan, as if to get confirmation.

"What did we get from the re-interviewing of all the people at the crime scene?" asked Mike after a short moment.

"I spoke with a nurse who recalled seeing Dr. Rupert the morning of the murders," answered Susan. She paused for a beat to look through her notes.

"What did you find out?" inquired Herb.

"Joan Wally was one of the nurses on duty the shift of the murders. She recalls seeing Dr. Rupert and thinking about how strange it was to see him there at that hour. It was a little before six o'clock in the morning. He had a small bag with him. He looked through the charts and heart monitors for several minutes. He paged Dr. Connor and asked him to come up to the unit. She recalls hearing him say that he wanted Dr. Connor to see Butterworth. She remembers seeing Dr. Rupert leave the unit with a small device in his hand. A few minutes later, Ms. Wally had to go to the blood bank to get two units of blood for her patient, Christine Rickman. The nurse recalls it was odd to see Dr. Rupert in the waiting room, hiding behind a large column. As she walked by, she noticed he was concentrating and working on a small handheld device. Why stand behind a column? There was no one in the waiting room. There was no one to hide from. She proceeded to the blood bank. When she was on her way back, she heard gunshots coming from the CCU. She ran away and called the police from a phone downstairs. Afraid of what was happening, she did not return to the crime scene. This is why we didn't interview her the first time. She was reported as missing at the time. I finally tracked her down and spoke with her."

"Good work, Susan," praised Herb.

"Any fingerprints on the gun or shell casings, other than the perp's?" asked Susan of the group, unsure who was handling that aspect of the investigation.

"No, none at all. I have also been checking our ballistic database, but the weapon continues to be a no show," answered Mike.

"Okay, let's keep up the investigation and search for the source of the gun. It does look like Rupert had the opportunity to have given Butterworth the gun," said Herb.

"Yes, but again, this is not conclusive. We need more." Mike was cocksure as he spoke.

"What should our next step be?" asked Susan.

"We'll re-interview the lab personnel. I would like to interview the nurse Susan talked about and see if I can get anymore from her," said Mike with confidence. After all, he was an agent of the FBI. All others were local small-town cops.

"Okay, Mike, go over and talk to nurse Wally again. Then

work on the gun aspect of things. We'll go to the research lab and see what we find there," said Herb authoritatively.

10:30 AM

The doors to the research lab were locked. The police, pending a search, had secured the department. Yellow tape crisscrossed the door, declaring it off limits to all but the authorities and their designees. Herb removed the yellow tape and unlocked the door. The animal cages were still there.

"I figured you guys took all the animals somewhere else," stated Jack.

"We don't have the facilities. We have the SPCA come here daily and take care of the animals. It's working out all right," answered Susan.

"What is the SPCA?" inquired Jack.

"The Society for the Prevention of Cruelty to Animals," she explained.

They started to snoop around in different directions as soon as the lights to the large room came on showering brightness everywhere. Herb and Susan searched the offices. The first of the offices was that of the Laboratory Chief James Miller. This was the second go around. The CSI people had been through taking pictures, drawing schematics of each room and taking inventory.

The invoices and requisition forms for the purchase of the animals necessary to run the lab were found here. This reestablished that the number of rats sacrificed in experimentation had spiked up tremendously earlier in the year, occurring right before the murders began. This lent confirmation to the notion that the murders were merely the continuation of a bleak killer experiment transferred from the animal lab to the male humans at large. Not actually at large, since the chosen ones had been selected from people that had required services at the hospital. The cardiac examination of these men had actually served to certify that they were indeed good specimens for research. Good enough to be killed.

While the detectives nosed around the offices looking for paperwork, Jack searched for the lab equipment, looking for something that might give him a clue about the macabre poisonous research efforts. The equipment in the lab was much like that of a surgical suite with which he was very familiar. Jack continued to browse.

Meanwhile in Miller's office, Herb came across a large folder of invoices from a company called MultiTech, Inc. Susan made note of this name. Looking through the invoices, it was clear that this company manufactured research drugs. She made a call to the station requesting that these folders and all others be taken to the police station for further detailed analysis.

"Herb and Susan look at this," requested Jack from the entryway into the office.

Intrigued, the detectives followed Jack, who appeared to be like the ten-year-old that finally discovered the location of his hidden Christmas present. Jack guided the cops to an area where a large ultrasound machine was the focus in the room. In a cabinet nearby, there were two devices. The larger of the two, labeled Bubble Maker, was used to compose tiny bubbles, which could be filled with any material or drug. Another small hand-held device was labeled Radiofrequency Sonicator. This small gadget comprised a small round dial demonstrating a series of frequencies. Both these units proudly displayed their maker was MultiTech, Inc. There were several vials of medications, some known to Jack, others not. The unknowns were research drugs.

"These vials of drugs with letters and numbers, like JMJ81661, LFJ659, and JAC21072, and so on, are investigational agents that don't have a real name yet. I have the paperwork for the experiments involving these," said Jack presenting the vials as he spoke.

"Can any of these make a man go crazy and start killing?" asked Herb, as Susan gazed at the drug vials pensively.

"That's the million dollar question," said Jack. "I don't know yet."

"I found purchase orders, delivery records, and invoices from MultiTech, Inc. about these contraptions. Here they are. They manufactured two of each of these units. I only see one pair here. Where's the other pair?" asked Susan looking through papers inside one of the folders then at the gaping eyes staring back at her. Silence ensued as the men shrugged their shoulders.

"Not sure what all this means, if anything," said Herb breaking the moment's silence.

"We'll look into MultiTech, Inc.," said Susan.

12:58 PM

The three musketeers Herb, Susan and Jack, walked to the cafeteria. Jack had a lunch date with his beautiful wife.

"Hi, Claire. Sorry I'm late." Jack took off his jacket and hung it over a chair next to Claire, who was drinking a glass of water.

"That's okay. I'm used to it by now." She smiled as she realized Jack had an entourage.

"These are the detectives I am working with. This is Detective Herb Fuller and this is Detective Susan Quentin." They shook hands and exchanged pleasantries.

The four walked through the cafeteria-style line and gathered their food. They sat down eating and talking about the weather, life in Evansville, Newton Memorial Hospital and what the institution has done for the community and county. Herb reminisced about the time before the hospital was built. He discussed how the land where the hospital stands used to be a huge farm, although he was too young to have any concrete recollections. After a few heartbeats of slightly uncomfortable silence, the conversation turned to the business at hand.

"What about Major Rooner and the other man, Muhammad Akrim?" asked Jack.

"We're still waiting on the full information. We might have something by tomorrow. So far, I know the major is a military career man who has been in several wars. He more or less fell off the end of the earth about three years ago. Apparently, he has been on some secret mission or assignment. The military is being hush-hush about the whole thing, but hopefully we can persuade them to give us more information. Our FBI connection, detective Mike Ganz, is pursuing that issue." Susan paused to take a bite of her burrito, then a sip of her iced tea.

Herb continued the conversation, "Muhammad Akrim is even more elusive. Apparently, he lives in the Middle East somewhere, probably Libya. Mike is also working on that through the FBI database." Now it was Herb's turn to have a bite of his pepperoni and cheese pizza and whet his whistle with Diet Coke.

"This thing is bigger than meets the eye, isn't it?" asked Claire.

"We think so," answered Susan.

"You know, Mrs. Norris, we really appreciate the help your husband is giving us. He has a knack for this type of work. If ever heart surgery doesn't suit him, he's got a full time job with us." At first Herb sported a serious look on his face, then a smile.

"Well, as a doctor, what I do isn't so different from what you do. It's all, how to figure out an unknown. Who dunnit? The heart? The stomach? The gallbladder?" said Jack with a faint grin on his face.

"I had never looked at it quite that way, but I think you're right," said Susan. The others nodded agreeably.

The focus of the conversation then led the group to discuss the differences and similarities between the different professions, such as cardiology, psychology, local police force, FBI, and so on. Once done with lunch, the group disbanded.

The detectives went back to the research lab to snoop around even more.

Claire had a couple of patients to see in her office. Jack decided to go back to his office and do the dreaded paperwork. He had files to sign and counter-sign, lab data to review and decisions to make about the care of patients that had called the outpatient clinic with problems. The in-stack was growing at an alarming rate, despite the hospital continuing to be on diversion. He would take this time to dwindle it down, before the deluge of hospital business as usual recommenced, expected in a day or two.

Around four o'clock, Jack walked down to his car. It was time to drive home. Claire would be done with her appointments by now.

"Hi, honey," said Claire when her cell phone rang. She was driving home.

"I finally think we're getting somewhere with this case," announced Jack excitedly.

"What did you discover in the lab?"

"They have been working on several experimental drugs. Wait a minute, baby." Jack looked in his rearview mirror. A dark sedan was behind him. He could make out the occupant. It was a well-dressed Caucasian man, wearing dark sunglasses.

"What is it, Jack? Are you okay?" Claire could not wait any longer, despite the request.

"I think I'm being followed. Oh wait, never mind," said Jack as the sedan in his rearview mirror turned right at the intersection.

"Being followed, did you say?" asked Claire worriedly.

"No, never mind. There was a big dark car behind me all the way from the hospital and I thought he was following me. But he turned off. He's no longer behind me." Jack was more relaxed now. The prospect of being tailed had momentarily made the hairs on the back of his neck stand out.

"Is this thing making you paranoid?"

"Why, do you know a good psychologist? I need some therapy."

"I know the type of therapy you want."

"I need a lot of therapy. I'm a basket case. Intense therapy."

"I better refer you to an experienced psychologist since you are such a far-gone case. How about Dr. Joel Garrison? He's older and wise in these matters."

"No, I gotta have you. No one else can make me sane. Only you."

"Okay, for a back rub I might see if my couch is free this evening."

Jack always joked that as a cardiologist and electrophysiologist, all he needed was a stethoscope, which he carried in the right pocket of his lab coat. As a psychologist, Claire really needed to carry a couch with her.

"It's a deal."

"Hey, let's watch Law & Order. It'll give us some clues and help us think like detectives. And let's go to bed early. We need to relax."

"Yeah. I know what you mean. I'll go flying tomorrow. That relaxes me more than anything else. Except sex, of course."

They both laughed aloud. Then, Claire rolled her eyes.

Six days ago

September 25

7:03 AM

Jack needed to unwind. Doctor's orders. The doctor ordered a trip to the clouds and beyond. Today was the perfect day to fill that prescription. The visibility was reported to be greater than six miles and the skies were touted to have an overcast ceiling at five thousand feet. Beyond the white fluffy cottony clouds, there was the promise of a beautiful sunny day.

While driving to Evansville Airport, Jack called ahead and asked the FBO personnel to pull his airplane out from its hangar into the apron. The FBO, fixed base operation, is the business that handles general aviation pilots and airplanes. They manage the hangars, fuel the airplanes, provide repair services and sell charts, maps, sunglasses and other flying paraphernalia.

"Hey doc," greeted Steve Peski. Steve was one of the managers at the FBO. His secret love affair with Jack's Bonanza was obvious. Well, actually, it was no longer a secret at all. Steve was in his mid-fifties with graying disheveled hair.

"Good morning, Steve." Jack walked towards the flying machine. Steve approached.

"She's a beauty, isn't she?" asked Jack.

"I heard about the mess you all had at the hospital. I'm glad you're OK. I was worried about you. I mean you could have been the one that was killed before you had a chance to leave me the Bonanza."

"Okay, Steve, if I ever get killed, I'll make sure to leave the airplane to you." Both men smiled. Jack was performing the pre-flight check, Steve right behind, attached at the hip.

"In my dreams."

"Steve, you know how I keep teasing you that I'll let you fly her? How about today?"

"Are you kidding? Doc, don't kid me like that. It's not healthy. I may have a heart attack on you."

"I'm serious. You take good care of her. You fly. I'll take the right seat."

In no time, both men were perched and strapped in their seats in the small cockpit. Jack gave Steve a quick once over the instruments. Steve had not flown the Bonanza, but he was rated in like airplanes. In no time, he was ready to go. He would require a little assistance for the first flight and Jack was happy to oblige.

"Niner-eight-gulf-kilo, ready to taxi with weather info Tango," announced Steve proudly into the microphone, roosted securely, admiring the instrument panel in front of him.

"Niner-eight-gulf-kilo, taxi to runway one-eight via taxiway Alpha then Charlie, hold short runway nine," instructed the Evansville Tower Ground Controller.

"One-eight via Alpha, Charlie, hold short niner," repeated Steve, increasingly proud and cocksure. With a little increase in throttle pressure, the beautiful airplane began to roll forward. Steve's smile was ear to ear, as he followed the Ground Controller's instructions. Soon the aircraft was positioned on Runway 18 awaiting orders to take off.

"Niner-eight-gulf-kilo, cleared for take off with right turn to 2–3-0, maintain VFR," commanded Tower. The flight had been filed as VFR, or visual flight rules. This indicated that navigation of the airplane had to consist of the pilot's ability to see outside the aircraft.

After repeating the instructions into the mike, Steve gunned the engine and the plane commenced its scamper down the runway. Soon they were airborne.

"Wow, she's fast and smooth," admired Steve.

"That she is, that she is." Jack smiled agreeably.

After about ten minutes of flying around three thousand feet, they managed to find a hole in the clouds through which they could climb above the cloud layer, remaining in visual meteorological conditions. Steve was not rated to fly by instruments alone. As such, he was not allowed to fly into the clouds and lose his ability to navigate without visual cues.

Now, they were on top of the world. Or, at least, the clouds that provided shelter from the scorching sun, like a gigantic pergola over Evansville.

"So, what the heck happened at the hospital?" asked Steve.

"A patient shot one of the doctors and a nurse. They were both my friends." Jack's eyes moistened with tears.

"I'm sorry, Jack. I should have realized it and—"

"That's okay. I should talk about it. It actually helps me."

"That's rough to lose your friends like that."

"Let me ask you a question, Steve. Do you ever get military aircraft landing here in Evansville?" asked Jack after a long pause, hoping to change the beat of the conversation. Oh yeah, and get some info. Jack felt like a detective.

"All the time. The military aviators have occasional drills around here and use the airport here in Evansville. Have you not seen them?"

"Yes, I've seen fighter jets flying around on occasion."

"We've even seen the top brass coming in. Now, they don't arrive in fighter jets. They travel in full comfort. A major with the Marine Corps, who has been here twice recently, flew in a fully loaded Citation X. What a beautiful airplane. Beautiful sight to see. That baby was equipped with—" the excitement in Steve's voice was interrupted by Jack, his interest piqued.

"What would a major want with Evansville, I wonder?"

"As a matter of fact, he wanted Newton Memorial Hospital. I arranged the limo transportation myself. He had meetings with some famous doctor at the hospital."

"And you say he came twice?"

"Yeah, a few months ago and again about a week later, something like that."

"Do you know who he came to see?"

"I don't remember now. I have the name on file. His last name is also a first name. I remember that. A bit of a weird name." Steve paused to attempt to retrieve the name from his memory-storing bin deep in the back of his brain.

"Was it Rupert?"

"Yes, that's it. Rupert."

"I wonder what he wanted with the military or what the military wanted with Rupert."

"And soon after the major, another even more impressive bird flew in an international businessman to see Rupert. I arranged his limo, too. And took care of his Gulfstream G550. Beautiful. You should see the inside. Very plush."

"What did he want with Rupert?"

"I don't know that. But, I can tell it was big business. This man was from another country. He looked like he was from the Middle East somewhere. I remember thinking he had to be a prince or some rich person. I remember, the pilot filed an IFR flight plan direct to Paris, when they left."

"How many times did this guy come see Rupert?"

"Just that one time."

"Anyone else unusual come to see Rupert or our fair little hospital?"

"No. Nobody. I have worked here for fifteen years. Nobody has visited the hospital. Not before, not after."

"Steve, will you give me a call if any of these two jets ever returns to Evansville?" Jack produced his card on which he wrote his cell number and handed it to Steve.

"It's the least I can do after you let me fly this beautiful bird."

10:10 AM

A more appreciative grown man, Jack had never met. Steve was so elated that Jack granted him his wish to fly the Bonanza that he would not shut up about it. With the single-engine Beechcraft now securely housed in the private hangar, Jack secured himself in his Lexus. After all, "Click it or Ticket." Besides being the law, Jack was a strong advocate of seatbelts and always used his.

During the drive to the hospital, Jack again had the premonition of danger. As he drove, he frequently scrutinized the rearview mirror. There was the large dark sedan. Was he becoming paranoid?

Jack dug out his Treo from his pocket and made a call.

"Hey, are you guys following me?"

"No, man. You're on our side, remember?" retorted Detective Herb Fuller, with a smirk.

"I keep thinking I'm being followed by a large sedan. Dark, maybe deep blue or black.

"Hmmm," returned Herb. "It's not us. I don't think."

"He just turned right. He was about three cars behind me. All the way from the airport. Maybe it's me just being paranoid."

"Hey, in our field paranoid is a good thing. Let me look into this a bit, see what I can find out."

"By the way, I have some stuff to talk to you about. Can I meet with you and Susan in a few minutes?"

"Sure, come on in. I'll have the Starbucks ready for you."

"Thanks, Herb. See you soon."

Jack drove to police headquarters. He walked straight to the detective office where Herb, true to his word, was stirring Jack's Starbucks coffee.

"We proudly serve!" stated Herb jokingly, as he handed Jack his coffee.

Jack took a long sip of the hot beverage, appreciating its rich flavor.

"Good to the last drop," said Jack.

"Wrong coffee brand. So, what did you find out? Herb said you had some news for us," asked Susan with a smile, sitting back on the sofa in the room.

"I went flying today. Steve Peski, who is the manager at the airport, told me a Marine Corps Major Rooner and a foreign executive have been in to see Rupert over the last few months. The major came twice, Akrim just once. These visits occurred after the first few murders. I have exact dates of their arrivals."

Jack pulled out some papers from his jacket's inner pocket. These were copies of the flight logs at Evansville Airport. Susan and Herb approached to look at the documents. Herb pointed to a large blackboard in the back of the room and the group walked in its direction. When they arrived, the blackboard displayed the time line of all the incidents they were investigating. The first unusual and unexplainable case the detective discovered was a bizarre medical situation which transpired on July 7 in Burkhart County, about fifty miles from Evansville. The victim's name was written in red chalk, Paul W. Clute. Under his name, was written the date of the occurrence and the manner of death—sudden cardiac death with no structural heart disease, a diagnosis obtained from the death certificate with an editorial from Jack's input. Under this was the location of the event, Redwood, Burkhart County. The other discovered cases of bizarre medical discrepancies and/or wacky homicide/suicides were likewise displayed in a timeline fashion to the right of the first incident. On that list were Floyd Sullivan, who died suddenly and unexpectedly on August 16 at Newton Memorial's emergency department; and Joe McIntyre, who perished from a massive brain bleed at home on August 26, but not until he ruthlessly killed his wife in cold blood.

"The first visit from Major Rooner was on August 14."

Jack paused looking through his papers. Susan stood up and picked up a piece of chalk. She added to the timetable: 8/14/06—Maj. Rooner visits Rupert. A drawn arrow indicated the point in time of the entry in relationship to all others. The other visit and that of Akrim's were likewise added.

"So, where does this take us?" asked Jack breaking the silence.

"We will talk to the DA and see if this is enough to get a warrant or at the least compel Rupert to come in and answer some questions. But first, we asked his head lab-tech to talk to us," said Herb. A short moment of silence ensued as Susan consulted her notebook, as anticipated by Herb.

"A Mr. James Miller," she said finally.

"I've met him at the research lab. He's a real nice older man. He's kind and helpful. Can I come along?" asked Jack.

1:07 PM

"Thanks for meeting with us with such short notice, Mr. Miller," said Herb. The two local detectives were joined by Jack and Mike in the pleasant surroundings offered by the plush conference room in the research laboratory. This site was chosen purposely, to allow Miller to be most relaxed and for all to have access to the lab equipment, should it become necessary. Miller waddled onto a chair with a glass of water in his hand. He yawned as he sat down, apologizing for the indiscretion as he did, his right hand covering his mouth. All others sat comfortably at the table, each with a drink perched on a coaster in front of them. Jack noticed a faint reddened area on James' right hand. The pleasantries and introductions had been completed a few moments earlier.

"My friends call me James. Please, call me James. It's my pleasure to help in any way I can. These atrocities really shook us all to the core." Miller spoke with a nasal tone of voice, but his words seemed true and from the heart.

"James, we have been chatting with hospital personnel from all departments, to learn about the routine here and try to find some clues into the murders," said Herb. Sitting back into the leather chair comfortably, his legs crossed, his hands on his knees, Herb continued in a calm, caring tone.

"Had you noticed anything strange or out of place before September 18, the day of the murders?"

"No, not at all." James seemed perplexed, speaking slowly with an inquisitive look of worry on his face. "Like what? I'm not sure I know what you mean," continued James.

"Anything out of the ordinary? Anyone or anything here that is usually not here? Anyone or anything missing that should have been here? Anything at all you can think of that might be a helpful clue for us," said Herb.

"None that I can think of. It all seemed usual and routine around here."

"What about the day of the murders or since then?"

"I can't think of anything unusual." James stopped for a moment to reach deep into the memory circuits of his brain. He shook his head looking at all present.

"What about Dr. Rupert? Has he seemed strange or anxious about anything?" inquired Herb.

"Oh, yes. Dr. Rupert is always that way. He is always worried about something. Always anxious that something will go awry. I have never seen a man with so much negative energy. He is just a worrywart; that's all there is to it," said James decisively, a yawn afterwards.

"Any recent changes?" asked Mike. All present had smiled at James' comments, save for the FBI agent, who pressed on.

"No, no recent changes. I've worked for that man for years and that's just the way he is. Very smart, but very nervous."

"James, what about the experiments and research trials you are doing here at the research lab?" asked Susan, attempting to move the questioning along.

"We are in the midst of many. I can provide a list of all of them, if you'd like."

"Yes, that would be great," interjected Jack before the other interrogators had a chance to reply.

"Give me a couple of hours and I will have a complete list detailing our efforts here at Newton Memorial," said James agreeably. He yawned again, putting his right hand in front of his mouth.

"We would greatly appreciate that. Of the research treatments and unknown drugs you are working with, any of them capable of causing paranoia and delusion?" persisted Jack, more to the point.

"No, not that I know," declared James, pensively and demonstrating little confidence in his answer.

"Are you experimenting with any drugs that affect the central nervous system?" persevered Jack.

"No, most of our research involves cardiovascular; some cancer, too, but not much. Dr. Rupert could give you a much more detailed analysis of the actual research being carried out," responded James.

"We will talk to him, as well," said the FBI agent.

"You mostly work with rats, huh?" asked Herb.

"We almost always start out with the rodent model, then either progress to small mammals like pigs or chimps, or go directly to humans, depending on the situation. Dr. Rupert and his research group make those decisions. I just make sure they have what they need to work with."

"We noticed that nine to twelve months ago, you went through a lot of rats. More than ever before in the history of the research lab. What was that all about?" asked Herb.

"Rat Poison," James said and smiled. "LFJ659 is a new drug for congestive heart failure that we were testing on rats. Instead of improving the heart failure, the stuff was killing rats. Dr. Rupert called the drug Rat Poison. Usually it takes us a couple of weeks to figure out the right dose, but this one is so potent that it can only be administered in minute quantities. We spent a lot of time and money buying rats getting to the right dose. They kept dying from what was subsequently found to be too high a dose. We now have it right and are getting great results. Dr. Rupert is satisfied with the progress we've made with this drug."

"How does the drug work and how is it administered?" asked Jack, fascination in his voice.

"The mode of action remains unknown and it is administered intravenously."

"Will you show us your records about the human phase response? Any human deaths?" inquired Jack.

"No, the patients so far have been all rats. No deaths recently. We will start the human phase soon." James knocked three times on the wooden table.

"Are you working on any drug delivery systems?" asked the young doctor.

"Yes, we are placing medications in tiny bubbles which can be administered intravenously or by inhalation. When the drug reaches the target organ or site, we can use ultrasound to disrupt the bubbles and deliver the material exactly where it'll do the most good. This is done remotely through a specific pre-determined high-frequency ultrasound wave."

"So you can burst certain bubbles with one frequency and others with a different frequency?" Jack was impressed.

"Sure, that way we can administer different medications simultaneously, but time the delivery of each agent by dialing in the desired frequency." James yawned yet again, covering his mouth with his right hand.

The two-sided conversation continued for several long moments, with the technical lingo increasing with each passing minute. At some point, the cops became totally lost with the medical jargon. Since Jack was on a roll, they remained silent. They would later ask for unriddling of all the scientific gobbledygook. While conversing enthusiastically, the two medical men walked to the area of the lab where the equipment in question was housed. The cops followed, still unsure of the details of the on-going dialogue. James showed the increasingly fascinated Jack the MultiTech RF Sonicator, Bubble Maker, and other units used in the different experiments. James demonstrated how they operated and explained their utility.

James was helpful, accommodating and courteous. And sleepy. It was clear, he truly wanted to be a positive factor in the investigation into the carnage of last week that had so devastated the hospital. The town. The county. The country. Unfortunately, the conversation with James, though informative, did not appear to be rewarding in advancing the hunt for the monster or monsters responsible for the bloodshed.

Five days ago

September 26

8:34 AM

By the time Jack arrived at police headquarters, the meeting had already begun. Herb was speaking to the group, which consisted of the usual faces: detectives Susan Quentin, Jim Franklin and Mike Ganz. Today's meeting also included a homely, stocky, well-dressed bald man with ill-fitting clothes and thick glasses. Jack would later find out this was Sebastian Ritter, the district attorney.

When Jack entered the room, the group was discussing

the mounting evidence against Dr. Ian Rupert. Ritter agreed Rupert was a person of extreme interest, but the evidence was circumstantial. They needed more to arrest him. Mike discussed his search efforts with the FBI database to see if the gun was tied to Rupert somehow. So far, the search had remained unfruitful.

"Let's bring him in for an interview," opined Herb.

"I don't think we have enough to compel him to do that yet," disagreed Mike.

"What do you think, counselor?" asked Herb of the DA.

"I will give him a call and invite him to come in. It doesn't have to be threatening. We're just asking for his help to solve the murders that occurred at his hospital. I know him personally from previous fundraising events for the research lab and hospital. It'll be better if I do it instead of you." This said, Sebastian excused himself and left the room to make the phone call.

The conversation then shifted to Major Rooner and Muhammad Akrim. Jack talked about his discussion with Steve Peski at the airport. Mike had not been able to find out much.

"Major Rooner is a military man who disappeared off the face of the earth seven years ago. This typically means he is deep undercover for the government. We're still trying to get more information and even speak with him directly about all this, but don't hold your breath. I have my FBI connections working on this and I'll keep you informed of their progress," said Mike.

"What about Akrim?" asked Jack.

"Akrim is a business man, but what his business is we

cannot say, as yet. He was born in Pakistan but has lived in Libya for several years," answered Mike.

"Is he involved with terrorism?" inquired Herb.

"We don't know yet," responded Mike.

Having murmured these words, Mike appeared microscopically edgy, thought Jack. If not for Claire's insistence that Jack learn to read body language so as to better understand what his patients were feeling, he too would have missed the nearly indiscernible signs. Mike clenched his jaw and his hands became fidgety. Mike tried to hide his restlessness by placing his hands under the table. Mike looked intently at Herb and Susan. As he did so, Jack fleetingly stared and concentrated on his forehead. A tiny bead of sweat had actually become visible, but barely. Mike was nervous. Something was bothering him. But what? And why? As Jack contemplated these questions deep in his head, he heard his name.

"Jack, what is your view of all this?" asked Herb.

"I think Rupert and his team, while investigating a new treatment, stumbled upon a way to kill people from a distance. I think the U.S. military is interested in it as well as some other foreign organization, either for military use or maybe even terrorism." As Jack spoke, he continued to notice the almost imperceptible physical and emotional changes in Mike.

"Interesting opinion," said Susan. Herb nodded with interest and agreement. Mike was still sitting on his chair quietly, endeavoring to remain inconspicuous, despite his internal agitation. Interestingly, besides Jack, no one else seemed to have noticed. For that, Jack had Claire to thank. Jack continued, "We need to find out more about the research projects Rupert has going on. It is conceivable that John

Connor found out and threatened to go to the authorities. So the hospital murders might have been a ploy to get rid of him with the others being innocent bystanders."

Jack paused, an eye still on Mike. At this point, Jack did not want to tip his hat anymore. He was no longer sure he could trust the FBI man.

"Great work, Jack. It is a great theory." Mike had gotten off his chair and was now walking slowly toward the young doctor. He rested his hands on Jack's shoulders, as he continued to speak to the group.

"I will send the gadgets we obtained from the lab to the FBI headquarters for further analysis. I bet the lab geeks will come up with a plausible theory as to the methods of the killers."

"I think we can do that here. I would love a chance to analyze the equipment," said Jack although he was quickly interrupted by Herb.

"I agree that the FBI is in a better position to make a determination, Jack. I know you are interested in looking at the stuff, but in the interest of time, I think we should send everything to the FBI lab. Mike, will you arrange that?" Mike nodded.

"Jack," said Mike, "Have you discussed any of our meetings with anyone outside these walls?"

"Claire, my wife," answered Jack in a serious tone.

"Anyone else?"

"No, just Claire."

"It is very important for you not to reveal our conversations to anyone. Anyone at all. Even your wife. Can we agree on that?" asked the FBI agent. Jack nodded. Mike's newfound sense of calmness was disconcerting, especially given his nearly indiscernible body language of a few moments earlier. Jack was now having second thoughts about his prior interpretative prowess. Maybe he had it all wrong. Or maybe he was right on.

The conference door opened and in came Sebastian wearing an ear-to-ear smile.

"I did it," he announced proudly to the group. "Rupert is coming in with his lawyer tomorrow morning at eleven. I've cleared my schedule so I can be here."

10:03 AM

After the meeting, all participants left the conference room. Jack sat in his car contemplating what to do about his new philosophy regarding Detective Mike Ganz.

He decided to talk to Herb. He dialed his cell number.

"Herb, it's me, Jack."

"Did you forget something?"

"No, I have to talk to you in private. Away from the rest of the team."

"What's the matter?"

"Can you come out to my car? It won't take long. I'm out in the parking lot."

"Sure, I'll be right there." The phone line went dead. As promised, Herb soon appeared. The parking lot was full of cars, but nobody was in sight. Herb entered Jack's car, when the doctor opened the door from the driver's seat.

"So, what's bothering you, Jack?"

"Mike."

"What about Mike?"

"I don't know. Herb, I get bad vibes from him."

"Really? What makes you say that?"

"I don't know, Herb. I just don't know."

"What do you think we should do about it?"

"Just watch him. Watch his body language. Watch his work. I don't trust him."

"Well, I guess I owe you that much. I will watch him closely."

"Herb, this is just between us. Don't say anything to Susan or anyone else. Let's see what you observe in the next twenty-four hours."

"Okay. Deal."

Reassuringly, Herb made a fist and lightly hit Jack's right arm as he exited the vehicle. As he disappeared from sight, Jack wasn't sure if Herb took him seriously or not. If he was having trouble coming to grips with his own observations of Mike, how would Jack expect Herb to take this cryptic request?

"Herb's probably having a good laugh with Mike right now, telling him about my amateurish conclusions," thought Jack with a smile. "Couldn't blame him, if he did."

Four days ago

September 27

9:52 AM

The room was quiet and dark. The man with the phone was standing, looking out the window. The light emanating from the outside and his reflection on the window would not betray his real identity. He was wearing a multicolored robe.

"Rupert is pathetic and jumpy. I don't trust him. Too itchy." The man paused, the phone receiver to his ear.

"That's a shame." A quiet moment ensued while the other party spoke.

"No. There's no way around it," he responded confidently to the voice on the line.

"No. I will take care of it. You find and bring to me all the paper trails. I want everything. He has contracts, letters, invoices. Everything." Another pause.

"I don't care how you do it. Just do it." Silence again.

"I will not tolerate sloppy work. We have too much riding on this." A long pause.

He slammed the phone down on the receiver, his anger erupting to the surface. His body tensed. The blood vessels on his temples engorged, visibly throbbing.

The man got a small suitcase from underneath the bed. On the bed, there was a suit jacket, neatly positioned to avoid wrinkling. He placed the suitcase on a nearby couch, dialed in the correct code on the combination lock causing it to fling open. He unzipped the valise. He pulled out a small contraption, about the size of a deck of cards. He quickly analyzed its small LED display to assure that the battery had sufficient power and that the unit would not fail the project at the appropriate time. After a quick inspection, he slid the unit into his right jacket pocket. Inside the suitcase, the man also found and removed a small tank and a small handheld nebulizer. He attached the tank to the nebulizer and turned the unit on. He pulled the trigger demonstrating that the nebulizer was operational. The man then pulled out a small leather box and removed from it an ampule, which he broke open. He carefully dripped its content into a chamber inside the nebulizer. Satisfied with the results, the man placed the contraption inside his left suit pocket.

The stranger got on his knees. He grabbed the suitcase,

ascertained that the padlock was properly and securely fastened and returned the baggage to its concealed nest under the bed. The man stood up, removed his multicolor robe and set it on the bed neatly.

10:41 AM

The doctors had just begun ward rounds. Jill Jeffries, a first year medical resident was discussing her patient.

"Mrs. Richardson is a seventy-two year-old woman who presented with atrial fibrillation. She has a history of CHF from a cardiomyopathy, which proved to be resistant to appropriate optimized medical therapy. She received a defibrillator with CRT."

"I'm sorry, a what?" interrupted Peter Joseph, one of the medical students.

"CRT is cardiac resynchronization therapy," answered Jill, hoping Jack would take it from there and explain the procedure to all.

Rounds were abruptly interrupted by a deafening uproar

coming from the room behind them. The loud noises became screams, which became progressively louder and real. Two people ran out of the room. They were John Connor and Heather McCormick.

"John. Heather. I thought you were ..."

These thoughts were broken up by thunderous gunshots. Red stains suddenly appeared on John's white lab coat, his face abruptly turning ghostly pale, and Heather's forehead, immediately disintegrating her stunning facial features. Both stopped running frantically and slowly fell forward, into Jack's arms. Jack felt helpless and powerless. As the two lifeless bodies fell at his feet, Jack stared at his hands, which had become blood-soaked, dripping crimson red.

"Is it the coronary sinus?" asked Jill, her voice miles away. Jill looked at Jack, noticing his pallor, air hunger and intense perspiration. Jack stood, looking frantically at his own hands, palms facing upward.

"Are you okay, Dr. Norris?" asked Taylor also noticing Jack's distress.

"I'm alright. Sorry. I missed what you were asking." Jack felt asinine and silly.

"I don't think you're okay at all. You're short of breath and broke out in a cold sweat." Jill appeared worried.

"I'll be okay. What were you asking?" endured Jack, feeling a bit better about his dreadful nightmarish fantasy of a few moments ago.

"I was asking about CRT. Jill was telling us how it is a procedure where three intracardiac leads are used to pace the right atrium, right ventricle and left ventricle to help synchronize the heart contractions in patients with cardiomyopathy resistant to medical therapy. The right-sided leads can be placed inside the right heart, but the lead that paces the left ventricle cannot be placed in there, so Jill was saying the lead is placed in the coronary sinus. I was hoping you could say more about it," explained Peter going back to business, as usual.

"Yes, the left ventricle is paced from the coronary sinus. Why don't you plan to observe a CRT implantation? I'll find out when we have a case and I'll let you know." Jack paused. "I'm not feeling especially well. Let me take a break. I need to go get some water. Stan, you go ahead with rounds and page me if you have any questions. I'll catch up with you in a little bit."

Jack did not look well. His customary olive-colored complexion was absent, leaving behind a weary paleness and cold beads of sweat dripping down his forehead and temples. As he walked away from the group, Jack looked outside the window to his left. From that vantage point, he could see the edifice that housed the Emergency Medical Service rigs, next door to the emergency department main entrance. He spied the ambulance bay door open and witnessed Rescue One depart the premises with lights and siren on the way to some mysterious catastrophe.

A feeling of doom came over Jack. He quickened his steps to the office where he would avail himself of cold fresh water. He needed it desperately.

10:42 AM

"Finally a break in the case," said an excited voice. Susan looked at Herb expectantly.

"What is it, Mike?" she asked into her cell phone.

"We finally got the son of a bitch. I found out about the gun. It was purchased illegally and without paperwork or registration by, you guessed it—"

"Dr. Ian Rupert," interjected Susan, pleased. Herb smiled imitatively.

"Dr. Rupert, indeed. We got him now. Will you file for an APB on him and get a warrant for his arrest?"

"We'll do it right now. We'll pick him up and call you when we have him." As soon as Susan ended the call with

Mike, she turned to Herb to give him details. His smile intensified.

Herb turned the unmarked police car towards the Evansville Court House. They were not far and would be there in no time.

Susan dialed the DA to get the necessary paperwork in motion. As she was waiting for the call to connect, loud sirens grew louder, indicating that emergency vehicles were approaching. It was a red Evansville Fire Truck. Behind this red truck was another and behind it a third one sped by, with lights and sirens. Hanging on were several firefighters with the typical hard hats and yellow Scott Air Tanks.

11:05 AM

After drinking some cold water and taking a break from work, Jack almost felt normal. He walked back and joined the others at ongoing ward rounds.

"Are you feeling better, Jack?" asked Jill.

"Much better, thanks." Jack did have some color back and the beads of sweat had dissipated from his face.

All looked concerned, but remained silent for a moment.

"Okay, what did I miss?" Jack broke the stillness of the moment.

"We were talking about Mrs. Agnes Baldwin. She is an eighty-eight-year-old woman who presented with fever and confusion." This patient had been relegated to Christopher

O'Neal, one of the medical students assigned to this team. Chris was presenting the relevant medical data.

"Okay, go ahead." Jack was back in his groove.

"On admission, her BP was 70 with a heart rate of 125. We were called for the rapid heartbeat. It was unclear what the rhythm was at the time." This said, Chris handed the electrocardiogram to Jack, who perused the tracing for a few seconds.

"What do you think it is?" Jack asked.

"I wasn't sure, but I was thinking atrial flutter," answered Chris.

"What else? Anybody have any other ideas?" inquired Jack.

"Atrial tachycardia," volunteered Pete.

"Both are possibilities. Do we have an old electrocardiogram?" posed Jack.

"Yes." Chris was ready for this eventuality and immediately produced a tracing from the old records. This EKG was obtained on the patient four months earlier.

"Now, let's compare P-waves between the two tracings. Look at the twelve leads and see which are different." Jack held up the tracing as the others approached to analyze and scrutinize them.

"The P-waves look exactly the same, then and now," said Jill, all others nodding in agreement.

"So, now what do you think about today's tracing?" solicited Jack.

"Since the tracing was definitely sinus back then and the P-waves are identical in all leads, this must be sinus tachycardia." Peter appeared confident and cocky, neglecting the fact that he was wrong the first go-around.

"Correct. Tell us what all this means now and how we should treat this lady." Jack looked at Chris.

"Since this is sinus tachycardia and not an arrhythmia, her low blood pressure is probably what is causing the rapid rate," said the medical student.

"This is an instant patient." Jack spoke as he approached the bedside and visually examined the elderly woman.

"What's an instant patient?" asked Chris.

"Just add water and she perks up. Look how dry her skin, tongue, and lips are. She has no edema and her jugular veins in her neck are flat. All signs of dehydration." He looked around the bed to find the Foley bag. He picked it up showing the scanty dark yellow urine.

"Low urine amount and very concentrated urine. Dehydration. You're right. Her renal blood work is also consistent with that." Chris seemed to have developed a light bulb over his head.

"That's why she has a rapid heart rate and hypotension. And that's why she is confused. Let's change her intravenous fluids to saline and start out with a bolus of five hundred CCs. What else do you want to do? Is she on a diuretic?" asked Jack.

"Yes, she's on Lasix. I'll stop it. She just had a normal echocardiogram. Let's just see how she is by tomorrow with intravenous hydration. We can follow her blood tests and clinical findings." Chris recommended.

"I agree. By tomorrow, she will be talking and telling us all kinds of tales. What tests will you order for tomorrow and why?" persisted Jack.

"I can get a BMP, TSH, BNP and—"

Christopher's statements were rudely interrupted by loud beeps in unison from all the pagers: "Code Blue, Emergency Department, Trauma Room 1. Code Blue, Emergency Department, Trauma Room 1. Code Blue..."

The group placed all the charts down and made a beeline to the ED. On their arrival, a bloody patient was receiving CPR. The ED staff was working diligently to save the man's life. His expensive suit had been extensively torn and cut up to allow rapid access to the chest and abdomen by the emergency personnel. Tubes entered the mouth and left nostril. An emergency physician was inserting a chest tube. He spoke first addressing the newly arrived cardiology team of doctors.

"Hey, Jack. He has a pneumo with tracheal deviation. We have two large bore IV's but could use a central line. His sternum is fractured, so he may have a cardiac contusion."

"Give me a central line. I'll get a subclavian line in." Jack took off his white lab coat and approached the dying man. Jack suddenly gasped as he realized whom he had in front of him. The man on the stretcher was Dr. Ian Rupert. Rupert, the man he could have sworn was the root of all the recent hospital killings. Wow. Jack paused for a brief moment.

"Here you go, Jack." Linda, the emergency room nurse assigned to Trauma Room 1 poured Betadine, a dark brown liquid used to disinfect the skin, generously in the area under the left collar bone. Another nurse with sterile gloves scrubbed the area vigorously.

By then, Jack had his sterile gloves on and was ready for action. In no time, a thin long intravenous tube was inserted into the main vein under the collarbone.

"Check the CVP, then let's hang O-neg. blood."

"What's a CVP?" whispered Peter in Jill's ear. She was standing next to him, observing and taking it all in.

"Central venous pressure. It'll give us an idea about how much blood volume is inside his central circulation and how the heart is dealing with it," answered the young doctor softly. The medical student nodded, satisfied with the answer. During the exchange, the students watched in awe the rapidity of the skilled actions of Jack and the ED staff, as they worked in harmony to accomplish the necessary tasks.

"CVP is zero," read one of the nurses.

"Give the blood wide open," commanded Jack.

"Are we getting any pressure with chest compressions?" asked one of the ED doctors.

"I don't feel much of a femoral pulse," replied an ED resident.

"He may have tamponade. Continue CPR and prepare for a thoracotomy. Page the CT surgeon on call, stat." Jack looked intense.

Betadine was again used to paint and scrub the chest. Sterile drapes were used to attempt some form of a sterile field, although at this dismal time, infection was the least of all worries. Jack and the ED attending proceeded to use a chest-saw to cut the breastbone and expose Rupert's dying heart.

"What are they doing?" asked Chris looking at Peter, then Jill.

"The patient is not responding to CPR, medications, or fluid and blood transfusions. They're checking to see if there is blood around the heart. Sometimes, if the heart is lacerated, blood escapes out of the chambers into the saç around the heart. This can squeeze the heart and prevent it from pumping. This is called cardiac tamponade. The patient may also be bleeding into his chest from a major vessel. They are going to crack the chest cavity open to examine it and try to stop bleeding and open the pericardium, if there is tamponade." Jill spoke softly, but concisely.

"I don't feel so good." Chris was pale and sickly looking.

"That's okay. Let's step outside and get you some water," commanded Jill with a motherly tone of concern, walking the lightheaded medical student out of Trauma Room 1.

The thoracic cavity was full of blood, which was quickly suctioned. The descending aorta was cross-clamped above the site of brisk bleeding. The pericardial sac was inspected and found to be normal. The heart itself was empty despite all the fluid and blood that had been administered. The team worked efficiently and without words.

"Nothing," said the ED resident palpating the pulse while Jack performed open massage of the heart. Bags of lactated ringers, saline and O-negative blood hung high and dripped fast.

"Flat line on the monitor," said the ED attending.

"What's the down time?" asked the ED resident.

"Sixty-three minutes," announced the nurse documenting all orders and procedures.

"Damn," said Jack in an audible whisper.

"We need to quit, Jack," suggested the ED attending doctor.

"Do we have an ID on this man?" asked the head nurse.

"Ian Rupert. Dr. Ian Rupert," declared Jack gravely.

1:32 PM

The medical team assembled in the solace room in the Emergency department. This room was decorated and comfortable and was utilized for the doctors to meet with the families, traditionally to give bad news. This time there was no family to receive the reports.

Claire had text messaged Jack about lunch an hour before. When the resuscitation efforts ended, Jack retrieved the message and called her. Claire arrived in the conference room a few moments later and was now at Jack's side. Susan and Herb walked in.

"Did you hear?" asked Jack solemnly, as the two detectives walked into the room and sat down.

"If you mean Rupert, yes. He had a car accident. Did he make it?" said Herb.

"No, we just pronounced him dead. Massive internal injuries." Jack appeared dismayed.

"I'm sorry to hear that. We had a warrant for his arrest. It turns out he was linked to the murders. He was the one that purchased the gun and presumably gave it to the killer," said Susan somberly.

"So, is the case closed now?" asked Claire.

A moment of silence ensued. The detectives were reluctant to discuss these matters in such an unprotected area.

"Does anybody else think it's strange that this man has a fatal car accident the moment you find out he is involved with the previous crimes and get a warrant for his arrest?" said Jack tensely.

"It is a coincidence, isn't it?" said Herb.

"Have you found out anything about the accident? Was it rigged?" asked Jack.

"We're still investigating, but it looks like it was a legit accident. There is no evidence of foul play, but we cannot rule it out as yet either," answered Susan.

"That leads us to our next point, Jack." Herb was serious as he looked into Jack's eyes. "This may be getting dangerous. For your protection, we do not want you involved with this case any longer. We will call you, if we need you or when we have news to tell you. You have been of great assistance thus far. We appreciate all you've done. But you need to go back to work and back to your normal life."

"Normal life? I don't think I can ever have a normal life anymore," said Jack poignantly. A long pause followed, terminated by the sound of the door to the room opening. James Miller was escorted into the small area by a nurse who accompanied the portly old man to where the others were. Once inside the room, James looked at all, one by one, with a serious concerned expression. The nurse closed the door behind her as she returned to work. For a short moment, the silence in the solace room was shattered by the distant loud buzz of the busy Emergency Department. When the door shut, silence and peace reigned once again.

"Is it true? Did Dr. Rupert have a car accident?" asked James, restless and apprehensive.

"I'm afraid so, Mr. Miller," finally volunteered Claire, wishing to terminate the awkward silence provoked by the question.

"He arrived with massive internal injuries and could not be saved," added Jack looking into the old man's eyes.

"Did he have any last words? Was he able to speak?" asked James.

"No, he came in receiving CPR. He did not say anything here at the hospital," said Jack.

The group sat in silence. With tearful eyes, James sobbed reticently, both hands covering his face. The reddened rash Jack noticed on the lab head tech's right hand was now a bit more prominent. Claire offered a much-needed tissue, which James appreciatively accepted, weeping gloomily.

3:09 PM

"So, where does this leave us?" asked Susan. The two Evansville detectives, Jack and Mike Ganz were gathered at Newton Memorial Hospital's walkway to the main parking lot. A nearby gigantic oak tree provided shade and respite from the otherwise bustling activities on campus.

"Well, the accident seems legit. We'll transport the car to our headquarters for further analysis. We'll see if there is any foul play but preliminarily, it seems like any other accident. The evidence against Rupert is strong, so the case may be closed," said Mike assertively.

"What evidence?" inquired Jack.

"Mike found out that Rupert had purchased the gun involved in the murder. We already knew Rupert was at the scene the morning of the shooting. So, he had the opportunity to give Butterworth the gun," answered Susan.

"What about Major Rooner and Muhammad Akrim? What have you found out about them?" persisted Jack.

"Jack, we really do appreciate your help on this case. But, for your protection, we must insist that you go back to work. We'll stay in touch with you and let you know how it turns out. If we need you for medical questions, we'll come find you, okay?" Herb spoke like a determined, concerned patriarch.

"Oh, and Jack, I cannot over-emphasize this. Please do not discuss anything to do with this investigation with anyone. Even your wife or friends." Mike was serious. Mike was always serious.

The three cops walked away still disputing the next step in the investigation. Herb and Susan got into their unmarked vehicle. Mike walked deeper into the parking lot in search of his car. Jack stood under the oak tree pensively, feeling unfinished. Unsettled.

Three days ago

September 28

8:05 AM

"Back to your normal life." Detective Herb Fuller's words resounded in Jack's mind.

The medical team was back in business. Morning Report was about to begin.

"Let's hear about Mr. Carl Morrison, Howard," asked Jack of the cardiology fellow on call and in charge the night before. Dr. Howard Hahn was a thin, muscular and bright young man, with the physical attributes of a marathon runner. His hair was cut short and he was clean-shaven, atypical for anyone just post-call. Howard gathered his papers and proceeded to the front of the room. After a moment, he commenced the case presentation.

"Mr. Morrison is a sixty-four-year-old diabetic man who presented to the Emergency department last night with congestive heart failure. This is a recurrent problem for him; he has had multiple such admissions. He is now on appropriate optimized medical therapy. His internist followed him for years with diabetes, hypertension and hypercholesterolemia. Despite many warnings of the dangers of nicotine, he continued to smoke for years, though he quit two months ago. He was admitted in June with CHF. At that time, an echocardiogram showed a LVEF of twenty- to twenty-five percent." Howard was interrupted.

"One of the students, remind us of what LVEF means." Jack looked around for volunteers. Taylor beat the others to the punch.

"Left ventricular ejection fraction is a measure of how strong or weak the heart contractions are. Normal is fifty percent; at twenty- to twenty-five percent, there is significant heart muscle weakening."

"Good, Taylor; please continue, Howard."

"A cardiac cath in June showed the coronary arteries to be patent, so he has a non-ischemic dilated cardiomyopathy which is resistant to medical therapy. His present meds are Coreg CR, eighty milligrams daily, Altace, ten milligrams daily, spironolactone, fifty milligrams daily and Lipitor, forty milligrams daily. We added Lasix, forty milligrams IV last night and an IV drip of Natrecor. His symptoms improved, though he remained short of breath."

"Good. What is the QRS duration?" asked Jack.

"It's wide." Howard paused to find the patient's electrocardiogram tracing in the folder. As he did so, Dr. Mark Holden, a medical resident assigned to Howard's on call group, placed a transparency on the projector so all could analyze the tracing.

"It measures 160 milliseconds," said Howard finally, while Mark concurred using his pencil to draw on the transparency, indicating where the QRS complex started and ended, allowing for proper measurement of its duration.

"What do you think we should offer the patient?" questioned Jack.

"CRT with ICD backup," answered the young doctor at the podium.

"Will you explain what that means?"

"Cardiac resynchronization therapy, or CRT, also called bi-ventricular pacing, is a procedure whereby we pace the right and left ventricles to force both sides of the heart to contract simultaneously. Because of an electrical delay, this patient's heart becomes inefficient. Instead of a coordinated contraction, the heart wobbles back and forth. CRT will correct this and make the heart more efficient. This has been shown to improve quality of life by reducing CHF symptoms and hospitalizations."

"Very good explanation. What about the ICD backup you talked about?" inquired Jack.

"Because his LVEF is less than thirty-five percent despite optimized medical therapy, he is at high risk for sudden cardiac arrest. An ICD or implantable cardioverter defibrillator, is a device that can be implanted to shock rescue the patient to normal rhythm if he should experience a lethal rapid heartbeat called ventricular fibrillation."

"Excellent. Does anyone have any questions for Dr. Hahn?" asked Jack, looking around the room.

"Is that two devices? One for CRT and another for ICD," asked Peter.

"No, one device will have both," answered Howard.

"Okay, let's round on him later today, see how he's progressing and talk to him about a bi-ventricular ICD. Let's discuss another case, Howard. How about Pennington?" proposed Jack looking at the form containing all the cardiac admissions of the previous night. Howard looked through the records on the platform in front of him and pulled out the folder labeled 'Randall Pennington.' After a short recess to review the data, Howard presented the information. At the same time, Mark replaced the electrocardiogram transparency with the new patient's.

"Mr. Pennington is a forty-five-year-old man with recurrent symptomatic palpitations. He presented to the emergency department yesterday evening with rapid regular tachycardia."

Jack visualized the middle-aged man complaining of the racing heart. As he did, Howard's voice became drowned in his thoughts. Abruptly, Jack beheld Rupert driving his 745 Li BMW, a bullet from nowhere hitting him squarely in his chest. Blood spurted out draining the doctor of his life essence, the car out of control crashing into a tree. More blood now soaked his entire body, although the spurting had become a trickle, as the soul of the man hastened into the beyond. Ambulance sirens grew increasingly loud culminating in a deafening cacophony of tuneless detonations. The scene gradually became that of an operating room where Jack, sterilely gloved and gowned, operated on Rupert, helped by John Connor and Heather McCormick. Rupert floundered helplessly on the operating table, like a fish out of water. Straps and restrains secured the man to the surgical slab. A scalpel in one hand, a stiletto in the other, Jack prepared to send Rupert to the after-life. John and Heather held the old doctor down with all their might, empowering Jack to precisely and skillfully perform the deadly feat. With a grin, Jack raised both his hands high in the air, to gather momentum in his effort to plunge the sharp objects deep into Rupert's carcass, finishing off that which the car crash had merely instigated.

"Jack, do you agree?" a distant faint voice penetrated the grotesquely and outlandish daydream.

"Jack. Are you all right?" asked Chris, the medical student sitting next to Jack. These words yanked Jack back into reality.

"Yes, I'm fine," whispered Jack guilefully.

"Do you agree, Jack?" asked Howard for the third time still puzzled with the tracing projected on the large screen.

"It's AV node reentry," responded Jack confidently merely five seconds after visually analyzing the rhythm strip. Jack was trembling, a cold sweat easily visible on his forehead.

"That's what I thought," agreed Howard, clueless to the outward physical signs displayed by Jack.

"Taylor, give us a brief report on this type of arrhythmia tomorrow, okay?" asked Jack, feeling somewhat better and trying to show a business-as-usual attitude.

"Sure, no problem," said Taylor.

Morning Report was over. The pack ambled out of Meeting Room 3 and separated into groups. Those assigned to Jack followed him up the stairs.

"We're happy to have you back, Jack," said Jill Jeffries, a medical resident.

The group of doctors and students followed Jack. The others conversed amongst themselves. Someone described an event; something funny about a TV program from the evening before. They talked and laughed. Jack was not listening. Deep inside, he was fearful that the sudden tragic loss of his friends was affecting him more profoundly than he had imagined. He was having vivid daydream nightmares. He was distracted. He was unfocused.

"Maybe it's time to take this seriously and get shrunk," thought Jack. Getting shrunk was Jack's usual comments when he thought the patient needed a shrink. A psychiatrist. A psychologist. Claire was right. He was going to need serious professional help. There was no denying it.

The group reached the sixth floor medical unit, the main place cardiac patients would be hospitalized. The group would start rounds there. As they walked, Jack's beeper beeped. He paused causing all others to stop.

"It's Dr. Vivian Wall, one of the EP attendings. I need to call her back." Jack walked several more steps to reach a phone on a desk at the Nurses' Station. Jack dialed and spoke for a few minutes. Once or twice, he looked at his wristwatch. Then, he put the phone back in its perch.

"Who wants to come see a device implantation?" inquired Jack of the group. They all raised their right hands blissfully, resembling a pack of elementary schoolers asked who would prefer recess to a pop quiz on multiplication tables.

"I didn't think you were assigned to the Cath Lab this month," said Jill inquisitively.

"I'm not. I'm on the clinical rotation service with you guys. Archie Patel has not returned to work since the murders. She was scheduled to perform this procedure with Dr. Wall, so I get to do it. Dr. Wall needs my help with the case.

The group made a beeline to the basement and entered the area marked: Cardiac Cath Lab.

9:34 AM

"Thanks for coming to my rescue, Jack. You have an entourage. Welcome everybody. I'm Dr. Vivian Wall and I'm one of the attendings in the Department of Electrophysiology."

Vivian was in her late fifties. She had long jet-black hair and dark brown eyes. She wore light green scrubs, surgical hat and mask. Her reception of the team made everyone feel at home, although the students appeared apprehensive even then.

"It's always a pleasure to assist you, Viv," said Jack. "We'll go get into scrubs and meet you at the sink." Vivian smiled. She was sitting at a table in the doctor's lounge. When the group disappeared, she went back to reviewing the patient's chart.

A few minutes later, one by one the group reassembled by

the older doctor. When they were all back, she spoke slowly and with intellectual poise.

"We are going to operate on Mrs. Genevieve Everton who is sixty-four and has a severe non-ischemic cardiomyopathy. Her ventricles are dilated, weak and out of synch. We are going to implant a device to resynchronize her ventricle and I hope we can help her feel better, and keep her out of the hospital. Do you all know about CRT and ICDs?"

"Jack has been telling us about defibrillators and bi-ventricular devices," responded Pete, proudly.

"Good. This woman, unfortunately, has had a sick heart for years. She was cared for by a family practitioner that saw her every three months, but did little for her. About six months ago, she was sent to me for management of her heart failure. I started her on medical therapy but she has continued to go downhill. We should have seen her a long time ago, before she got to this stage. Oh well, let's see what we can do to help her."

With these words, Vivian started her scrub routine at the sink. Jack took the sink next to her. As the two doctors vigorously brushed their fingers, hands, wrists and forearms under the running water, the others gathered around. Observing. Studying the moves.

"Why do we need generalists? Why not just have specialists?" asked Pete. A pause to ponder the question ensued. To break the silence and its awkward consequences, the medical student continued, "I mean, if we live in the boonies and there are no specialists for miles, I guess we need generalists. But in a city, where there are specialists, why do we need generalists? They seem to know very little about a lot."

"Pete, realize that the more one specializes, the more one knows about fewer things. At some point, some know everything about nothing." Taylor's joke was timely and rewarded by a hearty laugh by all. The question was sincere and left even the wisest of the doctors temporarily speechless.

"I'm serious, though. If I break a bone, what is the advantage of going to see a generalist when I can go see a specialist? If I have a heart attack, same question. There are data to show that the chances of survival and quality of life are better when a cardiologist as opposed to a generalist manages a heart attack victim. Studies show that more specialists than generalists use evidence-based medications. So, why do we need them? Why not make all doctors pick a field, have them concentrate on it, and learn it exclusively. Make everybody a specialist." Pete continued on his soap box as the two doctors scrubbed and walked into Cath Lab Three, hands dripping water.

"Hello, everybody. I convinced Jack to give us a hand with the case. This is his entourage. Did she get her antibiotic?" asked Vivian of the nurses in the lab, as she entered the room, back first, to avoid touching her scrubbed hands on the door.

"Yes, she received cefazolin. She is well sedated and ready for you to do your thing," answered one of the nurses in the room. She was covered head to toe with apparel including a lead apron, which covered her entire torso. A thyroid shield enveloped her neck. Her eyes were covered by protective eyewear. All wore similar garb, including the newly arrived.

The patient was totally submerged underneath a sterile light blue surgical cover. At the head, a nurse gave medications and monitored the vital signs. As the scrub nurse at the left side of the patient prepped the doctors, the conversations resumed.

"You ask an interesting question, Pete," said Jack pushing his right hand into a sterile glove held open by the scrub nurse using impeccable surgical technique. The left hand endured the same fate.

"Why do we need general doctors like family practice, internal medicine, pediatrics and so on?" reiterated Vivian for the nurses' sake. "Why not just have specialists caring for people?"

"What if I have a pain? Say in my chest or abdomen. How do I know whom to see? Should I see a cardiologist? A gastroenterologist?" asked one of the nurses in the room, facial expression and identity hidden perfectly by the surgical mask and hat.

"If I were the king of the world, I would make all doctors specialists. To answer your question, I would come up with a national computerized system that everyone would have access to, either by phone or online. You would give your age, gender, description of symptoms, and the computer program would analyze the information, ask a few questions and come up with a list of probabilities and what specialty you should see first. The computer could even give a list of referrals and even make you the appointment on the spot." Pete was on a roll.

"So, you'd put your faith on a computer program?" inquired a skeptical nurse who recorded information and data documenting the procedure at hand.

"Sure. I bet it would do as well as a general doctor who really is merely a glorified triage nurse," said Pete.

"Most patients have multiple problems. Who would coordinate care?" asked Jack. He was sticking a needle under the collarbone to access the subclavian vein. Blood return on the syringe indicated the needle had successfully penetrated the vein. A guide-wire was pushed through the needle, the needle was withdrawn and a peel-away sheath was slid over the wire into the blood vessel. Through this, a lead was advanced, soon reaching the right atrium. Fluoroscopy was used to visualize the procedure.

"All doctors would be connected through an electronic medical record, so exchange of information from doctor to doctor would be instantaneous. A computerized system would coordinate things better than any man," said Pete.

"Man, yes. But women would be even better," said one of the nurses. All laughed. By then, Jack had the three necessary leads inside the right heart.

"Okay, this is the part where it gets tricky," said Jack hoping to put the debate on hold. "I need to cannulate the coronary sinus," he said, pushing a button that caused the fluoroscopy tower to angulate to the patient's left.

"Who knows what the coronary sinus is and where it is?" asked Vivian looking directly at the medical students.

"It's a vein that dumps deoxygenated blood into the right atrium. It wraps around the left atrioventricular groove." Pete was amazing. He knew his shit. And his heart.

"Correct," said Vivian. "We will use it to pace the left ventricle and synchronize it to the right ventricle by force pacing both at the same time."

Silence ensued as the lights were dimmed. Jack looked intently at the fluoro-screen as he manipulated a deflectabletip catheter inside the right atrium, in search of the opening into the vein. After several minutes, he stood straight.

"Here it is. Let's do a venogram," said Jack.

"Good technique, Jack. Very nice," congratulated Vivian, with a reassuring and ingratiating stare.

The procedure went well and soon the operative wound was sealed closed with surgical glue. The patient began to wake up from conscious sedation. The doctors took off their surgical garb and walked outside the lab.

"So why do we need generalists?" reiterated Jack.

4:32 PM

Jack was worried. He was worried that his professional work was being affected by the murders. The daydreams of horror persisted and he wanted them to go away completely. He vowed to discuss the issue with Claire and seek her help. It was clear the dreadfulness of it all was not over for him, psychologically. He was also confident that his best way to cope with the situation was to help catch the mastermind behind it all. Rupert was most definitely involved. No question of it in Jack's mind. Now, he was dead. He was conveniently murdered. Who would gain from it?

Jack had taken time to catch up with the piling up work at his office. He reviewed laboratory results, signed previously given verbal orders and patient files, dictated patient histories and discharge summaries that had been neglected due to a busy case load and labored over the on call schedule for the doctors in training.

Keeping his mind busy was marvelous. It kept the Boogie Man away. It was time to go home.

The car ride was peaceful, chill time. Cars were moving rather well, although the peak hour of heavy traffic was still to come. The phone rang.

"Jack, it's Herb."

"Hi, Herb. What's up?"

"I did what you told me. I've been researching and watching detective Mike Ganz. You may have something with your suspicions. I think Mike has been giving us bad information. You know how he called us yesterday to tell us that he found out Rupert was the owner of the mysterious gun used to commit the heinous crimes at Memorial Hospital?"

"Yeah," said Jack perplexedly.

"That's the thing, Jack. We've been looking for where the gun came from. We all thought the gun was the key to the whole case. Mike volunteered to do a check of the FBI database and told us we didn't need to do our own check here locally. He told us repeatedly that the gun was not reported on the database. He finally discovers that Rupert purchased the weapon and calls us to tell us that the moment the poor slob shows up dead. How opportune. I went behind his back and found out he never checked at all. Also, he comes to the morning meetings everyday except for the day Rupert ends up dead."

"What are you going to do now?

"I'll talk to Susan first thing in the morning. I will interrogate Mike and see what he has to say. First, I want to gather as much evidence as possible. And Jack, thank you."

"No problem."

"Did I tell you that Rupert's home here in Evansville was ransacked?" asked Herb.

"No, I wonder why?"

"I don't know yet. The neighbors reported suspicious men at the house. On their arrival, the police officers found it totally rummaged."

"I wonder what they were looking for?" asked Jack rhetorically.

"Don't know. Jack, please do not talk to anybody about any of this for your own protection. I think whoever is behind all this is dangerous." He hung up the phone.

Jack glanced at his rearview mirror. He spotted the black sedan again a few cars behind him. Unsurprisingly, despite great efforts, Jack could not see who the driver was. Jack accelerated. The sedan followed suit. Jack suddenly turned hard right, almost recklessly. The sedan mimicked the turn. As the cars sped down the highway passing all other vehicles, a road sign gave Jack an idea. It read Evansville Airport. Jack pulled out his Treo and dialed.

The race continued with the mysterious vehicle closely behind Jack's car. The covert driver of the sedan was obviously a pro at this, pursuing with impeccable precision and timing. Despite best efforts, however, the distance between the two automobiles increased little by little. As he approached the airport, Jack spied a police car parked on the side of the road. Jack contemplated stopping and reporting his pursuer, but then thought better of it. There was no wrong doing yet, nor would he actually be able to prove he was being followed, although that was clear to Jack. He would persist with his plan. A traffic light turned red as Jack crossed the intersection. The dark car, now two cars behind, would be forced to stop, especially with the cop car nearby. Waiting for the light to turn green for what seemed to be an eternity, the man was able to see Jack turn left. A sign pointing in that direction, read Evansville Airport.

After several more minutes of street racing, the sedan arrived at the airport's parking lot and parked briskly without any delay. Jack's car was in one of the stalls. The mysterious man immediately got out of the sedan and ran towards the gate leading to the tarmac. As he did, the Bonanza slowly gathered velocity as it sped down the runway. In a few heartbeats, the airplane was airborne. The landing gear retracted as the aircraft disappeared into the beautiful blue sky.

Dispirited, the unknown man stood looking skyward for a long moment.

"Shit. Damn it!" he exclaimed in disappointment. The man made a cellular call, as he furiously walked back to his car. He opened up the trunk of the parked vehicle, removed a round object and carried it towards Jack's car. All the while, he appeared steaming mad. He got on his knees next to Jack's auto and attached the small round object to the undercarriage of the vehicle. He performed this task seamlessly in a matter of seconds. Before finishing the job, the stranger looked in all directions underneath the parked vehicles. Satisfied that no shoes were discernible near his location, he stood up inconspicuously looking in all directions through his dark sunglasses. Seeing no one in sight, he proceeded to his sedan.

Behind a parked truck, Jack kneeled down on the large protruding bumper crouching down to avoid detection. In a few heartbeats, the stranger entered his car and sped out of the parking area.

"I owe you one, Steve," murmured Jack to no one in particular, as he got on his feet and searched for his mobile phone.

7:53 PM

Several parked vehicles crowded the parking lot. Additionally, two patrol cars, one unmarked police car and one Crime Scene Investigation van loitered about displaying a myriad of flashing emergency lights resembling a kaleidoscope from afar.

Claire arrived, her speeding car rushing into the area. She stopped the vehicle, put it in park and rushed to Jack's arms.

"Are you okay, baby?" she asked anxiously.

"I'm fine. The police are investigating the object. They removed it from under the car. It appears to be some sort of tracking device. They are now getting pictures, fingerprints and so forth. But, I'm okay." Jack reassured and calmed her with his composed tone. Claire took a cleansing deep breath.

How good it felt to be in Jack's protective arms. As they hugged, Claire regained her sense of tranquility.

Herb, Susan and Mike walked towards the couple.

"Are you guys okay?" asked Susan.

"I'm still shaking, but I'll be fine," answered Claire.

"Good. There's no reason for alarm," reassured Susan, as the men looked on approvingly.

"Jack, for your safety, we'd like to give you police protection. I'll have a police car parked outside your house until we get to the bottom of this," declared Herb authoritatively.

"Okay, sure," answered Jack, looking at Claire for approval. She nodded.

"We'll take the device and your car to our station for full analysis," interjected Susan.

"Are we in danger?" asked Claire.

"I don't know, but we'd like to take precautions. Whoever is behind these heinous murders knows you are involved, Jack, and is following you. So, please be careful and stay out of the investigation," said Herb. Mike stood tall, in silence.

Susan took Claire by her arm and gently guided her to her car. Herb put his hand on Jack's right shoulder walking with him behind the women. Mike stood still watching all walk towards the vehicle.

"This may be an FBI-issued tracking device," whispered Herb, so that only Jack could hear. Jack remained quiet and continued to make full eye contact, as the detective spoke.

"Be careful. Don't take any chances. We'll talk tomorrow morning," continued Herb, sensing Jack's apprehension.

Mike Ganz looked on from a few feet away, where the group had initially met. He was calm, cool and collected.

Jack nodded slowly, as if in a trance. By then, they were by Claire's car. Jack helped Claire get into the passenger side of her vehicle then got in, sitting behind the steering wheel. The investigative crowd was not quite done poking and prodding at Jack's car. A police officer would drive the car to the police station and Jack agreed to pick it up the next morning. They slowly drove off in utter silence, mesmerized by the latest sequence of events. This had turned personal and the stakes had become much higher.

Behind them, in the rearview mirror, the misty autumn evening and the dimming sunlight exaggerated the luminous effects of the flashing emergency lights on the roofs of the police vehicles.

8:12 PM

Once the car carrying Jack and Claire departed the area, the detectives went back to work. Susan approached Todd Turner, head of the CSI team, and engaged him in professional conversation. Mike had attempted to follow her, but was asked to stop.

"Mike, I have some questions for you," said Herb.

"Yeah, what's up, Herb?" answered Mike turning back to face the older detective.

"I checked with the FBI headquarters in Indianapolis. You never accessed the database to check on the gun. How did you find out it was Rupert's gun?"

"I asked one of my cohorts to check. He finally did it and called me with the results."

"What's his name? Your cohort?"

"Are you checking up on me, Herb?"

"I guess I am," answered the local detective, slowly.

As they spoke, Mike turned his body away from the investigating crowd, causing Herb to naturally shift in the same direction. Mike put his hand on Herb's shoulder and gently guided him away from the area and into the darkness of the late evening. This was done with such flare and grace, that Herb never realized he was being escorted away from the others.

"I don't know what you think I did. I'm just helping you get the bad guy," said Mike with an angelic shit-eating grin on his face.

"I find that hard to believe. The gun was our main focus. You told me repeatedly you had checked on the gun and the ballistics and neither were in the database," persisted Herb. Incredulously, Herb grew increasingly astonished by Mike's testimony, becoming more convinced with each answer that Mike was implicated.

"I don't know what to tell you, Herb. I was busy."

As the dialogue progressed, the two slowly and imperceptibly walked deeper into the parking lot and away from the lighted area of intense investigation. Mike suddenly removed a mask from his right jacket pocket and placed it over his own mouth and nose. In rapid succession, he also withdrew an apparatus from his left pocket, which he pointed at Herb's face. An aerosolized mist swiftly entered Herb's nasal passages, causing an almost pleasant tingling cooling sensation. Mike removed another gadget from his right pocket. This had the appearance of a remote control which he pointed at Herb and pressed a button. The initial pleasant awareness in

Herb's nasal passages grew rapidly into a stinging impression, which Herb felt deeper and deeper into his airways. First the trachea, then bronchi, and finally the alveoli, where the chemicals would speedily enter the blood circulation en route into the heart then brain.

8:23 PM

"Jack, come back. Herb collapsed. Please hurry," yelled Susan into the cell phone, seeing her partner and best friend slip away in front of her eyes.

"Call 911. I'm turning back." Jack threw the phone at Claire, who sat apprehensively with growing agitation, looking at Jack.

"What's going on, Jack?" she asked as the car raced back to the scene where they left only minutes before.

Soon the vehicle entered the parking lot. To the side, a group of people gathered around. In the middle of it all, Herb lay on the ground motionless. Susan knelt down next to him supporting his head on her thighs. Concerned looks abounded.

"Give us some room, please. Will everyone step back?"

yelled Jack, taking control of the situation. A quick visual assessment of the detective clearly indicated that the man was in serious trouble. There was blood around his lips. His airway was patent but he was cyanotic, a bluish discoloration of his lips and tongue.

"Who can tell me what happened?" asked Jack of the audience then looking at Susan.

"He walked out here on his own. The rest of us were out by the car talking to the CSI people. We suddenly heard a grunting noise and ran here. When I got here, Herb was on the ground having a seizure. He was foaming at the mouth. These officers held him down and we placed him on his side to avoid aspiration. I called you right away. And 911. He stopped having a seizure as you arrived." Susan's words showed obvious distress and feelings of helplessness.

Jack took Herb's carotid pulse. His pulse was extremely rapid, but faint. Sirens in the distance grew increasingly louder by the second, alerting the group that an ambulance with paramedics would soon arrive.

Herb briefly regained consciousness becoming agitated and hyper.

"My guns, my gun, my guns," repeated the confused, combative patient, slurring his words, which were barely comprehensible.

"Herb, do you know what happened to you?" asked Jack hoping to assess Herb's mental status.

"Ma guns, ma guh…" persisted Herb with increasing difficulty in forming his words. His combativeness and agitation was waning rapidly as he faded.

The ambulance siren was now loud, as the emergency vehicle arrived. Two young men dressed in a blue uniform jumped out of the ambulance carrying a large container full of drugs.

"It looks like he had a seizure," said Mike to the approaching paramedics.

"Does he have a history of seizures?" asked Jack looking at Susan.

"No, he's been healthy all his life. He had a full physical three months ago and was told he was a picture of health," answered Susan.

The paramedics cut off Herb's shirt and placed skin electrodes on his chest.

"I'm a doctor. Jack Norris," introduced the young doctor.

"I recognize you, doc. I'm Ray, this is Bo," said one of the paramedics.

"Ma gun, mmm," continued Herb now even more feebly.

"Sinus tachycardia," said Jack, as the monitor unit came alive, indicating Herb's heart beat. It was racing. Racing at 220 beats per minute.

"Get a blood pressure, please," asked one of the paramedics of his partner who obliged.

"Let's administer verapamil and propranolol as soon as we establish an IV line," commanded Jack.

As this was being done, the monitor suddenly changed. The extremely rapid QRS sharp waves, indicating each heart beat, suddenly slowed to 100 then 40 then became a straight line. Simultaneously, Herb, took a deep last breath.

"Start CPR. Let me help you get a line. Get ready to give one milligram of epinephrine and one milligram of atropine," commanded Jack authoritatively.

Susan started chest compressions. One of the police officers had obvious first aid training, grabbed an Ambu bag and placed the mask over Herb's mouth and nose. At his request, another officer brought an oxygen green cylinder closer. This was attached to the Ambu via the appropriate clear tubing. He squeezed the bag every five seconds forcing air into Herb's lungs. Susan continued chest compressions like a pro.

In no time at all, and with the expertise of a magician, Jack had intravenous access. A bag of five percent dextrose in water was held by one of the medics. The tubing from the IV bag was hooked to the IV port, which was taped securely to the skin.

"Epinephrine and atropine are in," yelled one of the paramedics. CPR efforts continued for a minute. The monitor was reassessed but still showed a flat line.

"One more round of epi and atropine," ordered Jack.

Instantaneously, the paramedic giving drugs complied.

"No response," said one of the paramedics despondently.

"Continue CPR to the hospital. Let's move fast and give another round of drugs," commanded Jack with sorrow. Jack realized that the chance of a successful outcome was nil.

The group positioned Herb on the stretcher, placed it in the ambulance and sped to Newton Memorial Hospital. A radio announcement to the emergency department's personnel would facilitate the transfer on arrival. In the rig, Susan continued CPR, Jack, at her side, had taken on the task of breathing for Herb. More drugs were administered intravenously in the hopes of restarting the heartbeat. None did any good.

As the ambulance sped away with lights and sirens blaring, Jack could not stop hearing Herb's last words in his head: "My guns, my guns!"

Strange. "Why would he want his gun," thought Jack.

"Did he want to commit suicide? Kill people around him? Was he poisoned like the others?"

Two days ago

September 29

12:36 AM

A nurse led Claire, Susan and Mike to the solace room. Anxious and concerned, none of them could sit still. Instead, they stood outside the door to the solace room, gazing at the door to the room where Herb was taken. Jack and the emergency department's personnel continued resuscitative efforts on Herb.

Ten minutes later, the door to Cardiac Room Three opened, allowing Jack to exit. For the brief moment the door was ajar, the commotion inside the room became visible. The dreaded reality they all feared was now on display as a white sheet, a telltale sign of the unsuccessful resuscitation covered Herb's total body, including his head. Jack's body language was revealing of the anguish and sorrow he was feeling inside.

Jack joined the group. They entered the solace room and sat down. This time, they were there to mourn one of their own.

"I can't believe he's gone. I must call his family. What will I tell them?" asked Susan rhetorically.

"I know it's tough. I'll do it with you, Susan," offered Claire, sympathetically.

"Thank you so much. I have done this so many times with so many different people. But now, it's one of our own." Susan's eyes were moist, tears flowing down her cheeks. Claire sat by her silently, holding a box of tissues.

"I'll be with you for as long as you need me," said Claire.

"I should tell his wife in person. I think that's what he'd want," alleged Susan.

"I'll go with her," said Mike before Claire could speak.

"Thanks, Mike. You two go on home. Mike and I will take care of this. You need some rest. We'll talk in the morning," offered Susan appreciatively, looking at Jack and Claire.

The river of tears flowed even more briskly now. The two couples exited the emergency room and walked outside towards the parking lot. Susan and Mike entered a waiting police car and soon were on their way.

Jack and Claire exited the ED main door and prepared to walk towards the car she had driven back from the airport.

"Claire, give me a minute. I need to run downstairs. I'll be right back," said Jack as he ran off into the guts of the hospital. In a few minutes, Jack returned with a large shopping bag full of medication vials, syringes, needles, a tourniquet and alcohol swabs.

"What's all this stuff for?" asked Claire intrigued by the sack of drugs.

"All these people that have died, either in the hospital or at home, have done so in a cardiovascularly hyper-stimulated manner. Herb tonight had a heart rate over 200 beats per minute. That is incredibly difficult to fathom unless there are stimulatory drugs in his system. So these vials of medicines in here are drugs that block the cells in the body from being stimulated."

"Are you saying Herb was poisoned? I thought he had a seizure," asked Claire puzzled.

"He did have a seizure, but why? With a seizure, the heartbeat may quicken a bit, but not that fast. He had to be poisoned with the same stuff as the others," concluded Jack.

"Rat Poison?" asked Claire.

"Yes."

"But who?" Claire seemed perplexed and troubled.

"Herb and I have been suspicious of Mike Ganz. He's an FBI agent working on this case. He could have done it. He was there and—," Jack paused, then continued.

"I think so, I think it's Mike Ganz. He's an FBI agent . . . " Jack suddenly stopped talking, a look of elation in his eyes, as if to say 'Eureka!'

"What's wrong, Jack?" asked Claire.

"Mike Ganz. Mike Ganz," repeated Jack with a progressively excited tone. "Mike Ganz!"

"What about him?"

"Don't you get it? Mike Ganz. My guns!" Jack sounded like he had lost it.

"No, I don't get."

"Herb was trying to tell me Mike Ganz. I thought he was saying my guns but he was telling me the name of his killer. Mike Ganz."

"Well, Mike is on the way to Herb's house with Susan. What should we do about it?" asked Claire vexed by how the situation had unfolded.

"I don't think he'll do anything to her. Not right now. He knows Susan doesn't know anything. I think Herb found out and that's why he killed him. Herb and I had been talking about Mike. We suspected him; Herb was going to approach Mike. I think he did tonight and paid the price. Claire, if something happens to me, I will use these drugs in the bag. I think they'll help me." Jack stopped for a moment to search his wallet in his back pocket. In it, he removed two business cards. He put one back into his pocket and handed the other to Claire.

"This is Susan's card. Her cell number is on there. Call her, if something happens to me."

"What's going to happen to you, Jack? I'm scared," said Claire.

"I know you are, sweetheart. We'll be all right."

As they approached their house, Jack and Claire noticed a police car in the driveway.

"Good evening officer, we're Jack and Claire Norris," explained Jack after he parked his car next to the police car and opened up his window. It was a beautiful dark evening. The temperature was comfortable. The officer sat in the car with the windows open enjoying the cool delightful mist the autumn evening offered.

"Welcome home. Rest assured I'm on the job. Nobody will bother you while I'm here. I know a lot has happened, but you can feel safe. Sleep well," reassured the cop. He was young, but extremely well built; the kind of body structure that could only come from repeated trips to the gym.

"Can we offer you anything? Some coffee?" offered Claire leaning down to see the cop from the passenger's seat.

"No, thanks, Mrs. Norris, I'm fine," he said lifting up his large cup of McDonald's coffee. He smiled reassuringly.

Jack drove on with a polite nod and wave of his left hand. Once in the garage, the automatic door closed. Jack watched as the garage door locked firmly in place. As Claire prepared to go to bed, Jack went around the house, door-to-door and window-to-window, making sure they were all properly and securely locked. As the last window was tested, Jack looked outside into his driveway. The police officer was now standing outside the car leaning on the driver's door smoking a cigarette and sipping his coffee.

5:30 AM

“Two thousand dollars to each of you,” offered the man in the dark room as he spoke into the cell phone. After a long pause, the mysterious man continued to speak. He sported a comfortable multicolor robe and was sitting on a divan, his feet up on an ottoman. He was wearing his bedroom slippers and sipped coffee as he spoke.

“Okay, make it five thousand, total. Dead or alive, it doesn’t matter to me. But I don’t want any screw-ups. No mistakes.” The incomprehensible distant words emanating from the cell phone was the only sound that disturbed the calmness and silence of the night.

“No, five includes all.” The other party interrupted his words, for a short moment.

"Don't forget, you owe me. That's my final offer. If you're not interested, I'll go somewhere else," continued the man pausing to hear a reply.

"When can you get here? I need this done right away." Another break while the other voiced his viewpoint.

"Not soon enough. I need this job done now." The mysterious man commanded respect and fear.

"Okay, tomorrow night. Don't be late or you'll be sorry."

2:12 PM

Jack and Claire felt safe with the police protection. The officer had proven respectful and sympathetic. In the morning, another policeman arrived to relieve the one that spent the night on sentinel duty. The newly arrived man seemed just as competent and professional as the other. The two cops were rewarded with coffee, bagels, muffins and orange juice for breakfast.

Around mid morning, Jack left for an hour to purchase an alarm system. There was no time to have it done professionally, but Jack thought, "I'm an electrician of hearts. I'm not all together unintelligent. How difficult could it be to wire this house safe?"

Jack tried to contact Susan. Several voice messages were left on her cell number. Finally, she called back but Jack was on a ladder wiring the upstairs windows. He didn't hear the phone ring. Later, when he realized he missed a call, he heard the voice message left by Susan. She said she was sorry she had not answered her phone calls, but that she was busy comforting the Fuller's. They had been close and Susan felt it was her duty, as a friend and colleague, to be with his family. She vowed to call later in the evening or the next morning. Jack understood the pain and anguish they were suffering. He felt it, too.

When lunch was served, the police officer was invited inside to experience Claire's wonderful culinary skills. The guard expressed his appreciation for Claire's superb talents and stated that this was the best fried-chicken he had ever had. Throughout the meal, he gave his thanks for Claire and Jack's hospitality many times.

Jack spent the rest of the day installing the alarm system. The task proved arduous and grueling.

"Why don't we just get a dog?" he asked Claire.

"Is it working yet?" she inquired.

"What, the dog?"

"No, the alarm system?"

"It's all installed, but I need to plug into the electrical. You know, a dog doesn't need electrical. They work on kibble, which is easier to install. I need to research this some more. I don't want to short out the whole Evansville board. I'll finish this tomorrow."

"You call yourself an electrician? That's a joke." Claire smiled as they made eye contact, dirt and oil stains all over Jack's face and clothes.

"Heart electrician! Not house electrician," he amended.

"Doctors," Claire shook her head, a faint smile on her face.

"Do you know how many psychologists it takes to change a light bulb?" asked Jack.

"No, how many?"

"Just one, but the light bulb really has to want to change."

"Jack, do you know how many cardiac electrophysiologists it takes to change a light bulb?"

"No, how many?"

"Two. One to hold the bulb, the other to rotate the house."

3:52 AM

During hospital rounds, Jack had begun to regain his confidence. Things were definitely resuming some degree of normalcy. The medical group had entered Room 622 as they discussed the intricacies of the patient's medical problems. An elderly man lay in bed under the covers, on his back, his hands under his head. The young doctors continued the discussion about the patient's medical ailments. Barely noticeable, the man slowly moved both his arms to under the linens. Engaged in the conversations, Jack and the other doctors hardly became aware of the patient's activities. Subtly and covertly, the old man pulled his right arm out from under the bed sheets, exposing the small revolver. Suddenly, the patient sat up in bed, holding the firearm with both hands, the muzzle pointed at Jack. A loud gunshot was heard, the bullet traveling directly towards Jack's forehead at 2,000 feet per second. The earsplitting sound caused Jack's body to jerk awake from his nightmare. Jack sat up in bed, sweating profusely, heart pounding and breathing rapidly. He looked over at Claire, who slept peacefully, like an angel.

Despite trying, Jack could not fall back asleep, his nightmare and the events of the last few weeks were playing wildly in his mind. He got up as slowly and as silently as he could, not to disturb Claire. He glanced out the window to see the police car parked on his driveway, a reassuring detail. A spotlight mounted high under the roofline illuminated portions of the front yard, driveway and police car. A quick shadow passing over the driver's door disappeared as rapidly as it had appeared.

"What was that?" thought Jack curiously. "Maybe it was a blowing tree branch shadow?" Whatever it was, it caught Jack's eye. Jack strained to listen for unusual sounds. Nothing. No wind blowing, no dogs barking, no coyotes howling, no ghosts jingling. Nothing at all, just weary utter silence.

Jack walked out of the master bedroom and took the steps stealthily to avoid making any sound. He opened up the kitchen door into the backyard and paused to soak in the calmness of the night. He turned on the flashlight he picked up in the kitchen and headed for the police car. He was deliberately strident and conspicuous as he approached the vehicle parked on the driveway, lest he would find the police officer fast asleep at his post. That would be not only awkward for both men, but more importantly, it would irreparably diminish the incredible reassurance the police car represented for him and Claire. On the other hand, maybe the officer would be super efficient and shoot him dead as he approached unannounced.

As he converged upon the automobile, he could see the officer sitting comfortably inside. He was still and quiet, his left arm hanging out the window, his head resting snugly on the headrest. Jack continued to approach, ensuring that he stepped on a small, dry, fallen tree limb to proclaim his arrival. The officer remained silent.

Now ten feet from the police officer, Jack took a whiff of a smell he recognized only too well. Fresh blood. This was a scent he was accustomed to in the operating room and emergency department, but not on his driveway and not emanating from a professional dispatched to protect him and his wife. Surprised at the sensation and curious to learn more, Jack quickened his step towards the car.

Jack gasped uncontrollably. The police officer bled profusely from his neck, ear to ear. Jack noticed that the blood, though freshly spilt, had stopped spurting indicating death had arrived for the police officer. Jack entertained the thought of checking for a pulse to be sure, but this impulse was immediately interrupted by thoughts of Claire. Jack ran into the house. Before he entered through the kitchen door, he first stopped in the garage to pick up a baseball bat. Then, he made a quick stop by his cell phone, charging in a cradle on a table nearby. He dialed 911 and put the phone down. The police would get the call and dispatch help to the signal beacon.

Jack now frantically raced up the stairs toward the master bedroom. He took the stairs two by two, then three by three. He did so silently, hoping to use the element of surprise to his advantage. However, it was he who was surprised. When he arrived, he saw two men in the bedroom, both wearing black clothing and hoods covering their entire heads, save for the eyes. Tight surgical rubber gloves covered their hands. One of them was holding a gun, the other detained Claire with his brawny, muscular right arm, his hand over her mouth. Aware that Jack entered the room, the man with the gun, looked to his right to search for and turn on the lights in the room. As he did so, Jack knew this move would likely occupy the man's attention for a split second. Jack took the opportunity to strike first. This was probably the only break he would have to defend Claire. The baseball bat was hidden from sight at his side when he entered the room. With the speed of a Bonanza A-36 airplane on steroid-laced fuel, Jack raised the Louisville slugger and struck the gunman with all his might. Surprised by the rapidity of the attack, the man took it on the left side of his skull, dropping the revolver. The blow was hard and bulls-eye, causing the villain to experience severe dizziness and shock. The man would remain in a daze and stupefied for some time, leaving Jack to contend with his counterpart. Astonished by the surprise attack on his partner, the second hooded man released Claire. Unimpeded, she could now breathe deeply. Her hands were hogtied and she had a gag over her mouth.

The gun now lay on the carpet near the foot of the bed, equidistant to Jack and the second assailant. Wishing to take possession of the weapon, both dove for it and both grabbed at it simultaneously. A struggle ensued between the two men. In the thrash about, the gun fired striking Claire in the left upper chest, momentarily stealing her breath away. Blood gushed out the wound instantaneously as she gasped for air.

The gun fell on the carpet again. For a split second, Jack became paralyzed with fear. Fear that he might lose the love of his life. This momentary distraction was what the second man needed to take possession of the gun. As he attempted to do so, Jack's thoughts became again of his safety and that of Claire's. Rapidly, Jack picked up the baseball bat and struck the gunman, hitting him on the head. He fell to the floor like a sack of potatoes, barely conscious. By now, multiple angry sirens could be heard approaching in the night. The first man had recovered sufficiently from his T-ball experience, where his head provided the ball and his body the tee. He was able to stand up straight, though wobbly, and help his buddy to his feet. Given the severe vertigo and nausea, the first intruder had significant difficulty helping his cohort out the door and down the stairs. The second man continued to be nearly dead weight. Though the exit from the scene was arduous and complicated, the men were unimpeded by Jack, who held Claire in his left arm while holding pressure over the bleeding dike on Claire's upper left chest. Her radial pulse remained strong, a good clinical sign. Her breath was rapid and short, no doubt a sign of a pneumothorax. Sobbing, Jack sat impatiently, waiting for the cops to arrive. The adrenaline rush caused him to breathe quickly.

Police officers with guns drawn ascended the main staircase. As each cleared a room, the procession progressed towards the master bedroom. When he could get his breath, Jack yelled for help indicating he was in the master bedroom and that the scene was safe for them to enter. When the troops stormed in, Jack immediately asked for an ambulance. One was already on the way, although its intended patron would not be requiring it any longer. The officer in the police car on the driveway was DOA. An ambulance soon arrived.

Earlier today

October 1

10:02 AM

"I used to say I had no use for baseball. It wasn't a sport. Well, I changed my mind. That baseball bat John gave me for my birthday as a gag, really came in handy, huh?" said Jack jocularly, sitting at Claire's side. She was lying in an ICU bed, a bag of red blood transfusing into an IV and a chest tube protruding from her left ribcage. This tube was hooked up to a suction apparatus helping her left lung to re-expand. The bullet had caused her lung to collapse and she lost a lot of blood, but luckily, it had missed all the major blood vessels or organs. Surgery to repair her insides was uneventful and she was on her way to a speedy and full recovery. She would be transferred out of ICU in the morning and home soon thereafter.

"Don't make me laugh, Jack," said Claire wincing with pain.

"Sorry, honey. Can I get you anything?" asked Jack concerned.

"Yes, a husband that doesn't feel he needs to keep me laughing all the time," she said sticking her tongue out at him.

"Okay, meet the new me. I will be boring and serious. No more joking. No, not me," said Jack, making her wince yet again.

"Quit it, Jack. Don't make me get up and hit you with my chest tube sucker thingy. I'll do it, so help me," she threatened.

"Hey, who's 'so' and why should he help you?"

"See, you can't stop it, can you?"

Susan, who cleared her throat when she entered the small cubicle, interrupted the playful dialogue.

"Hi, Susan, come in," invited Claire, smiling.

"Well, you got some color back. You were so ghostly pale last night," said Susan.

"Amazing what a little hemoglobin can do for your complexion," joked Jack. "Sorry, baby," he said, then turning to Susan, he whispered, "I'm not supposed to make her laugh; it hurts her."

"I don't think you can do it, Jack. You're a stand-up comedian masquerading as a cardiologist," entertained Susan with a smile. "I mean that in a good way," she continued.

"Thank you ladies and germs. Don't forget to tip your

waitresses and if you liked the show, I'll be appearing at the Holiday Inn in Cincinnati, Ohio next Thursday," said Jack holding up a banana as a microphone.

"So, what did you find out, Susan," asked Claire, trying not to encourage Jack any further.

"Well, no fingerprints. We're waiting on ballistics from the bullet extracted from Claire's chest. The police officer killed on duty had a large gash—"

Claire gasped. "What?" she said sorrowfully.

"I hadn't told her about that. Sorry, honey, I was waiting until you were stronger. The officer that was outside on the driveway was murdered. I went out to talk to him because I couldn't sleep. I found him dead in the car. That's when I called 911 and got the baseball bat."

"Good thing you did, Jack. These people are professional assassins. We are still looking for them, but they're long gone. We have no clue as to who they are or where they went," lamented Susan.

"Wow. Professionals. When will all this be over?" asked Claire.

"Soon, baby. Really soon," answered Jack reassuringly.

"When you leave here, we got you two a hotel room out of town and police protection there, too. The two rooms surrounding your room are occupied by on-duty cops who will watch over you," said Susan.

"Susan, did Herb talk to you about Mike?" asked Jack.

"Yeah, he didn't like him. He was jealous of him. Mike and I have been dating for three months now and—"

"No, it's not that. Herb and I believe Mike is involved with all this, Susan," interrupted Jack abruptly.

"What? Mike has been helping us. Why would you say such a thing?" asked Susan, astonished.

"Herb was in on this. He wanted to gather more evidence against Mike before telling you and bring him in for interrogation. I believe Herb was killed by Mike because of it." Jack was serious as he spoke.

"Mike was with me when Herb died. He was at my side, holding hands with me. He helped me hold Herb and tried to save his life. What you're saying is impossible. It makes no sense." Susan was visibly upset. She wasn't ready to accept the truth. With dogged persistence, Jack continued.

"What about the gun used for the hospital murders? Why hadn't he found out about it until Rupert died? Herb found out that Mike hadn't accessed the FBI database at all. He was telling us the gun was not in the system, but had done nothing at all to check on it."

"I don't believe that for a minute. You're crazy, Jack. You are delusional." Susan dropped a card she was holding on the hospital table in front of Claire and exited the cubicle.

Jack and Claire looked at each other, unsure as to what to do.

"Let her go, Jack. She needs time. This is too much for her to accept right now. She'll come around," said Claire clinically.

Jack nodded.

Hope you get well soon! read the caption on the card, under the cartoon of a mouse sick in a hospital bed, with his little leg in a cast.

"Cute," said Claire passing the card to Jack.

"Yeah, cute." Jack's face was serious.

After a long moment of silence, during which a nurse arrived to take Claire's vital signs then left, Jack spoke again.

"A lot has happened over the last several weeks and we need to think of a unifying theory to explain it all. These things aren't just happenstance. How can we explain this whole scenario?" Jack was intrigued. He considered this as a diagnostic dilemma, a patient with multiple seemingly unrelated complaints for whom the physician has to put it all together, deriving one unifying diagnosis.

"Okay, so what do you think happened?" asked Claire. She knew Jack was capable of many great things when he put his brain to work. Jack felt the same about Claire. They needed to put their brainpower together and come up with something.

"The evidence is strong that Rupert was involved. It also indicated Mike is involved. They are two different people, with different backgrounds and somehow they seem to be intertwined in this catastrophic series of events. What are the possibilities that would bring them together?" posed Jack.

"Money," exclaimed Claire, without much thinking.

"I agree. So, where would they get money out of this?" asked Jack.

"I don't know."

"I don't either. What are the possibilities?"

"We know the hospital is involved and people are getting murdered because of it. The research lab has to be part of this whole scheme." Claire remained pensive.

"I think you're right."

"The research people come up with a drug that somehow makes them money, but it involves murdering people," continued Claire.

"But why is an FBI agent involved at all?" asked Jack.

"That's a puzzler. Why would an FBI agent become

involved? FBI is involved when State lines are crossed, otherwise the local or State law enforcement agencies are drawn in."

"So, something involving multiple States brought in Mike. Mike sees the opportunity to make some dough and takes over the project?"

"Killing people was a necessary part of the experimentation?"

"Or maybe an undesirable side-effect."

"A side-effect would lead to discontinuation of the experiment, or drastic change in protocol to avoid the deaths. This experiment seems to be about killing people."

"That may be the Major Rooner's connection. Remember how the military was involved? Rooner came out here and met with Rupert. That must mean there is a military application for the experiment. In the military, you look for ways to kill people."

"In wars, not in Evansville."

Jack continued to speculate.

"Imagine a killing machine. A medication that is probably administered by inhalation; what's it called?" A pause. "Ah yeah, Rat Poison. In the lab, there was an aerosolizing device. There was also a device that made bubbles. John was telling us they were putting drugs into these bubbles, which could be destroyed remotely with an ultrasound device. So, if the medicine is aerosolized into the air consisting of bubbles of a drug and multiple soldiers breathe it in, at the appropriate time the bubbles can be disintegrated remotely causing the soldiers to become acutely paranoid and agitated with a particular drive to kill fellow soldiers. A small group, or even one soldier, could cause destruction of an entire platoon given enough ammo and a target-rich environment. What do you think?" asked Jack.

"Sounds about right. What about the other man? What was his name? Akrim?" asked Claire.

"I'm not sure how he fits in to all this."

"Do you think John found out about the deadly scheme and was neutralized to keep him quiet?" asked Claire.

"I'm sure of it. That explains why he wanted to talk to me at the end of the soccer game. I blew him off and he was murdered the next morning. I could have prevented his death." Jack became somber again, a guilt-ridden expression all over his face.

"Jack, you can't blame yourself for John's death. But your theory makes sense. Rupert gave the patient a gun and the aerosolized drug. He then burst the bubbles inside the poor man. He gets paranoid and starts shooting people, including John. It's not your fault. It's Rupert's and Mike's and whoever else is involved in this tragedy."

"Was Rupert killed or did he just have a car accident?" asked Claire.

"I'm sure he was murdered. The accident was probably a manifestation of the Rat Poison. If you get the drug while driving, in your paranoid agitated state, you'll probably want to kill others by using the car as a weapon. The police had a warrant for Rupert's arrest. They were going to interrogate him that day. So, his accomplices killed him off to avoid complications and possible condemning testimony," postulated Jack.

"Some of the patients just had a cardiac arrest. They didn't become paranoid and agitated, at first," interjected Claire.

"I've been thinking about that. I believe that was the

early experience with the drug or an exaggerated response in some individuals. For instance, Herb just collapsed, had seizures and rapid heartbeats. That's probably an exaggerated response, maybe a double dose."

"So, how is Mike Ganz involved? And how do we get Susan to see the truth about him? We need foolproof evidence," said Claire.

"I'm not sure how that piece fits yet. I imagine Mike met Rupert. Maybe Rupert calls the FBI initially to see if there is a potential role for this drug. Sell it to the good guys. The local FBI agency would probably be a good place to start. Mike sees the potential financial gains and approaches the U.S. military. They say, 'Okay, give us more evidence of what it can do.' Rupert and Mike go out testing the drug. Killing people to prove their drug is worth buying. On the other hand, maybe the military says, 'No, thanks,' and they go to the other side. I bet you Akrim is a terrorist or something like that. As such, he sure would want it. Money keeps coming in for further research and improvement in the weapon manufacturing devices. And here we are now."

"So, where do we go from here?" asked Claire.

"I think Rupert has some documents about this whole thing. He was a documentation fanatic. John told me so several times. If he did, where would he keep them safely? Mike went through his belongings at the hospital. His home was ransacked I bet looking for documents. I bet you Rupert has important files hidden in his cabin."

"Oh yeah. I remember he invited us and all the new cardiology fellows to a Fourth of July picnic there a couple of years ago. Do you remember where the cabin is?"

"No, but the GPS does. I marked an away point when we were there and it's still in the GPS database. I can drive to it by following the pink line. All the way to the front door."

"You're such a geek. How does it feel to be a geek?" asked Claire with a feeble laugh causing her to wince in pain at the same time.

Jack got up and grabbed his jacket. He was anxious to check out his new idea.

"See you later. I'll call you."

"Be careful."

They kissed and Jack left the room. Outside ICU, two uniformed police officers sat on a chair drinking coffee, flirting with a nurse. Jack waved as he passed. The officers waved back.

2:14 PM

The trip to the cabin was uneventful. The day was clear with practically no wind. Moderate temperatures were typical for early October. As he drove out of the city and into the country, a feeling of peace overcame Jack. He got off the highway and entered a smaller thoroughfare that eventually led to an even smaller side road. From there, the GPS led him to a path, which was paved only for a while. As he penetrated deeper and deeper into the woods, Jack found himself on a dirt lane lined with trees, meandering through the forest. The leaves had started to turn into beautiful brilliant colors of autumn. The sunlight pierced through the foliage giving the area a serene glow. As he approached the log home, Jack glanced around looking for anyone that might later identify him on this clandestine mission. Nobody in sight, but the out of sight potential hideouts abounded. Constant vigilance for a prospective witness was in order. It was quite feasible that Rupert would have someone, perhaps a neighbor farmer, minding his infrequently visited cabin. Meeting this someone today would be less than ideal.

He arrived at the cabin, parked the car and surveyed the area. Swirling dust clouds kicked up by the moving vehicle were uncontestable proof that he had arrived in the country. Jack exited his ride and walked to the front door, looking side to side and behind as he went, still paranoid that he might be spotted. The front door was locked. Well, no surprise there. Jack looked under the welcome mat. No key. He looked around for a logical area to hide a key. None was apparent. Jack walked around the log home and entered the back porch. This looked out onto a winding stream with a waterfall, the perfect picture of serenity and tranquility. The back door was also locked. A large rustic square wooden box on the porch contained logs for the fireplace. This would make a perfect place to hide a key. Despite a thorough search, none was discovered. Imitating his moves earlier, Jack walked around inside and outside the porch assessing for what would make a good place to hide a key. There were beautifully decorated pots with plants, rocking chairs and even a hammock. All were potentially capable of hiding treasures.

An abrupt loud noise from behind startled Jack, causing his heart rate to suddenly quicken and his hands to quiver. A sinking feeling appeared in his chest and his face turned pale. All his muscles tensed, as he experienced the primitive flight or fight reflex. Shaking all over, Jack turned to the location of the clatter. It was a raccoon that had just pushed over a garbage can. The animal fled the area, likewise disturbed by the sudden clang. The mystery of the clamor solved, the nerves began to unruffle. Jack took a deep breath. The search for an entry into the cabin resumed. No key could be located. Discouraged that he made the trip for nothing, Jack started to walk back to the car. Doing so, he recalled there was another porch upstairs, off the master bedroom, yet another vantage point to admire the strikingly beautiful meandering brook and falls.

Jack took off his jacket and placed it over one of the rocking chairs on the downstairs porch. He climbed up a nearby large oak until he reached a limb that coursed near the upstairs veranda. Stretching his right arm as far as he could, he placed his fingertips in close proximity to the edge of the balcony. Before attempting the transfer, Jack spied in all directions looking for potential witnesses. He smiled realizing he was in the middle of the wilderness. No human souls for miles. He took a deep breath and jumped. With all his might, Jack held on to the railing to the veranda and got his knee onto the ledge of the woodwork. From there, it took little effort for him to climb onto the upstairs porch. He took a few seconds to admire and enjoy the awesome view and collect himself.

He took another deep breath and walked to the sliding door leading into the master bedroom. Darn it. The door was locked as well. Jack tried with all his strength to slide the door open but to no avail. He looked at the locking mechanism through the glass door, but he soon gave up. To the right of the doorway, there was a small window. He would try that next. He breathed a deep sigh of relief when the window gave to his pushing. He slid the window open and entered the master bathroom.

Jack spent twenty minutes snooping around inside the cabin. He wasn't sure what he was looking for, but he hoped he would recognize it when he saw it. Nothing visible. He thought about moving things and potentially finding a hidden closet. He looked at his watch dispiritedly. A strong gut feeling that he had been wrong about the whole thing began to arise. This cabin was too far to come out and hide important things. He would snoop for fifteen more minutes then call it all a useless trip and colossal waste of time. After a few more minutes of further search, a large beautiful painting of a civil war scene, which served as a door to a hidden safe, rewarded Jack. He slid the painting to the side exposing the miniature-cloaked vault.

"Oh, please be unlocked, please," pleaded Jack. It was not. The strong thick metal door would not give an inch.

"What is your secret combination?" asked Jack of the safe. The combination to the locking mechanism involved three rows of numbers, two digits each totaling six digits. He stared at it for a long moment, pensively. He noticed the numbers as he found them and made a mental note: first row, 52; second row, 27; third row, 23. He tried 12–34–56. No go. Then backwards. Locked.

"I wonder how I can find out what his birth date was? Or his wife's measurements?" Jack smiled faintly. "He didn't have a wife. Mistress then." Another grin.

Staring at the combination lock, he had an idea. He removed his cell phone from his pocket and figured out which numbers corresponded to the word LABRAT, Rupert's license plate number.

"LA is 52, BR is 27 and AT is 28. Okay, let's try it. Don't let me down?" said Jack to no one in the room. As he started to turn the dials, he grinned. He knew he was right on. The dial had initially displayed 52 on the top row, 27 on the middle and 23 for the bottom. The only number that was off was the third row, 23 instead of 28. Jack did that, too, in similar circumstances. Only one number to remember and change. Jack turned the dials accordingly and paused shortly to compose himself. He took a deep breath and tried the door. Voila! The lock gave way and the door opened with little effort.

"Come to Papa!" said Jack cheerfully. Inside the tiny vault, there was a small envelope marked First Federal Bank of Evansville. In the envelope, there was a small key with the number 232 imprinted on it. There was also a small thumb drive labeled Research Log—LFJ659. Jack smiled big as he held the small envelope and the tiny USB computer drive in his right hand.

He exited the house, making sure that everything was as he found it. When he arrived in his car, he called Claire and filled her in on his discovery. He began his trip back home.

"Will you please find out how many First Federal Banks there are in Evansville?" he asked her. A few minutes later, Claire called back and indicated there were five branches and gave him the addresses and phone numbers. He wrote them down.

"Good afternoon. I would like to rent a safe deposit box. What time do you close today?" asked Jack deceitfully. There was a pause.

"Oh, all your deposit boxes are at your main branch on

Green River Road? Okay, thank you," said Jack when the other party was finished speaking. As he drove toward the city, Jack entered the address information into the GPS. He sat back and drove on, content with the results of this trip.

On his arrival, Jack got out of the car and brushed off the dirt from his clothes.

"You can take the man to the country, but you can't take the country out of the man," he said, smiling to no one in particular.

He walked into the bank, greeting an elderly security guard at the entrance. A doorway to his left displayed a sign overhead: Safe Deposit Boxes. He entered the room and found box number 232. He opened the drawer and removed all its contents. He closed the deposit box and returned to his vehicle. He needed a safe place to review the documents. He drove toward Newton Memorial Hospital. First, he would stop to get dinner and the essential post-prandial Starbucks coffee.

Stomach full and back in the car driving to Newton Memorial Hospital, Jack removed the Treo from his pocket and dialed.

6:42 PM

Susan felt betrayed by Jack and Claire. She was starting to fall in love with Mike. He was kind, smart, devoted to his job and treated her like a lady. As a police detective, she would know if Mike was involved with such heinous crimes. Wouldn't she?

Right here and now it was time to put all that aside. Mike was at her home and a romantic dinner and evening were in the cards. Nothing was going to ruin that, not even Jack and Claire's assertions that Mike could possibly be a mass-murderer.

"Ridiculous. My God, he's a decorated FBI agent. He's here helping us with this difficult case," she thought as she prepared the dinner table. Mike was right behind her. He looked particularly attractive. He wore a well-fitting, expensive suit and tie, attire that would leave most cops envious. She smiled at him lovingly.

Mike opened up the bottle of red and struck a match to light up the candles on the dinner table, bringing Susan's attention back to the moment. Everything was set. Everything was perfect. They sat down, soft music playing in the background. Susan looked into Mike's eyes from across the table and saw love and irresistible passion. Mike might very well be the one.

"Great music, great food, great company, great, well, everything," said Mike tenderly, taking a sip of merlot. She imitated him, eyes still locked on one another.

"I love this song," she managed to say finally, hoping this moment would never end.

"Would you like to dance?" asked Mike getting up from his chair. Lou Rawls' You'll Never Find Another Love Like Mine played softly on the CD player.

"I thought you'd never ask," said Susan shyly. He helped her up, like the gentleman he was and soon they embraced to the rhythm of the music on the makeshift dance floor.

"I'm just glad the case is finally closed," he whispered in her ear.

The statement surprised her. Whether the case was closed or not was impossible to say at this time with any degree of confidence. It was so complex and involved, who knew what else was yet to come? Jack and Claire's words hypothesizing Mike's involvement echoed vividly in her mind.

"Me, too," she replied softly going along with Mike.

"I'm sorry about Herb. I know the two of you were close."

"We were. Herb was my bud. I'll miss him terribly," said

Susan, a tear down her check. Mike wiped the tear then held her tightly, dancing to the music.

"He had this case almost completely wrapped up. How sad for him to die of a seizure. I heard the doctors say he may have had a stroke that caused the seizure. I am so sorry, Susan."

"You don't think he was murdered, do you?"

"Absolutely not. I was looking at him in the parking lot when he collapsed. Poor guy. Great cop. I know I'm gonna miss him," said Mike. Susan remained subdued and pensive. The two continued dancing without saying a word until the song was over and then kissed passionately. Mike helped Susan to her seat at the dinner table. Susan served herself mashed potatoes and steak and then passed the plates to Mike.

"You know," Mike paused for a beat, then continued, "I'm not so sure Jack Norris isn't involved with the crimes. I've been thinking a lot about it lately. I might just snoop around a bit and see if I can find any connection between him and Rupert," said Mike convincingly.

Susan was intrigued by the possibility. Herb and she had been so sure of Jack's innocence that it was hard to fathom anything else. She would go along with Mike, for now, and see where this conversation was going.

"Interesting thought," she said, taking a forkful of mashed potato.

"This food is delicious, Susan," said Mike appreciatively.

"Thanks."

"So, what will you do now?" she probed.

"I'll follow Jack around for a bit and see what he does and where he goes, as we wrap up the case. Then I'll need to go back to Indianapolis. But I'll be back. For mashed potatoes like these, you'd better believe, I'll be back. If you'll have me, that is," offered Mike with a smile.

"Sure, I'll have you back. I was hoping you'd be back for me," said Susan, bashfully.

"Of course, it's you, silly girl." The two sat in silence and ate for a long moment, while Lou Rawls sang 'Georgia on My Mind.'

"You did a great job on the grill. My steak is impeccable," said Susan, interrupting the peaceful quiet.

"Thank you. I learned grilling from my dad. It's a family secret." Both smiled. Susan felt herself fall for the man. Suddenly her cell phone rang. She excused herself, walked to the kitchen, found her purse and fished out the mobile device.

"Hello," she said pleasantly.

"Susan, it's Jack," she heard on the telephone. She wanted to hang up and go back to the unfolding romantic evening. But she did not. She struggled to remain calm and polite as she spoke, and, for the sake of the ongoing investigation, inconspicuous.

"Yes." She purposely left out the caller's name.

"Susan, I wanted to keep you in the loop. I went to Rupert's cabin in the woods and found some files. I haven't looked through these yet, but I'm going to. I'm headed to my office at Newton Memorial Hospital. I think these files will answer many questions for us. Are you interested in joining me? I can meet you at police headquarters and—"

"No, this is not a good time," she interrupted. After a short pause, she continued. "Give me a call tomorrow and we'll discuss your findings."

She hung up the phone, returned it into her purse and

rejoined Mike. She felt confused and alone. Vulnerable. How she wished Herb was there to give her advice. Ever since her father passed away from cancer five years earlier, Herb had taken his place in her heart. She had learned so much from him. One lesson she would always cherish and remember was how to follow her gut instinct. Her gut was telling her Mike was a good person.

"Who was that?" asked Mike, nonchalantly.

For a short moment, Susan struggled as to whether to and how to answer. Then, she replied: "That was Jack Norris."

"Oh, what did he want?" The topic had obviously piqued Mike's interest.

"He found some files that he thinks might be important in the case. He's looking them over at Newton Memorial," she answered truthfully.

"Found files? Where? What kind of files?" persisted Mike, taking a sip of the red wine.

"Rupert had a cabin in the woods somewhere. He found them there. I didn't get much information. I wanted to get back to you quickly," she finished with a smile.

"Of course. Please forgive me. Where were we?" With this Mike stood up, gestured for Susan to get up and they returned to the area in front of the fireplace, the designated dance area. They danced, now closer than ever, her head resting on his upper chest. No words. They kissed tenderly.

"This feels so right," reflected Susan. They kept on dancing.

Susan couldn't remember ever having felt this way. She had been able to put work completely aside and enjoy the here and now. Having lost Herb so tragically made her feel vulnerable and alone. Mike was providing her with the strength she so needed and desired.

When they were done eating, she excused herself to change into something more comfortable. Mike was sitting on the sofa in front of the fireplace, a glass of Merlot in his hand. A log crackled noisily in the hearth, adding to the romantic ambiance.

Susan exited the room and made her way to the master bedroom. Her first stop was the bathroom. While sitting on the commode, she barely noticed the music had been turned louder. She thought nothing of it. She washed her hands and reentered the bedroom. She took off her dress and put it on the bed.

She thought she heard Mike speaking. She put on a robe and sneaked out of the room essentially to ascertain if Mike was talking to her. He was not. The stereo had been turned up and Mike was not in the living room anymore. The door to the guest bedroom was now closed. Susan knew it was open before and surmised he went in there.

"Why would he go in there?" she thought to herself. She walked towards the closed door to the guest bedroom deviously. He was definitely in there talking to someone on his cell phone. She couldn't make out any words.

Intrigued, she went back to the master bedroom. As she took off her robe and put on her comfy jogging pants, Mike returned to the TV room. The stereo music volume was again lowered little by little, as if to avoid perception.

"Why did Mike make a phone call he didn't want me to know about," she asked herself. "Maybe he received a private call? From the FBI? From another woman? Should

I approach him about it? No. I'll let it go and enjoy the moment," concluded Susan, still in deep denial.

She entered the living room. The door to the guest bedroom was open again, as she had left it before Mike's arrival. The FBI man stood up, a glass of wine in each hand, one of which he delivered to Susan.

"You are so beautiful," he declared.

6:57 PM

Jack was sitting at his office when his cell phone rang. It was Claire.

"I thought I'd hear from you by now. I got worried. What's up?"

"I'm in my office at the hospital looking through all the documents from Rupert's deposit box. There is a lot of stuff in here. I want to go through each piece carefully."

"What have you found so far?"

"There are a series of letters from the U.S. Marine Corps. From Major Rooner, saying that they are interested in pursuing and learning more about the potential military value of the aerosolized bubbles, but they required more animal research. They point out that it is unethical to experiment with humans. They weren't willing to fund the project. There are invoices and documentation about the equipment they are using to deliver LFJ659, which Rupert coined Rat Poison, as we already knew. There are notes about the meetings with Akrim. That is where I am now."

"What about Susan. Will you call her?"

"Yes. I called her earlier and told her I am reviewing this stuff in my office. I'll call her with details tomorrow morning. There might be evidence against Mike Ganz in here. I don't want her to know about any of this until I understand it myself. Let me call you later, when I figure out everything." Jack was anxious to get off the phone and continue his investigation.

As soon as the call ended, Jack's attention was again focused on the documents in front of him.

The administrative offices of the Department of Medicine and Cardiology were located in a separate wing of the hospital. There were no clinical services provided in this location. As such, the place was already deserted. The lights were off in the halls, which were illuminated only minimally from the dim sunlight peeking through the windows. The hallways were silent. Eerie. Spooky.

Down the hall, exceptionally soft footsteps approached. A man walked slowly and soundlessly, every step a bit closer to Jack. Unhurriedly, the man continued steadily on his path, advancing at snail's pace, ascertaining along the way that he remained unnoticed. Like a ninja warrior in the dark, the man was now just outside Jack's office door.

The mysterious figure placed a protective transparent mask over his face and mouth. He removed an aerosolizing device from his left pocket and another apparatus from his right pocket. Armed and ready, he covertly and slowly sneaked into the office. Due to his enthusiasm and focus, Jack remained clueless to the man's presence for a long moment.

7:42 PM

"Hi, I didn't hear you come in? What's with the mask?" asked Jack, totally surprised, as he finally saw the man in his office, now only a few feet from him.

The assailant did not speak. He remained serious. By the time Jack realized what was going on, it was too late. The man was rotund of body, giving his identity away easily. He sprayed into the Jack's mouth and nose, using the element of surprise to his advantage. After spraying the deadly microscopic tiny aerosolized bubbles for a few seconds, the man stopped and smiled. Mission accomplished. All that was left to do now was to allow a few more seconds for the bubbles to descend into the alveoli sucked in by an obligatory breath and enter the circulatory system. At that point, the proper frequency would be dialed in and the ultrasound device would be activated, creating a supersonic, indiscernible beacon that would travel several yards. This would penetrate the human tissue unimpeded and disintegrate the bubbles releasing their lethal toxins. Given the certain death about to come, Jack would not divulge any information about what he found regarding the Rat Poison project. The prosperous venture would lead to great riches beyond anyone's dreams.

As soon as the spray was directed at him, Jack knew exactly what was happening. His first reaction was to hold his breath and flee. He did. He grabbed his white lab coat and ran towards the emergency department. During the spraying, the young doctor detected a red rash on the perpetrator's right hand. He had observed this unusual rash beforehand.

Jack first noticed a slight pleasant tingling sensation in his nostrils. This awareness sunk deeper into his respiratory tree and soon it could be felt in his chest. Jack knew the drug had been successfully deployed and was now inside of him. Should he run to the emergency department where he could get help? Should he inject the drugs he gathered earlier, now in his lab coat pocket? How quickly would he have symptoms and become incapacitated? His heart started to race. Was this the result of excitement and running or the bubbles expelling their noxious content?

Considering that the effects of Rat Poison were swift, Jack decided he should try to help himself and start his own treatment. He stopped suddenly and looked behind him. No one was chasing. Good. He briefly considered the elevator but thought it would be smarter to take the stairs. Pushing past a door, he entered the staircase and hurriedly descended two floors. Now on the sixth floor, he listened for chasing footsteps. Nothing. He sat on the stairs, removed the tourniquet from his pocket and tied it around his left arm, just above the elbow. He quickly removed a syringe and needle from his pocket and assembled the two. He withdrew five milligrams of propranolol into the syringe and stuck the needle into a forearm vein. Having accomplished this seemingly monumental task, he repeated the process with ten milligrams of verapamil. He took a breather to assess his condition. He could still think rationally and, so far, the only person he'd like to kill was the son of a bitch who sprayed him in the nose. He retrieved the midazolam vial and injected two milligrams into his vein. Given his hyperdynamic circulation, three blood geysers thrived in the front surface of his forearm. Having injected the three medications, Jack removed the tourniquet and held pressure over the puncture sites, still holding the syringe. His heart hammered hard in his chest and his breath quickened. He could feel his mind slipping away. He descended one more flight. Still, there were no signs of a pursuer. His right-hand fingers were bloodied from holding pressure over the venipunctures. He stopped the descent and sat down on a stair. Using his blood as ink, he wrote some words on the wall. This accomplished he stood up again and stumbled erratically down the stairs. The disorienting effects of the poison were becoming increasingly prominent, surfacing sporadically in waves.

Where am I going? Where am I supposed to be, contemplated Jack, gradually more confused. He looked around wildly to get his bearings, unsure of what to do.

Ah, yes. The emergency department. I must get there

fast and get help, thought Jack. He continued running down the stairway, now almost on the second floor. Suddenly, he stopped, reflecting on the situation at hand. He felt a wave of nausea and dizziness.

"I'm getting worse. At this rate, I won't reach the ED." He sat on a step and procured the drug vials again. He managed to inject another round of the medications, this time having more difficulty obtaining venous access and deciphering the necessary dosing. He put all medical instruments back into his pockets and took off running again down the stairs. He felt a little better. He had to reach the emergency department.

When he arrived on the first floor, a wave of confusion and disorientation hit him again, more intense this time than ever before. Perplexed, Jack had the distinct impression that there was somebody or something running after him. He felt threatened. He could swear somebody was hunting him trying to kill him. A deep-down sentiment he could barely explain, told him he had to fight the assailant. He frantically looked all around him for the anticipated threat. Moving in all directions rapidly caused him to feel dizzy and nauseated. He sat back down on the steps. A large heavy door at the bottom of the steps and now in front of him was labeled: Exit. He pushed past that door winding up in the doctor's parking lot. The cool breeze on his face helped him feel better physically, but increased his confusion and unsettlement.

He had a deep need to escape. Run far and fast. He pushed past several parked cars and came to an open area in the parking lot. Where was he going? Confusion and disorientation reigned.

He stopped for a moment and looked around dazed. He shed his lab coat and kept on running.

9:09 PM

"Claire, I found out where he is. It sounds like he's been poisoned with the Rat Poison drug," declared Susan gloomily, as she drove to the scene.

"I know, Susan. I know. Please hurry," implored Claire.

"I will. I promise. We'll take him to the hospital immediately."

"I'm being realistic. I'm prepared for the worst. You know, we have not seen anybody survive Rat Poison yet. But, he's young and strong.

"Let's remain positive, Claire."

"Susan, who knew where we live and knew Jack was in his office tonight?" asked Claire rhetorically, hoping the question would spark something in Susan.

The young detective reflected.

The cell phone call in my guest bedroom. He arranged this attack, thought Susan, as she sped to the scene.

The day after

October 2

7:30 AM

"Did you see today's headlines?" asked the man wearing a plush multicolor robe. He was sitting in a beautifully decorated room on a divan, his feet up on an ottoman. He sipped from his cup of coffee and put it back down, his Bluetooth receiver hanging on his right earlobe. There was a short pause and then he spoke again.

"Young doctor shot dead by police. That's the title. Apparently, he survived until he got to a neighborhood behind the hospital. Somebody called the cops. They found him under a tree agitated and frantic. He fought the law and the law won. It says here they shot him when he attacked one of the police officers. Who said cops are good for nothing? They thought he was drunk and on drugs." The man was obviously elated about what he was reading on the front page of the Evansville Courier & Press.

"By the time they find out, we'll be way gone, sipping on a cool red drink with a small umbrella." A fake smile and a pause.

"I don't know what she knows. We'll assume she knows enough." Another long pause.

"Find out where she is and take care of it," he commanded. "And, no screw ups. Call me later and I'll give you information about the flight. They should be picking you up around noon today." A short break.

"I'll meet you later. In about a week. There are a few loose ends I need to take care of first."

He hung up the phone and took another sip of coffee, overjoyed. It was going to be a good day and it would be even better tomorrow.

10:02 AM

The two men in green scrubs exited through the door labeled Doctor's Changing Room. They first looked to the right, then left. Side by side, the two continued down the corridor to the right. A sign on the wall indicated the direction to the post-op unit.

"First, we'll make sure she's asleep and quiet," said one of the men.

"Yeah, either by herself or with this stuff in the bag." He raised his right hand showing a small black doctor's bag.

"I know, I know. You worry too much."

"Yeah, right. I'll take care of the anesthesia. Do you know your part?" inquired the other man with a wry smile.

"Yeah. When she's asleep, I inject this stuff in her IV," he replied lightly tapping on the back pocket of his scrub pants.

"Do you push it in slow or fast?"

"Fast. Don't worry. I know what to do."

"What if she doesn't have an IV anymore?"

"I help you find a vein and inject the stuff directly into the vein."

"I have a tourniquet in the bag."

"What about the cops outside the door?"

"The most important thing is for her not to make any noise. When we get in, you distract her. I'll come from behind with the anesthesia."

"Pretty easy work for five thousand bucks, huh?"

The two men walked several more yards in silence, as they entered the nursing unit. Having taken a corner to the left, they could now see the door leading to the room down the hall. A police officer sat at the entry reading a magazine. Hospital personnel were busy going in and out of patient rooms, a clear sign that business was again booming at Newton Memorial Hospital. The hospital was no longer on diversion and the daily routine had returned to normal.

"She recuperated well from the surgery and will be discharged later today," said one of the two men to the other, as they approached the cop, ascertaining that they could be heard. They nodded at the officer politely as they opened the door.

"Hey, doc? Are you going to be in there a few minutes? I gotta take a leak. Can you wait for me to come back? I ain't supposed to leave my post," said the police officer to the two men in scrubs.

"No problem. We'll wait. Take your time," replied one of the men.

"You gotta go, you gotta go, right?" said the other. Both men smiled at the cop, then at each other.

"It must be our lucky day," whispered one of them, as both men entered the hospital room.

Inside, the two assailants ceased talking, surprised not to find Claire in bed. She was nowhere to be found. On the bedside table, papers with discharge instructions declared the patient ready to go home. Walking towards the closed door into the bathroom, one of the goons craned his neck to listen. Assured that she was in there, he thumbed towards the door, gazing at the other man.

"She's taking a shower," he finally whispered.

"We'll wait," responded his cohort, while opening up his black doctor's bag, placing it on the unmade bed.

Claire was taking a much needed steamy hot-shower. The surgeons said earlier the bullet missed all the important parts. Unfortunately, the slug had traumatized enough unimportant parts that her shoulder muscles throbbed in pain. Well, at least everything still works, she pondered, wincing as she slowly moved her left arm and shoulder. She experienced a lot of discomfort and agony.

"This too shall pass," she stated convincingly, to no one in the bathroom. Slowly and gently, she would take her first shower. Alone. She was not about to have a nurse help her through it, as had been suggested by the medical staff.

The events of the last few days had been torturous and maximally stressing. Dense smog now emanated from the shower stall. The water stopped running and the shower door opened. Claire slowly grabbed a towel and put it around her wet body. She wiped the mist off the bathroom mirror and gave herself a reassuring wink. She opened the bathroom door causing dense vapor to escape into the hospital room. As she walked into the hospital room, she saw the two men dressed in scrubs.

"Good morning. Did somebody change their mind about letting me go home today?" she inquired perplexedly with a fake smile.

"No, nothing like that. We're here to give you instructions," said one of the men turning to his right, while the second one conspicuously went the other way.

"Well, I got all my instructions earlier from Dr. Watson," Claire stated, now with a suspicious tone. She had not met these doctors before and something inside told her they were not who they appeared to be.

Rapidly, the second man advanced towards Claire without warning. In his hand, he cupped a small towel. A small bottle labeled Chloroform leaned on the doctor's bag, on the bed. Before Claire could scream or the towel made contact with her nose, four undercover police officers forced the door open and entered the hospital room, guns drawn. One of the cops was detective Susan Quentin.

"Cuff them and read them their rights, boys," she said authoritatively, winking at Claire.

One of the detectives holstered his weapon and approached one of the men in scrubs. With the speed of lightening, he grabbed the man's hands, forced them behind his back and placed the handcuffs around them, a well-rehearsed practice. Another cop repeated the process, cuffing the other criminal.

A quick search of the criminals produced a syringe with a capped needle. Inside the doctor bag, a small nearly empty medicine bottle was labeled Potassium Chloride. All would be subsequently bagged and inventoried as evidence.

The police officers escorted the detainees out of the hospital room, one of them reading the Miranda rights: "You have the right to remain silent, anything you say can, and will, be held against you in a court of law. You have the right to an attorney…"

Claire was stupefied and stunned. Her heart pounded in her chest. When Susan came to her and hugged her tightly, she found the solace she needed at that moment. Claire broke down, and commenced to sob incessantly.

"It's all over, now. It's over. You're okay," repeated Susan assuringly, patting Claire gently on the back. Claire wept but remained motionless for a long moment, not sure of what to say. She hugged back, tears flowing onto Susan's shoulder.

"What will happen now?" sobbed Claire, barely able to form words, dabbing, yet again, her tear-soaked eyes.

"We'll take these two to police headquarters and interrogate them. We'll get them to tell us who's behind all this!"

"I want to go see him now," said Claire tenderly, changing her tone.

"I'll take you to him right now," said Susan helping Claire walk. Slowly, they exited the hospital room.

10:29 AM

The group of cops and the two criminals arrived downstairs. Multiple marked and unmarked police vehicles were parked in disarray, red and white emergency lights still revolving. Many other officers loitered the area.

"Good work, guys. Susan asked me to take these two to headquarters; you can go back to patrol. I'll book them and start the interrogation." Mike showed his FBI badge as he spoke. The officers helped place the two crooks inside the backseat of the unmarked car. Mike got in the driver's side and drove off. The officers gathered around detailing the adrenalin-rich incident they just experienced to those unlucky enough to not have partaken.

"You assholes. You're such imbeciles. Incompetent assholes!" yelled Mike once the car was far enough away from the crowded parking area. Once out of sight, he turned off his emergency light, previously stuck on the roof of the car. He brought it in and placed it on the front passenger seat. Mike was steaming mad. The assailants remained silent.

He drove ten minutes out of town and stopped the car on the side of the road.

"Let's go for a walk," he commanded the others.

"Mike, what are you going to do? Don't be crazy, man. We can still fix this," begged one of the men, obviously aware of Mike's plans. The other soon realized it, too.

"Mike, don't ruin everything, man. Give us a chance to fix everything. We can do it," he pleaded.

Once out of the car, Mike pushed the two men down an embankment and into a heavily forested area. Realizing their fate, the two men started to run. Mike reached underneath his jacked and produced his weapon. Effortlessly, he fired double tap once, then again, in rapid succession.

He approached the fallen men. Each of the recently departed had two bullet holes, in close proximity, on their skulls, blood and brain matter spurting onto the mattress of fallen, yellow leaves of autumn. Unperturbed, Mike returned to his car and drove off.

11:09 AM

Evansville Airport was quiet, which was not atypical for this time of day. Steve Peski sat with his feet up on his desk, reading the September issue of AOPA Pilot Magazine. An article on short runway landings caught his eye and he was now engrossed in its message. Not so engrossed that his heart didn't skip a beat or two when the radio squawked ending the hush of the late lazy morning. Steve immediately stood up and monitored the conversation.

"Gulfstream, Four-two-tango-juliet, visual runway one-eight."

"Four-two-tango-juliet, Evansville Tower, clear to land, one-eight," responded the air traffic controller, authorizing a landing.

Gulfstream jets were exceptionally rare in Evansville, particular the G550, la crème de la crème. The expensive business jet was too rich for the small industry that abounded in the area. Steve knew exactly whom that plane was carrying. He hoped this didn't mean trouble; trouble with a capital T. He searched in his top drawer for a business card and sat back down on his desk. He dialed, all the while spying outside his window, tracking the beautiful taxiing jet.

"Who's this?" The woman's voice shocked him. After a moment, he lowered his head, a somber look all over his face.

"I'm sorry to hear that." Another short pause ensued.

"He wanted me to notify him if the Gulfstream Jet ever returned to Evansville. And it just did." Silence for a beat.

"Best of luck to you. I'll keep you all in my prayers," said Steve, sorrowfully.

Slowly, the FBO director walked outside to supervise his linemen as they serviced the newly arrived luxurious jet. Three of his best employees were on the job. The occupants of the jet had requested fuel, but no luggage needed to deplane. The stairs from the main exit of the jet were deployed and the two pilots descended onto the tarmac. They were dressed in their blue blazer pilot uniforms and caps. They nodded pleasantly as they walked by Steve who acknowledged them with a wave.

At the pilot's request, the airplane was readied for quick departure by the ground crew. The aviators entered the FBO but soon returned to the aircraft with a man that had driven in by himself and had parked his car right outside the building. He was wearing an expensive suit and carrying a briefcase. His name was Mike Ganz. Steve noticed that one of the pilots had politely offered to carry his small suitcase, but he vehemently refused.

"What's he carrying in there, gold pieces?" thought Steve, amusingly.

The three men boarded the plane and soon the door was retracted and locked from inside the aircraft.

The vicinity of the jet was vacated in anticipation that the crew would soon be firing up the engines with a noteworthy increase in decibels. Before long, the jet engines came alive.

"Gulfstream, four-two-tango-juliet, ready to taxi for immediate take-off," announced the loud speakers mounted outside the building, echoing the conversation between the cockpit and ground control.

"Gulfstream, four-two-tango-juliet, negative on taxi; we are awaiting clearance for your IFR file." The two pilots looked at each other, perplexity painted on their faces. An airport of this size, would rarely delay taxiing to the runway. Clearance for a flight from here would inevitably take a few computer keystrokes and a few seconds.

"What's wrong? Why aren't we moving?" asked Mike, impatiently after a minute.

"They're asking us to hold here until we get clearance, sir. It shouldn't be long," said the pilot in command, sitting on the left seat in the cockpit.

A few more tense moments passed. By then, Mike was irritated, rubbing his hands on his knees forcibly.

"What's going on? Let's go. Now!" he commanded.

"I'm sorry, sir. We cannot taxi without instruction from—" The pilot stopped talking as he felt the barrel of the revolver touch his right temple.

"Let's go, damn it. Now!" screamed Mike.

The pilots glanced nervously at each other. They had no choice. The jet began moving forward as the throttle lever was advanced slowly.

"Gulfstream, four-two-tango-juliet, you do not have permission to taxi," warned the ground traffic controller noticing from his high perch that the aircraft was moving forward, in clear violation of FAA regulations.

"Ground control, Gulfstream four-two-tango-juliet, I am being forced to taxi. We are taxiing to runway one-eight." The pilot sounded petrified as he spoke into the microphone.

The jet slowly made its way to Taxiway A, then B and finally Taxiway E. Another right turn and they would take the runway marked eighteen.

"Gulfstream, four-two-tango-juliet, hold short of runway one-eight," yelled the controller.

The jet did not obey and soon, the airplane was lined up with the center dashed line.

As the airplane approached the runway, Mike returned to his seat, although he could still spy the two pilots, the cockpit door ajar. He looked out his window, apprehensively. Seeing the airplane take the runway, he sat back and took in a deep slow breath. He fastened his seatbelt.

It was at that time, that multiple emergency vehicles sped onto the runway. Susan's unmarked car was leading the procession. In moments, the cars barricaded the plane on all sides. The officers got out of their cars, guns drawn.

12:22 PM

The hospital room was quiet, save for the rhythmic sounds of the respirator pushing air into the sedated patient. Multiple IV bags dripped medicines into his veins. At his side, a woman sat gloomily, holding the patient's hand, staring at his face. The woman was Claire.

A loud ring upset the stillness and monotony in the room. It was Claire's cell phone, located in her purse at the foot of the bed. Startled, Claire sat upright and answered the phone.

"We got him!" exclaimed Susan.

Claire, noticing that the loud ring awakened the patient, passed the word on to him.

"Jack, they got him. Susan arrested Mike Ganz. He's in

police custody," she repeated felicitously. Claire closed the cell phone after telling Susan she would call her back later.

Despite the deep sedation, Jack seemed to smile. Maybe even nod. He had an endotracheal tube in his mouth, which was attached to a respirator, metrically pushing oxygenated air into his airways and lungs, necessary due to high-dose of sedatives required.

Jack's brain was in a deep fog, due to the intense intravenous medications he was receiving. Once Claire's message registered in Jack's brain, adrenaline commenced to outpour into his circulatory system. Inside his body and mind, turmoil was afoot. Jack fought the heavy sedation, wanting to shout and scream. There was more to be declared. There was much more to be done.

Stop these drugs. Let me speak. I have to speak. I have something I have to say right now, Jack wanted to yell. But he could not. His muscles were paralyzed and his mind was blanketed by the sedatives. Sitting right next to him, Claire could not perceive any change whatsoever. All was calm.

Jill, Jack's nurse, strolled into the ICU cubicle.

"What's going on?" she inquired looking around the room, then at Claire.

"Oh, nothing. He seems to be doing okay." Claire was a bit intrigued with the question. Jill had just checked on him about ten minutes before and all was stable. All was well.

"We just picked up an increase in his heart rate and blood pressure on our monitors up front. His oxygen levels are still fine. I wonder what caused the sudden changes in his vital signs." Jill continued to snoop around looking at all instruments and assessing all the information she could glean from them. The monitor indicated a heart rate of 92 beats per minute and the blood pressure monitor showed 168/92.

"Is that bad?"

"No, no. Nothing bad. Just a change is all. Hmmm." Jill placed the stethoscope in her ears and listened to Jack's heart and lungs. She felt his extremities, then his forehead. She took his temperature. She assessed the tiny tube in Jack's groin artery, allowing for constant monitoring of his blood pressure. She flushed the line. She inspected all the intravenous lines for signs of irritation or infection. All seemed intact. All was registering properly.

"What do you think?" inquired Claire not sure of what to think herself.

"It's all normal," reassured the young nurse.

"I just got great news on the phone. I shared the information with Jack. Do you think that caused his pulse and blood pressure to go up?"

"Maybe. Yes," answered Jill hesitantly. "Could it have been bad news?"

"Great news. Why do you ask?"

"Well, bad news would be more likely to cause this. Not so much good news. It's more of a distress response. I'll increase his sedation and paralyzing meds. We'll watch him carefully for now." Jill dialed in the higher drip rates for the intravenous agents and documented the changes in the electronic medical record. She walked around the bed again. The effects of the drugs would be instantaneous. The nurse observed for a few minutes as the higher dose entered Jack's blood stream noticing the change in vital signs. Happy with the results, Jill walked out of the room.

Jack felt himself start to drift away deeper yet into unawareness. Blissfully, a tear escaped from Jack's right eye cascading down his cheek. Claire immediately wiped it off then squeezed his hand. They locked eyes for a short moment, until Jack slipped again into much needed deep sleep.

After five minutes, the heart rate had begun to drop back to the fifties, Jack's baseline. His blood pressure was back down to 102/56. Claire decided to call Susan back.

"As I told Jack the good news about you arresting Mike, he first appeared happy then became a bit agitated. He is so drugged up that the only hint of his restlessness was that his heart rate and blood pressure temporarily increased a little bit. His nurse told me this usually means bad news rather than good news. Go figure. She sedated him more heavily and he's back totally asleep and unaware. His vitals are back to baseline." Claire waited for a reply from Susan for a moment.

"I wonder if Jack was trying to tell us something. Some bad news. I wonder if he knows something. If he was trying to speak. I'm on my way in. Will you talk to the doctors and see if it's safe to stop the sedatives for a little while?" said Susan excitedly.

"Sure, I'll page Dr. Irvin and discuss this with him. I'll see you here soon."

Claire asked Jill to page Jack's doctor. Twenty minutes later, Susan arrived and hugged Claire. Four minutes later, Dr. Irvin arrived. Introductions were made and the three stepped outside to talk away from the patient. Jill took Claire's place at Jack's side and re-evaluated him once over again.

"It would be potentially dangerous to stop these medications. Especially if that was done suddenly. When we do it, we have to wean them over about twelve hours." Dr. Jeff Irvin was an older intensivist with many years of experience. Jack thought the world of him and had so told Claire many times. When he was assigned to his care, Claire felt very comfortable.

"I understand, Dr. Irvin. I appreciate your time," said Susan shaking the doctor's hand. She hugged Claire again and departed the area without a word.

The detective walked back to Jack's office. The area was deserted, as it had been designated a crime scene, yellow police tape closing off access to this wing. She sat at Jack's desk. She felt it necessary to recreate the situation when Jack was attacked.

"Okay, I'm sitting here reading a whole bunch of files and documents. Some guy enters and sprays me in the face. I know it's a poison that's going to kill me. Now, what do I do?" Susan conversed with herself, no one else in the room. She stood up and held her breath.

"I know this stuff enters my body as I take breaths. So, I hold my breath and run out of the room. Where do I go?" She stopped for a second. She exited the small office and looked to the right and left.

"To the left, there are only other offices. Dead end. I go right. I run fast. This guy may be chasing me." She walked to the right, down the hall, past several offices and a conference room. She arrived at the elevator she had used to come up to the office. She pushed the Down button and the light became illuminated. She crossed her arms and waited.

"I'm not going to wait. I've been poisoned. A bad guy may be chasing me." She looked around and found the door to the stairway.

"No, I take the steps. I'm used to taking the steps and they're faster." Susan recalled briefly the day she met Jack. They walked up these stairs to go to his office. She pushed through the door and stopped.

"I go downstairs." She climbed down the stairs. She continued until she arrived. Arrived at the message on the wall. Astonished, she used her cell phone as she reread the blood-written memo:

J MILLER = RAT POISONER! CHECK CPAP STORES

1:21 PM

The multicolored robe was the last thing to pack. This done, all bags were packed and James Miller was ready to go. Leave forever. Never to return. On the positive side, he had a one-way ticket to Jamaica, where life was easier, beer smoother, and the ocean waves soft. With time, he would even learn to enjoy watching a game or two of cricket.

He closed all his bank accounts. He would invest his money overseas. He would drive the rental car to Miami then fly to Jamaica. It was all planned out.

James got into the car and placed the key in the ignition. He started up the car and drove on. He turned right at the second light, en route to Newton Memorial.

At that exact moment, an unmarked car arrived at his

house. Two detectives got out of the vehicle. Wordlessly, one of them walked to the front door of the home while the other strolled towards the back of the property. There, a separate smaller structure served as the garage, being occupied by James' car. The detective walked around the vehicle making observations. He used a flashlight to illuminate the semi-dark environment. The garage and car were impeccably clean. He felt the hood of the car. It was cold, a sign that the engine had not been turned on for several hours. Meanwhile, the cop on the small front porch looked around for clues. Once at the main entrance, the officer pushed the doorbell.

"Police department. Open up," he said, knocking on the door. Nothing. Nobody.

Moments later, the officer tried the doorknob. It was unlocked. He opened the door and prepared to enter the residence when he heard a distinct noise. A click. Quickly, the detective shut the door and ran away from the house.

It was at that point the earsplitting explosion occurred, heard many blocks away. The officer was thrown several feet in the air landing on his side, temporarily stealing his breath. With all his might, he fought to drag his body as far from the burning structure and scattered flying fiery debris as he could. By then, his partner was at his side, helping him escape from the house ablaze.

"Dispatch, Delta-seven-six, officer down. We have an explosion and fire at this location. Send the fire department and EMS," shouted the cop anxiously.

"That was quick," thought James, hearing the blast, driving down the street. "That was way too quick."

An instant later, multiple sirens could be heard converging on the scene of the burning house. James pulled over to the side of the road as a red fire truck sped by, going in the opposite direction. Then another. Then an ambulance.

"The only connection to me is Norris. Maybe he's come back from the dead," whispered James to his own face displayed on the rearview mirror. He spied the emergency vehicles as they sped away.

James drove to the Home Medical Equipment facility, near the hospital campus, where he would make a quick stop on the way to Florida. As he turned the corner, he noticed a police car parked in front of the store.

James kept on driving past the establishment. When he turned south onto Interstate Route 41, he accelerated, pulled out his cell phone and dialed.

"Marlene, I won't be needing that CPAP equipment after all. I'm all better. Goodbye, darling." James closed the phone, opened up his car window and tossed the mobile device.

He turned on the Rolling Stones CD, picked the seventh song, sat back comfortably and prepared for the long trip to paradise, while Mick sang his heart out: You can't always get what you want! But if you try sometimes, you might just find, you get what you need!

Two days after

October 3

2:33 PM

The Rat Poison was now out of Jack's system. The weaning process from the sedatives, other intravenous medications and respirator had been initiated earlier in the day. As this process was carried out, Jack's awareness of the world around him would slowly return. When his brainpower sufficiently came online punching through the fog, Jack anxiously signed to Claire and his nurse that he wanted to write something down. The endotracheal tube was still in his lungs bypassing his vocal cords and, as such, he was unable to speak. As soon as he was provided with a clipboard, paper and a pen, he wrote:

"Get James Miller!" Jack wrote, and handed the clipboard to Claire forcefully and repeatedly pointed to the words.

"I'll call Susan right now," she said. Claire fished out her cell from her purse and dialed. After a short phone conversation between the two women, Claire closed the mobile phone and placed it back in her purse.

"Susan already knew it was Miller. She told me to thank you for your message on the wall. The police have been trying to find him but he's nowhere to be found. He may have left the city, maybe even the country. She's on the way here and will fill us in when she arrives," said Claire. Somehow, this seemed to have had a soothing effect on Jack. He took a deep sigh.

Jack tolerated the slow discontinuation of the sedatives and other medication drips and was taken off the respirator. It felt good to be alive, to breathe slowly, and not to feel his heart hammering away inside his ribcage.

Susan walked in the room, greeted Claire and hugged Jack tightly.

"Thank you, Jack. Thank you," said Susan appreciatively. "We couldn't have done it without you."

"If medicine doesn't work out for me, maybe I can come work with you?" asked Jack, his voice still a bit raspy from the recently removed endotracheal tube.

"Don't make me laugh, it still hurts," said Claire, holding on to her left side.

"Jack, how did you know James Miller was involved with the murders?" asked Susan.

"He was the one that sprayed Rat Poison in my face," answered Jack.

"I got your message," said Susan. "We've been looking for Miller ever since. We have every cop in the state looking for him. We're checking airports, bus and train terminals all over the state, but so far, we've not found him. He booby-trapped his house to explode. It went up in flames when the front door was opened. One of our detectives got minor burns, but he'll be okay."

"If I was him, I would change my name, my appearance, and leave the U.S.," offered Jack.

"I agree. I'd be gone by now," said Susan. There was a pause.

"Did you check stores that carry CPAP equipment?" inquired Jack.

"Yes. It took me a while to get that part of the message, but ain't Google great?"

"CPAP? What's that?" asked Claire, wearing an expression of puzzlement.

"Continuous positive airway pressure," answered Jack.

"Why were CPAP equipment stores places to look for Miller?" asked Susan.

"Miller has obstructive sleep apnea," said Jack.

"He has what?" asked Claire.

"Obstructive sleep apnea is a condition where people stop breathing when they enter deep sleep. That makes them feel very tired all the time since the quality of sleep is very poor."

"How do you know he has sleep apnea?" asked Susan.

"He's obese, speaks nasally, looks tired all the time and I've seen impressions on his face from the mask," answered Jack.

"What mask?" questioned Claire.

"Patients with sleep apnea have to wear a CPAP mask attached to a pump that pushes air into the mouth and/or nose during the night, so the patient will continue to get oxygen and breathe even when they stop breathing on their own. That way, the patient gets restful sleep and they can function during the day. The mask is attached with straps, which leave an impression on the face, if you look carefully. He had them."

"So what? How does this help?" inquired Claire.

"If you depend on a CPAP machine to sleep well and you're about to leave the country permanently, what do you do?"

"Hmm, you need to get equipment and supplies to last you awhile. You're pretty smart." answered Claire.

"That was great thinking. You were thinking like a detective. But we checked all the places. I sent a police car to all stores and nothing. One of the store owners told one of the officers that they had an order to be picked up by Miller, but he canceled that same day. Somehow, Miller figured us out."

There was a long pause after Susan spoke.

"Jack, I need to know everything you know. Will you start from the beginning," asked Susan, breaking the silence.

"I knew Rupert had a cabin in the woods. He had invited the cardiology fellows there for a Fourth of July party. On a hunch, I went there. I found some files, which I was reading in my office. James Miller walked into my office with a mask and sprayed me in the face. I knew it was Rat Poison. I ran away from there and injected myself with propranolol, verapamil and midazolam twice, I think, to try to overcome the effects of the poison."

"How did you know to use those drugs?" asked Susan.

"Observing Herb and the other victims, I noticed Rat Poison was a stimulating agent to the cardiovascular and central nervous systems. It caused rapid heart racing, agitation, paranoia and so on. It made sense to use drugs known to impede those processes. The drugs I used are known to do that."

Susan and Claire nodded understandingly. Jack continued.

"I knew my mind would fail me. The last thing I remember was writing you a message with my blood about Miller. I'm not clear at all about the rest. I just remember waking up here."

"You ended up calling my cell phone, fortuitously. All you were doing was grunting. I called Susan. She found you." Claire finished her sentence and looked at Susan.

"You were acting like a mad man. The cops found you in a subdivision behind the hospital. I met them there and we brought you here. We told the press you were dead." Susan paused as she looked through her purse to find the Evansville Courier & Press newspaper and held it up so Jack and Claire could examine it. The headlines read in large bold letters: Young doctor shot dead by police.

"This was designed so that those responsible would think you were out of the way," she continued.

"I was never shot," stated Jack with diffidence. "Was I?"

"You know, as a matter of fact, you were almost shot by a rookie," confessed Susan. "But no, you weren't shot. Thank God for that. You were saved by the shift commander."

"Why did you want the news to say I was dead?" asked Jack.

"For two reasons. First, so they would quit coming after

you. Second, we knew that the next target would be you, Claire." Susan looked at Claire. "They would think you had some knowledge of the events and would want to get rid of you, as well. So, we covertly guarded your room heavily, knowing they would come after you." Susan turned to Jack.

"You should be proud of Claire. Two men walked into her hospital room and tried to abduct her. We were all over them, but she was so brave. She did great. We owe you, Claire." Susan exchanged glances with Claire and squeezed her hand appreciatively. Claire smiled.

"The two men we apprehended were later murdered by Mike. He still had gun residue on him when we caught him at the airport." Jack looked confused.

"Airport?"

"Well, Steve Peski called you to tell you the Gulfstream Jet had landed. You asked him to tell you if that airplane returned to Evansville. Claire got the call and told me. At that point I suspected that the jet was here as the get-away vehicle. Fortunately, we were able to stop the plane from taking off. I called and asked the Evansville Tower to hold them on the tarmac for as long as possible. Mike held a gun to the pilot's head and made them taxi, but we got there in time. I arrested the fabulous FBI man, Mike Ganz, myself."

"I thought the two of you were dating," exclaimed Jack.

"We were. Well, I was. I thought he was coming to Evansville to see me, but all along he was coming here to take care of his business. Now that I think about it, every step of the way, he was trying to throw us off the case." Susan shook her head in disgust, and then continued, "I broke it off. I don't date scumbags. It was hard for a bit, but I'm already over him. What a fool I was!" Susan paused briefly. Then smirked.

"At least you caught him," offered Jack, trying to reassure her.

"I was angry at myself. I let myself be blinded by my feelings for Mike. I let Mike kill the one man in my life who really mattered. I wasn't seeing what you two could plainly see," said Susan regretfully.

"Don't blame yourself for having feelings, Susan," interrupted Claire.

"I know. I understand now. I'm over it." Susan sat up straight.

"Good. You have a healthy attitude, Susan," said Claire approvingly.

"Can you explain to me how the Rat Poison works exactly?" asked Susan, a ravenous appetite for more information.

"Sure. They developed this agent for congestive heart failure patients. A drug designed to stimulate the heart to work more efficiently. As they tested it on rats, they noticed that the drug, at high doses, made the rats die suddenly of cardiac arrests or bleeding in the brain. At lower dosages, it made rats aggressive toward each other. The drugged rats would just go helter skelter on the others. The lab was also developing an unrelated system to administer drugs by inhalation in the form of tiny bubbles. When desired, an ultrasound device is used to burst the bubbles releasing their contents into the circulation. This was designed to deliver medications into precise areas of the body, such as chemotherapy into cancer cells. They combined the two experiments and made a weapon out of it. After the rats, they started to test

Rat Poison on humans. Just like the rats, men would just die suddenly. As they figured out the right dose, the men given Rat Poison would become agitated and paranoid with a desire to kill those around them. A pretty good weapon to sell to the military."

"Rupert was a greedy sick bastard," interrupted Susan.

"That's the funny part. Rupert was against it. He kept notes on all of it. He had copious entries on his computer log on Major Rooner, Muhammad Akrim, James Miller, and Mike Ganz, saying he would not agree to run tests on human. He said it was unethical. He told them that the prime directive of medicine is Primum, non Nocere."

"English, please," interrupted Susan.

"First, do no harm," translated Claire with conviction.

"James Miller and Mike threatened to kill Rupert if he wouldn't go along with them. James administered Rat Poison to Rupert to coerce him to continue the research on humans. At any point, James or Mike could kill Rupert with a touch of a button. And Rupert knew it," continued Jack.

"You think Rupert was killed remotely by bursting the bubbles in his body, while he was driving?" solicited Susan intrigued.

"I'm sure of it. When the time came, Mike knew the correct frequency used to burst Rupert's bubble. Excuse the pun," answered Jack confidently, with a grin.

"How did Mike get involved?" asked Susan.

"When they first wanted to see if there was a military application for Rat Poison, Rupert approached Mike. He was here in town helping the Evansville Police with a federal case. Mike met with Rupert and became enamored by Rat Poison and it's potential to make him millions. Rupert tried to back out, but James and Mike wanted to pursue the project."

"Is all this information in the files you found at the cabin?"

"Yes. Speaking of the files, we need to check my office." Susan slowly shook her head disappointedly and interrupted Jack.

"I already checked. There are no files. James Miller must have taken them after he poisoned you. Mike claims he knows nothing of them. We'll keep searching. Something will come up," interjected Susan.

"So, was the military sponsoring the project?" asked Claire, after a long pause.

"No, the military didn't want anything to do with it due to its unethical nature during testing. I'm sure they wouldn't mind it after it was tested. Akrim, who is probably a radical terrorist or something like that, was funding them. Did he arrive in the jet today?"

"No, he's too smart. However, we do have his Gulfstream. Do you want to buy a slightly used, beautiful, well-equipped jet?"

They all chuckled.

"What about John Connor and the others murdered at the hospital?" asked Susan.

"John must have discovered what was going on with the project. He was trying to tell me. Mike found out about it and made Rupert kill John. Mike got the gun and gave it to Rupert who, in turn, gave it to Butterworth with a hefty dose of Rat Poison. He called John to come in to the unit to sign up a patient for one of their trials. When John arrived, he detonated the bubbles and Butterworth did the rest. Heather

McCormick and the security guard were just collateral damage; in the wrong place at the wrong time."

"That's a damn shame," said Susan. Saddened by the remembrance of unnecessary loss of life, the group sat in silence for a moment, shaking their heads slowly.

"Yes, it was. Rupert had all this in his journal," offered Jack.

"And somebody stole it all. We'll see if we can recover this important evidence." Susan paused.

"You'll get it when and if you get James Miller," said Jack.

"Either that or it all went up in flames with his house," lamented Susan.

"You know, I just had another thought that may be useful in trying to catch Miller," supposed Jack.

"Watch out, he's thinking like a cop again," said Claire smiling.

"I noticed Miller had a rash on his right hand when he sprayed me. I noticed it before but it was faint. It's raised, scaly, red and itchy. I noticed scratch marks on and around the rash. I think it's a fungal infection the name of which I can't recall. It's almost exclusively diagnosed in people who work with lab animals." Jack remained pensive for a beat. "Will you get me a computer so I can do a quick Internet search?" he continued.

Susan made a phone call and a policeman carrying a laptop computer arrived in Jack's room in no time. After a few clicks on the keyboard, the conversation resumed with newly found enthusiasm.

"Wherever he's going, he'll need to take care of this soon. It's very itchy. If he's planning to leave the country, he'll see a doctor here in the United States before he leaves. The treatment is a specific antifungal agent that gets little use otherwise. Is there a way, you or the FBI can track the sale of this medicine around the U.S.?"

"I'll find out." Susan dialed her cell phone and spoke for several minutes. During her phone conversation, she paced around the small hospital room. At one point, she paused to ask Jack to spell the name of the antifungal agent. When she hung up the call, she sat on the bed and looked at Jack and Claire, who had remained intrigued and quiet.

"Let's see where this takes us. So, when are you leaving this joint?" inquired Susan, breaking the silence.

"Leave this joint? I work here, you know," stated Jack.

"Are you guys ready to go back to your normal lives?" asked Susan.

"I don't know that we'll ever be normal again, Susan," proclaimed Jack.

"What is normal, anyway? Normal is what you make it to be. We will be richer and poorer by the experiences of the last few weeks. But we must go on with our lives," said Claire.

"Claire, you're such a psychologist," said Jack, picking up a pillow and throwing it at Claire. Susan imitated the gesture.

"Don't make me laugh. I was shot in the chest, you know," screamed Claire, trying desperately not to chortle. The three laughed for a long moment.

The few days later

October 6

2:40 PM

The mysterious man was James Miller, the Research Lab Head Tech and the mastermind of the Rat Poison operation. He talked quietly on his cell phone. He was wearing his plush multicolor robe and occasionally sipped from his coffee mug, waiting on a table within reach. He was sitting on a divan, his feet up comfortably on the ottoman. He was wearing slippers. The Bluetooth device was attached to his right ear, the cell phone on his lap.

"We were found out, Mr. Akrim. The police caught us. They arrested Mike Ganz and confiscated all the equipment and drugs." His words were remorseful. A short pause ensued.

"No, we can't make the drug or the equipment needed to weaponize it. Rupert's company, MultiTech, Inc., has been taken over by the police and the FBI. All assets frozen." James rubbed and scratched the reddened rash on his right hand.

"They confiscated the airplane. Do the pilots know anything?" Another pause. Another scratch.

"Oh, good." James nodded slowly as Akrim spoke on the other side of the call.

"Mike will give me away, but he doesn't know anything about you. He doesn't know your name or where you are. Only Rupert and I knew about you. I made sure of that." A long pause while the other party talked.

"I have all the documentation. All the records. Everything. There is nothing else out there." The room was overcome by silence for a short while again, save for the sound of the right hand being vigorously scratched.

"Well, investments sometimes are like that, Mr. Akrim. Do all your investments always make you money?" inquires James.

"Well, this investment didn't. Think of it as a bad investment. We all have those, sometimes."

"Yes, sir. I understand. But, you'll have no trouble. I promise you that."

"I can't implicate you without implicating myself. You only provided research money; I masterminded the whole operation." Another pause while excited gibberish was barely audible through the mobile device. James remained tranquil.

"I will leave the United States. I'll change my name and

have surgery to change my appearance and voice. Nobody will ever find me." Another long pause ensued.

"With all due respect, Mr. Akrim, you won't be able to find me either, so your empty threats don't scare me." James continued to stay composed.

"The cell phone is untraceable. You're welcome to try, but you'll be wasting your time."

"We have nothing else to talk about. Goodbye forever, Mr. Akrim." Calmly, James closed the cell phone, hanging up the call.

After a few seconds of deliberation and grins, James sipped from his coffee cup. He dialed again. His first call was to sever ties with one rich partner in crime. The second call was to secure a different, even richer, associate. While waiting for the connection, James smiled ear to ear, delighted by how well things were going. The future appeared bright. Very bright indeed.

James was getting sick and tired of the rash on his right hand. Periodically, he would scratch at it, but it never seemed enough. He would have to go see a doctor about it. And soon.

He made an appointment with a dermatologist using the name Joshua McCarthy. He was diagnosed with a rare fungal infection and was given a prescription. He stopped at a pharmacy and returned to the hotel with the hopes for a cure from his dreaded itching.

"It always pays to be ready. Prepared. Plan for every contingency," whispered James to no one in the hotel room as he looked around visualizing every corner of the large room.

"This may very well be a total waste of time and money. But it can also save my life," murmured James to himself. He made sure the door to the next hotel room was unlocked. He had taken the time to rent three rooms in a row, under different names. All rooms had adjoining communicating inside doors, the last room being around the corner the outside door of which led to the back parking lot. In that lot, Miller parked his second vehicle, which he rented under an assumed name.

Like a lunatic, James kept working, walking place-to-place, planning, scheming, all along talking quietly to himself. Satisfied with his progress, at 7:02 p.m. James was ready to relax. He made a call to a nearby Chinese restaurant and ordered food to be delivered to his hotel room. At 7:18 p.m., there was a knock on the door. James got up to open the door, anticipating crab Rangoon and Mongolian beef. Instead, two well-dressed men sporting an FBI badge asked politely to enter the room. The agents crossed the threshold with the left hand holding up their ID and right hand on their side revolvers, still holstered. They were also armed with a picture of Mr. James Miller. This was the seventh such incursion by the Bureau over the last three days, the others occurring in St. Louis, Denver, Boise, Seattle, Austin and San Diego. The other victims of the fungus had no resemblance to the man in the picture, so an arrest had not been made. No arrest until this time. Within seconds, James found himself on the floor with his hands behind his back. One of the agents pressed down hard with a knee on Miller's back, assuring he would not resist or attempt to get up. He was cuffed and Mirandized. As the agents aided the seemingly helpless man to his feet, James extended his right arm allowing the remote device to fall from his long sleeve and reach his right hand. That's when his preparedness began to pay off dividends. An explosion behind the sofa was loud and of sufficient magnitude to nearly completely pulverize not only the couch but also a nearby television and desk. The men had remained physically unharmed by this. A plume of thick smoke emanated from the area of the detonation. Most importantly, the blast provided a momentary diversion allowing James to escape from the distracted agent's grip and progress to stage two. A touch of a second button resulted in the dissemination of Rat Poison micro bubbles into the smoke-filled room, quickly penetrating into the detectives' respiratory tree. The two men would later be found dead in the hotel room, one having succumbed to a large brain hemorrhage, the other to a massive heart attack. The dose had been precisely and accurately calculated to achieve a drastic and rapid response. Mr. James Miller was, of course, nowhere to be found. The FBI placed the fugitive on its Most Wanted List.

Three years later

July 8

10:30 AM

Jack and his medical team, consisting of three medical students, two medical interns and one cardiology fellow were making rounds. Of the six, two were women and all were new at Newton Memorial Hospital. July 1 was their first day. They entered Room 615 to see a patient. Jack, now a staff-attending electrophysiologist, had been informed of the patient's status. Jack gestured for the others to enter. He went in last.

On arrival in the room, a beautiful woman was visiting the patient. They were talking joyfully, although the conversation came to a halt when the group entered.

"Can we talk outside, doctors?" After exiting the room, she continued: "What is the patient's condition?" asked the attractive lady looking at Rod Elmer, a medical student.

"Well," stuttered the student, hesitantly. "He is doing a little bit better. His heart rhythm is better controlled and—"

"You know you have beautiful eyes," interrupted Jack looking intently at the attractive young woman.

"Why, thank you," she whispered shyly. She looked at Jack for a short spell and then looked at the ground bashfully.

"Yes, I was saying the heart rhythm—" continued the student who was interrupted again in mid-sentence.

"No, I'm not kidding. I believe you're the most beautiful woman I have ever seen," persisted Jack, rudely disrupting the conversation between the two.

"Thank you," said the woman reservedly, blushing.

"Would you go out to dinner and a movie with me? Tonight?" persevered Jack.

The others were flabbergasted and unsure of what to think or say.

"I appreciate the offer," whispered the beautiful woman, "but I'm married." She lifted up her left hand, showing her wedding ring for all to see.

"So am I. Look," Jack showed the group his wedding band. "It's okay. We're both married, right?" asked Jack. With this, Jack approached the woman and dipped her backward with a passionate kiss. After a long and awkward moment, the couple got up.

"Guys, this is my wife, Claire. She's a cardiac psychologist here at the hospital. Let's be aware of our patient's emotions and see if some of them need support. Claire can help them and their families, if needed. Claire, say hey to my new group."

Claire looked up from the ground momentarily to wave to all with a forced smile. Her face was blushed, a clear demonstration of her embarrassment, having participated in this eccentric scene.

"Do we have to do this every time? You know he makes me do this. I swear. It's not my idea," she explained, apologetically.

"This is my way of making sure my students and trainees never forget the clinical pearls I teach them. Will any of you ever forget this moment?" he asked of the group. All nodded no.

"Okay, let's finish rounds. Want to do lunch?" he asked Claire.

"Sure, you're buying. And, not just for me. For all of them. Deal?"

"Deal."

6:30 PM

Jack and Claire had moved into a gorgeous home on Bell Road, the neighborhood behind Newton Memorial Hospital, not far from where Jack was first temporarily placed under arrest.

A beautifully manicured backyard served as a soccer pitch for Jack, his two-year-old son, Nick, and Trinity, his three-year-old dog, a Vizsla the couple purchased immediately after the incidents at the hospital. Despite multiple tries, Jack remained unable to turn on the alarm system he purchased that fateful day. From then on, Trinity would serve as the warning method for strangers or unwanted trespassers. Of course, the new home had a working sophisticated alarm system, which the Norris' were yet to turn on. Trinity was all the forewarning and protection they required.

"Jack, come quickly," yelled Claire from the kitchen door to the backyard.

"What is it? We're in the middle of a soccer match." Jack picked Nick up lovingly, helping him kick a goal.

"And he scores. The crowd goes wild," yelled Jack running to the house, Nick in his arms and Trinity running behind.

They entered the home. The HD-TV image was on pause. Claire had the remote in her hand.

"You won't believe this. Are you ready? You'd better sit down for this one," she commanded. Jack sat down, Nick in his lap and Trinity at his side.

"Look at what CNN just reported. I got it on TiVO. She pushed play and sat down next to Jack.

The headline read: "Terrorist group steals materials from North Korea to assemble a WMD then self-destroys."

The international reporter described an incident, where days ago, a yet unknown terrorist faction was able to enter the Yongbyon Nuclear Research Center facility, in the Pyongan Province of North Korea and abduct uranium and plutonium. An unnamed CIA source claimed intelligence had demonstrated the terrorists desired to assemble a nuclear weapon of mass destruction to be aimed at the United States. For reasons that remain unexplained, the group's headquarters in Afghanistan was discovered earlier today when massive gunfire was heard. All the terrorists in the group were found dead. The insurgents appeared to have annihilated each other, without cause or outside interference. The nuclear materials were recovered undamaged. An international investigation into this incident was ongoing.

Several retired military and CIA distinguished men then

took turns telling the world that they had never seen anything like this, and that they had no idea as to what could have caused this incident.

Jack winked at Claire.

"A covert operation, huh? Looks like the CIA's got the Rat Poison," postulated Claire. "Hope they put it to good use."

"They will. I have no doubt they will," said Jack with a grin on his face.

A few hours later, the baby was asleep. The dinner dishes were washed and put away. The beautiful sunny day had been replaced by a calm dark evening. All was calm. All seemed right.

Right outside the house, a dark sedan drove by slowly. Calculating. Scheming. The car stopped for a few seconds in front of the mailbox bearing the Norris family's address. Then continued. The car and its passenger remained unnoticed. And it disappeared into the night.